THE RETURN
LORD!

Energy bolts crackled wildly in all directions as the battle raged in the tunnel. Luke cut through the armoured legs of one soldier before the latter could bring his pistol to bear . . . Turning, Luke plunged back into the thickest fighting. He was hunting for one figure. It finally showed itself, standing aloof near the rear of the fighting crowd.

'Vader! Darth Vader!'

A wounded Imperial trooper charged Luke and he had to pause to deal with the more immediate threat.

But the Dark Lord had heard him. Surprised, the giant black shape activated his own lightsabre and strode into the mob, trying to cut his way clear to Luke Skywalker . . .

Also in Sphere Books
STAR WARS by George Lucas
THE EMPIRE STRIKES BACK by Donald F. Glut

Splinter of the Mind's Eye

From the Adventures of Luke Skywalker

by ALAN DEAN FOSTER

Based on the characters and situations
created by George Lucas

SPHERE BOOKS LIMITED
30/32 Gray's Inn Road, London WC1X 8JL

First published in Great Britain by Sphere Books Ltd 1978
Reprinted 1980, 1981

Published by arrangement with Del Rey / Ballantine Books, a division of Random House, Inc., New York, N.Y., USA.

For Dad & Mom Oxley, Louis & Ellie;
with all my love, which would fill several universes . . .

TRADE
MARK

Set in Intertype Baskerville

Printed in Canada

□ I

HOW beautiful was the universe, Luke thought. How beautifully flowing, glorious and aglow like the robe of a queen. Ice-black clean in its emptiness and solitude, so unlike the motley collage of spinning dust motes men called their worlds, where the human bacteria throve and multiplied and slaughtered one another. All so that one might say he stood a little higher than his fellows.

In depressed moments he felt sure there was no really happy living matter on any of those worlds. Only a plethora of destructive human diseases which fought and raged constantly against one another, a sequence of cancerous civilisations which fed on its own body, never healing yet somehow not quite dying.

A particularly virulent strain of one of those cancers had killed his own mother and father, then his Aunt Beru and Uncle Owen. It had also taken from him the man he had learned to respect more than any other, the elderly Jedi knight Ben Kenobi.

Although he had seen Kenobi struck by the light-sabre of Darth Vader on board the now obliterated Imperial Deathstar battle station, he could not be certain the old wizard was truly dead. Vader's sabre had left only empty air in its wake. That Ben Kenobi had departed this plane of existence was unarguable. What no one could tell was what level of existence he had passed into. Maybe death and . . .

Maybe not.

There were times when Luke experienced an agreeably crawly sensation, as if someone were lurking just behind him. That unseen presence occasionally seemed to move arms and legs for him, or to supply suggestions and thoughts when his own mind was helplessly blank. Blank as that of the former farm boy of Tatooine's desert world.

Unseen spirits or not, Luke reflected grimly, if there was one thing he was sure of it was that the callow youth he had once been was dead and dry as dust. In the Rebel Alliance of worlds struggling against the corrupt rule of the Imperial government he held no formal title. But no one taunted him or called him farm boy – not since he had helped destroy the bloated battle station secretly built by Governor Moff Tarkin and his henchman Darth Vader.

Luke had no experience with titles, hence no use for them. When the Rebel leaders offered him any reward within their ability to grant, he had asked only to be permitted to continue piloting a fighter in the Alliance's service. Some thought his request unduly modest, but one shrewd general disagreed, explaining how Luke might be more valuable to the Rebellion without a title or commission which, the veteran pointed out to his colleagues, would serve only to make the youth a prime target for Imperial assassination. So Luke remained the pilot he'd always wanted to be, perfecting his flying skills and always, unceasingly, wrestling with the Force Ben Kenobi had enabled him to begin to understand.

No time for meditating now, he reminded himself as he studied the instruments of his X-wing fighter. A glance forward showed the brilliant pulsing sunball of Circarpous Major, its devastating radiance stepped down to viewable intensity by the phototropic material of the transparent port itself.

'Everything okay back there, Artoo?' he called into his pickup. A cheerful beep from the stubby 'droid locked in position behind the cockpit assured Luke that it was.

Their destination was the fourth planet out from this star. Like so many others, the Circarpousians were appalled by the atrocities perpetrated by the Empire, but too paralysed by fear to openly join the Rebel Alliance. Over the years, a burgeoning underground movement had arisen on Circarpous, an underground needing only enough aid and encouragement from the Alliance to rise and swing their world to the cause of freedom.

From the tiny, hidden Rebel station on the outermost planet of the system, Luke and the Princess were racing to a critically important meeting with the heads of that underground, to offer the necessary promise of support. He checked his console chronometer. They would arrive in plenty of time to reassure the highly nervous underground chiefs.

Leaning slightly forward and glancing to starboard, he could admire the sleek Y-wing fighter cruising alongside. Two figures sat silhouetted by instrument lights within its cockpit. One was the gleaming golden shape of See Threepio, Artoo's 'droid companion.

The other . . . whenever he looked at her, the other caused emotions to boil within him like soup too long on the fire, no matter if she was separated from him by near vacuum as at present or by only an arm's length in a conference room. It was for and because of that individual, Princess and Senator Leia Organa of the now-vaporised world of Alderaan, that Luke had originally become involved in the Rebellion. First her portrait and then her person had initiated the irreversible metamorphosis from farm boy to fighter pilot. Now the two of them were the official emissaries from the ruling council of the Rebel government to the vacillating underground on Circarpous.

Sending her on so dangerous a mission, Luke had thought from the first, was a risk. But a second system was ready to commit itself to the Alliance, *if* it was announced that Circarpous had also joined. At the same time, if that second system would declare its defiance of the Empire, then the Circarpousian underground would undoubtedly come over to the side of the rebellion. So not one, but two systems waited on the outcome of this mission. And if it failed, Luke knew, both systems would probably lose heart and withhold their desperately needed aid. They *had* to succeed.

Luke had no doubts, as he silently adjusted his ship's attitude a quarter of a degree to the plane of the solar ecliptic, about the outcome of this mission. He couldn't imagine anyone who could not be persuaded by Princess Leia. She could convince *him* of anything. Luke treasured those moments when she forgot her station and titles. He dreamed of a time when she might forget them forever.

A beep from behind woke Luke from his daydreaming, wiping the smile from his face. They were preparing to pass close by Circarpous V, and Artoo was reminding him of it. A vast, cloud-shrouded globe, the planet was listed in Luke's library as being mostly unexplored, save for a single early Imperial scouting expedition. According to the computer readout, it was also known to the Circarpousians as Mimban, and ... His intership communicator dinged for attention.

'I'm receiving you, Princess.'

Her reply was filled with irritation. 'My port engine is beginning to generate unequal radiation pulses.' Even when bothered, to him that voice was as naturally sweet and pleasing as sugar-laden fruit.

'How bad?' he inquired, frowning worriedly.

'Bad enough, Luke.' The words sounded strained. 'I'm losing control already, and the inequality's getting worse. I don't think I'm going to be able to compensate. We'll have to stop at the first base down below on Mimban and have the problem corrected.'

Luke opened his mouth to reply, did so after hesitating briefly. 'You can't possibly make it safely to Circarpous IV?'

'I don't think so, Luke. I might make near-orbit, but

then we'd have to deal with official repair systems and couldn't set down as planned. We'd miss the meeting, and we *can't* miss it. Resistance groups from all over the Circarpous system are going to be there. If I don't arrive, they'll panic. We'll have one *Stang* of a time getting them to surface again. And the Circarpous worlds are vital to the Rebellion, Luke.'

'I still don't think . . .' he began.

'Don't make me make it an order, Luke.'

Biting back his initial response, he hurriedly began a check of visual readout charts and records. 'According to my information tapes, Mimban doesn't have a repair station, Leia. In fact,' he added with a glance at the murky green-white sphere below and to one side, 'Mimban might not even have an emergency standby station.'

'It doesn't matter, Luke. I have to make the conference, and I'm going down while I still have some real control. Surely, in a system as populous as this one, any world with a breathable atmosphere's going to be equipped with facilities for emergency repair. Your data must be old or else you're searching the wrong tapes.' A pause, then, 'You can prove it by shifting your communicator monitor to frequency oh-four-six-one.'

Luke adjusted the requisite controls. Instantly a steady whine filled the small cabin.

'Sound familiar?' she asked him.

'That's a directional landing beacon, all right,' he replied, confused. Several further queries, however, revealed no records of a station on Mimban. 'But there's still nothing in the listings on either Imperial or Alliance tapes. If we . . .' He broke off as a puff of gas glowed brightly from the Princess' Y-wing, expanded brightly and vanished. 'Leia! *Princess Leia!*'

Her small ship was already curving away from him. 'Lost lateral controls completely now, Luke! I've got to go down!'

Luke rushed to match her glide path. 'I don't deny

the presence of the beacon. Maybe we'll be lucky! Try to shift power to your port controls!'

'I'm doing the best I can.' A brief silence, followed by, 'Stop moving around, Threepio, and watch your ventral manipulators!'

A contrite, metallic 'Sorry, Princess Leia' sounded from her cabin companion, the bronzed human-cyborg relations 'droid See Threepio. 'But what if Master Luke is correct and there is no station below? We could find ourselves marooned forever on this empty world, without companionship, without the knowledge tapes, without . . . without *lubricants*!'

'You heard the beacon, didn't you?' Luke saw a small explosion whereupon the Y-wing dived surfaceward at an abruptly sharper angle. For a few moments only static answered his frantic calls. Then the interference cleared. 'Close, Luke. I lost my starboard dorsal engine completely. I cut port dorsal ninety per cent to balance guidance systems.'

'I know. I've cut power to slow with you.'

In the Y-wing's tiny cabin Threepio sighed, gripped the walls around him more firmly. 'Try to set us down gently, please, Princess. Rough landings do terrible things to my internal gyros.'

'They're not so good on my insides either,' the Princess shot back, lips clenched tightly as she fought the sluggish controls. 'Besides, you've nothing to worry about. 'Droids can't get spacesick.'

Threepio could have argued otherwise, but remained silent as the Y-wing commenced a stomach-turning roll downward. Luke had to react rapidly to follow. There was one tiny positive sign: the beacon signal was not imaginary. It was really there, beeping steadily when he adjusted the controls on his board so that the signal was audible. Maybe Leia was right.

But he still didn't feel confident. 'Artoo, let me know if you spot anything unusual on our way down. Keep all your sensory plug-ins on full power.' A reassuring whistle filled the cockpit.

They were at two hundred kilometres and descending when Luke jumped in his seat. Something began pushing at his mind. A stirring in the Force. He tried to relax, to let it fill and flow over and through him just as old Ben had instructed him.

His sensitivity was far from perfectly attuned and he sincerely doubted he would ever attain half the command of the Force that Kenobi had possessed ... though the old man had expressed great confidence in Luke's potential. Still, he knew enough to categorise that subtle tingling. It sparked an almost palpable feeling of unease in him, and it came from something (or several somethings) on the surface below. Yet he wasn't sure. Not that he could do anything about it now. The only concern of the moment was hoping the Princess's ship could set down safely.

But the sooner they left Mimban, the better he'd feel.

Despite her own problems, the Princess was taking the time to relay coordinate information to him. As if he couldn't plot her own course himself. Instead, he tried to identify something he'd just spotted below them as they entered the outer atmosphere. Something funny in the clouds here ... he couldn't decide just what.

He voiced his new concern to the Princess. 'Luke, you're worrying too much. You'll worry yourself to death at an early age. And that would be a waste of ...'

He never did find out what worrying himself to death would be a waste of because at that moment they entered troposphere for the first time and the immediate reaction of both ships to the thicker air and air to ships was anything but normal.

It seemed as if they'd suddenly plunged from a cloud-dotted but unexceptional-appearing sky into an ocean of liquid electricity. Gigantic multicoloured bolts of energy erupted from empty air, contacted the hulls of the two ships and fomented instrumental chaos where order had reigned seconds before. Instead of the blue- or yellow-tinged canopy they'd expected to sail through, the atmosphere around them was drenched with bizarre, perambulating energies so wild and frenzied they bordered on the animate. Behind Luke, Artoo Detoo beeped nervously.

Luke fought his own instrumentation. It flaunted a farrago of electronic nonsense at him. The madly bucking X-wing was held in the grip of unidentified forces powerful enough to toss it about like a plaything. The chromatic storm vanished behind him as if he'd suddenly emerged from a waterspout, but his controls continued to exhibit what were probably permanent manifestations of the electronically addled.

A quick verbal survey revealed what he most feared: the Princess's fighter was nowhere in sight. Trying to control his drunken ship with one hand on the manual controls, Luke activated the communicator with the other.

'Leia! Leia, are you . . .?'

'No . . . control, Luke,' came the static-sprinkled reply. He could barely make out the words. 'Instruments . . . replonza. I'm trying to get down in . . . one piece. If we . . .'

Gone, no matter how frantically he cajoled the communicator. His attention was diverted as something in one overhead panel blew out in a shower of sparks and metal fragments. The cockpit filled with acrid fumes.

Impelled by desperate thought, Luke activated the fighter's tracker. Part of the little ship's offensive armament. It was among its best-built and sealed components. Even so, it had been overloaded by the fury of the peculiar distorting energies, energies which its designers had never anticipated that it would encounter.

Useless now, nonetheless its automatic record was intact and playable. It showed for several moments the falling spiral which could only have been left by the Princess's ship. As best as he could without auto-enhancement, Luke set the X-wing on a pursuit course downward. There was little to no chance of following the Princess precisely. He simply prayed that now they might land somewhere other than on opposite sides of the planet from each other. Then he simply prayed they might land.

Swerving slightly like a crippled camel in a sand-storm, the fighter continued to drop. As the lush surface of Mimban rushed up at him Luke caught rolling, twisting glimpses of mountainless green swaths interwoven with veins and arteries of muddy brown and blue.

Though he was utterly ignorant of Mimbanian topography, the green and the blue-brown of rivers and streams and vegetation seemed infinitely preferable as landing sites to, say, the endless cerulean of open sea or the grey spires of young mountains. No rock is as soft as water and no water so soft as a swamp, he reflected, trying to cheer himself. He was starting to believe he actually might survive the touchdown, and the Princess might do likewise.

Frantically he fought to discover a combination of circuits that would reactivate the target tracker. Once he partly succeeded. The screen showed the Y-wing still on the course he'd just plotted. His chance of setting down close to her ship was looking better.

Despite the demands on his mind, he couldn't help but consider the energy distortions that had ruined their instrumentation. The fact that the rainbow maelstrom was confined to one area – an area very close to the location of the landing beacon – raised questions as intriguing as they were disturbing.

Trying to minimise the effects of his insane controls, Luke switched off his engines and continued down on glide. Back on Tatooine he'd plenty of practice idling in his skyhopper. But that was considerably different from doing practically the same thing in a vehicle as complex as this fighter. He had no idea if the same thought would occur to the Princess, or if she had had any experience in powerless flight. Anxiously chewing his lower lip, Luke realised that even if she tried gliding, his own craft was far better suited to such a manoeuvre than her Y-wing.

If only he could see her he'd feel a lot better. Strain his eyes as he might, though, there was no sign of her. Soon, he knew, all chance of visual contact would vanish. His ship began plunging recklessly into a floor of dirty grey cotton, thick cumulonimbus clouds.

Several rumbling flashes crackled through the air, only this time the lightning was natural. But Luke was deep in clouds by then and could see nothing. Panic hammered at him. If the visibility stayed like this all the way to the surface he'd locate the ground a bit too late, the hard way. As he considered switching back to auto, distorted as it was, he broke out of the bottom layer of clouds. The air was thick with rain, but not so bad that he failed to make out the terrain below. Time was running out faster than altitude now. He had barely enough of either to pull back on the atmospheric controls before something jolted the fighter from below. That was followed instantly by a series of similar crackings as he clipped off the crowns of the tallest trees.

Eyeballing his airspeed indicator, Luke fired braking rockets and nudged the ship's nose down ever so gently. At least he would be spared the worry of igniting the vegetation around the landing site. Everything hereabouts was drenched.

Again he fired the braking rockets. A series of violent jolts and jounces shook him despite his battle harness. A green floral wave crested ahead and overwhelmed him with darkness. . . .

He blinked. Ahead, the shattered foreport of the fighter framed jungle with crystal geometry. All was quiet. As he tried to lean forward water caressed his face. That helped to clear his mind and bring the scenery into sharp focus. Even the rain was falling with caution, he mused, that is if it were indeed a light rain, instead of an exceptionally heavy mist.

Craning his neck, Luke noted that the metal overhead had been peeled back neatly – as if by some giant opener – by the thick, now cracked limb of an enormous tree. If by chance the fighter had slid in here slightly higher, Luke's skull would have been peeled off just as neatly – a bit more to port and the broad bole of the tree would have smashed him back into the power plant. He had escaped decapitation and fatal compression by a metre either way.

Water continued to drip into the broken, open cockpit from the wood above. Luke suddenly realised he was parched and opened his mouth to let the water quench his thirst. He noticed a slight saltiness that didn't seem right. The rain (or mist) water looked clear and pure. It was. The saltiness, he realised, came from the blood trickling down from the gash in his forehead. It ran down the left side of his nose and on to his lips.

Undoing the g-locks, Luke slipped free of the harness. Even moving slowly and carefully, he felt as if every muscle in his body had been grabbed and pulled from opposite ends to the near-breaking point. Ignoring the pain as best he could, he inventoried his surroundings.

Between the distortions generated by the electronic storm he'd passed through and the more prosaic results of the crash, his instruments had become candidates for the secondhand shop. They would never operate this fighter again. Turning to his left, he keyed the exit panel but was not surprised when it failed to respond. After throwing the double switch on the manual release he jabbed the emergency stud. Two of the four explosive bolts fired. The panel moved a few centimetres, then froze.

Pressing himself back in the pilot's seat, Luke braced himself with both hands and kicked. That accomplished nothing save to send shooting pains up both legs. All that remained was the standard exit, if it hadn't been too badly jammed. Reaching up with both hands, he shoved the release mechanism, then pushed. Nothing. He paused, panting as he considered his alternatives.

The cockpit hood began to lift by itself.

Squirming frantically, Luke tried to find his pistol. A querulous beep reassured him.

'Artoo Detoo!'

A curved metallic hood looked down at him, the single red electronic eye studying him anxiously.

'Yes, I'm okay . . . I think.'

Using Artoo's centre leg as a brace, Luke pulled himself up and out. Clearing his legs, he got to his feet and found himself standing on top of the grounded X-wing. He rested his back against the curve of the great, overhanging branch.

A mournful whistle-honk sounded and he glanced down at Artoo, who clung securely to the metal hull nearby. 'I don't know what you're saying, Artoo, without Threepio to translate for us. But I can guess.' His gaze turned outward. 'I don't know where he and the Princess are. I'm not even sure where *we* are.'

Slowly he took stock of the surface of Mimban. Dense growth rose all around, but it was clumped in large pockets, instead of presenting a continuous front like a normal jungle. There was ample open space. Mimban, or at least the section where he'd come down, was part swamp, part jungle, part bog.

Fluid mud filled most of a languid stream to the right of the ship. It meandered in slow motion. To his left the trunk of the enormous tree he'd nearly hit towered into the mist. Beyond lay a tangle of other tall growths fringed with bushes and tired, drooping ferns. Grey-brown ground bordered it. There was no way to tell from a distance how solid the surface was. Bracing himself with a hand on a small branch, Luke leaned over the side of the ship. The X-wing appeared to be resting on similar terrain. It wasn't sinking. That meant he might be able to walk. This was some comfort to him, since without a ship he was a rotten flier.

Smiling slightly to himself, he crouched and peered under the limb. The double wing on the port side of the ship had been snapped off cleanly somewhere back in the forest, leaving only twin metal stubs. Both engines on that side, naturally, were also missing. Unequivocally, he was grounded.

Carefully crawling back into the ruined cockpit he unlocked the seat and shifted it to one side, then began rummaging in the sealed compartment behind it for the material he'd have to carry with him. Emergency rations, his father's lightsabre, a thermal suit ... the last because despite the tropical appearance of some of the vegetation, it was decidedly cool outside.

Luke knew there were temperate rain forests as well as tropical ones. While the temperature would probably not become dangerously cold, it still could combine with the omnipresent moisture to give him an uncomfortable and potentially debilitating chill. So he took the precaution of packing the thin suit. The survival pack for his back was strapped to the backside of the seat. Unbuckling it, he began to fill its copious interior with supplies from the compartment.

When the rip-proof sack was stuffed, he tried to seal the cockpit as best he could to protect it. Then he sat on the edge of the seat and thought.

His preliminary observations had revealed no sign of the Princess' Y-wing. Yet in the damp, foggy air it could have touched down ten metres away and still be effectively invisible. She probably had landed or crashed slightly ahead of him, according to his estimate of how rapidly he had set his own ship down. Lacking any other information, he had no choice but to continue on foot along his last plotted course for her.

It had occurred to him to stand on the nose of the ship and shout, but he'd decided it would be better to locate the ship visually first. The cacophony of cries, hoots, howls, whistles and buzzings which seeped out of the encircling bog and thick vegetation didn't encourage him to make himself conspicuous. Shouting might attract all sorts of attention, some of it possibly carnivorous.

Better to find the Princess's ship first. With any luck she would be seated sensibly in the cockpit, alive and intact and fuming with impatience as she waited for him to arrive.

Pulling himself clear of the cockpit again, Luke used branches for balance as he climbed down to the broken stub of the port double wing. He lowered himself carefully to the ground, which was soft, almost springy. Pulling up one foot he saw that his boot sole was already coated with sticky grey gook that resembled wet modelling clay. But the ground held, supporting him. Artoo joined him a moment later.

Thanks to the abruptness of his forced landing, he didn't have to search for a walking-stick. There was an abundance of shattered, splintered limbs strewn in the fighter's wake. He selected one which would serve both for support and for testing the ground ahead.

Using the nose of the ship as a crude guide, he set his tracomp and they started off, angling a few degrees to starboard.

It might have been a movement of bush branches in the forest, it might have been the Force, or it might have been an old-fashioned hunch, but even Ben Kenobi would have admitted that Luke had only one chance of finding the Princess's ship. If it didn't lie close along the path he was taking, if he missed it and passed on, he could continue treading the surface of

Mimban for a thousand years without ever seeing her again.

If his original plotting tape had been accurate and if she hadn't altered her course of descent at the last moment for some strange reason, he ought to find her within a week. Of course, he considered, she might not have been able to prevent her fighter from changing its angle of fall. He shunted that possibility aside. The situation was grim enough without such speculations.

The fog-mist-rain altered its consistency but never dried up completely. So it wasn't long before the exposed portions of his body were thoroughly soaked. At present, he thought, it was more of a belligerent fog than a real rain.

His suit kept his body moisture-free, but face, hands and scalp soon had rivulets of their own as water accumulated. There were rare, almost clear-dry moments, but he still spent a lot of energy regularly wiping the accumulated water beads from his forehead and cheeks.

Once he saw something that looked like a four-metre-long pale snake slither off into the underbrush at his approach. As he strode cautiously over the path it had taken, he saw that it had left a grooved track lined with luminous mucus in the soft earth. But Luke wasn't impressed. He had spent little time in zoological study. Even on Tatooine, which harboured its own protoplasmic freaks, such things hadn't interested him much. If a critter didn't try to eat you, claw you or otherwise ingest you, there were other things to absorb one's interest.

Nonetheless, he now had to direct all his attention to keeping to his predetermined path. Despite the tracomp built into his suit sleeve he knew he could easily lose his way. A deviation of a tenth of a degree could be critical.

He mounted a slight rise during one of the rare, almost clear periods. Through the fog and mist he glimpsed monolithic grey battlements off in the distance. It seemed likely to him that those walls had not been raised by human hands.

Their uniform steel-grey colour made them look as if they'd been constructed of a child's toy blocks. Luke couldn't be sure, this far away, whether their colour was true or distorted by the shifting fog. Soaring grey towers were inlaid with black stone or metal and boasted misshapen domes.

He paused, tempted for the first time to change direction and explore. There were discoveries to be made here. However, the Princess waited not in that eldritch city but somewhere farther on, in an environment which at any moment might prove hostile.

As if in response to his thought, he noticed a stirring in a clump of rust-green bushes ahead. Straining every sense, he dropped to one knee and removed the lightsabre from its place at his waist. The vegetation began to rustle violently. His thumb slid over the activation stud. Artoo beeped nervously alongside.

Whatever was in there was moving towards him. He thought about testing the wind, remembered sheepishly that there wasn't any. That, however, might not prove an inhibition to the creature approaching him.

Quite abruptly the greenery ahead parted. Out walked the Mimbanite. It was a large dark brown furry ball, with patches and stripes of green covering its body, roughly a metre in diameter. Four short furry legs supported it, ending in thick, double digits. Four arms poked clear of the upper surface. The modest tail was naked like a rat's.

Two wide eyes peering out from among the bristly fur were all that showed of a face. They grew wider as they settled on Luke and Artoo Detoo.

Luke waited tensely, finger poised over the lightsabre switch.

The creature did not charge. Instead, it produced a startled, muffled squeal and whirled. With all eight limbs propelling it, the creature shot back into the protective brush.

After several minutes of silence, Luke rose. His finger slid clear of the sabre stud and he reattached the weapon to his belt, smiling somewhat hysterically.

His first confrontation with an inhabitant of this world had sent it fleeing in terror from him. Maybe the wildlife hereabouts, if not actually benign, was something less than dangerous. With that in mind he continued on, his stride a bit longer, a touch more self-assured. His posture was straighter and his spirits considerably higher, raised up by that stoutest of buoys, false confidence. . . .

□ II

LEIA Organa made another half-hearted try at adjusting her rain-slicked hair, then gave up in disgust and peered out at the lush growth surrounding her.

After losing all contact with Luke, she'd managed to land hard in this wet hell. She took some measure of comfort in knowing that if Luke had also survived setdown, he'd try to reach her. After all, his job was to see that she arrived safely at Circarpous IV.

Angrily she mused that now she was going to be rather more than slightly late for the conference. A quick examination had indicated that she would no longer have to worry about the malfunctioning port engine which was now a crumpled oblong metal shape, incapable of propelling itself or anything else across so much as a light-second. The rest of the Y-wing was in little better shape.

She considered looking for Luke. But it made more sense for one of them to wait for the arrival of the other, and she knew Luke would come for her as soon as he was ready.

'Pardon me, Princess,' said the metal form behind her, 'but do you think Artoo and Master Luke set down safely in this awful place?'

'Of course they did. Luke's the best pilot we've got. If I made it down, I'm certain he had no trouble.' That was a slight lie. What if Luke was lying injured somewhere, unable to move, and she simply sat here awaiting him? Better not to think about that. The vision of a twisted, broken Luke, bleeding to death in the cockpit of his X-wing, made her insides spin tightly.

She slid back the roof of the cockpit once again, her nose wrinkling at the rankness of the dripping morass encircling them. Plenty of noise assailed her from hidden things moving stealthily through the undergrowth. Nothing larger than a couple of brightly hued quasi-insects had shown themselves thus far, however. Her pistol rested comfortably on her lap. Not that she'd need it, secure as she was in the cockpit whose sliding roof panel she could throw back in place and lock in seconds. She was perfectly safe.

Threepio felt otherwise. 'I don't like this place, Princess. I don't like it at all.'

'Relax. There can't be anything out there,' she nodded towards the densest growth, 'that would find you digestible.'

A shrill, hooting cry sounded like a sick trumpet close on her left. She jerked around sharply, sucking in a startled breath. But there was nothing there.

Her face pressed close by the open port as she strove to penetrate the green-brown wall of vegetation with anxious eyes. When the noise did not recur, she forced herself to relax.

'Do you see anything, Threepio?'

'No, Princess. Nothing larger than a few small arthropods, and I'm scanning with infrared also. That doesn't mean something large and inimical couldn't be out there.'

'But you don't see anything?'

'No.'

She was furious at herself. A simple noise had panicked her. Probably only the forlorn cry of some harmless herbivore, and she'd panicked like an infant. It would *not* happen again.

She was angry because whatever had caused them to crash would certainly cause her to miss her scheduled arrival demonstration on Circarpous, possibly aggravating the government officials assigned to greet her. She was twice over angry at Luke. Angry for not performing a navigational miracle and following her safely down without instruments or control, and angry most of all because he'd been right in insisting they ought not to land here.

So she sat and fumed silently to herself, alternately conjuring up the curses she'd employ when he finally did arrive and worrying about what she'd do if he didn't.

Aahhh-*wooop*!

Again the trumpeting sound. Whatever had produced it had not left after all. If anything, the sharp hooting sounded closer. This time her hand tightened around the pistol. Once more she examined the surrounding jungle, saw nothing.

As she stared she theorised. Suppose she had misinterpreted that landing beacon somehow? Suppose it was only the barest of automatic installations and this world was devoid not only of mechanics but of facilities for organic travellers as well?

If Luke was dead she'd be marooned here alone, without any idea of ... There was a loud crashing off to her right this time. Swinging around in the seat she instinctively fired off a burst through the cracked port and was rewarded with the odour of burnt, wet vegetable matter. The muzzle of the pistol remained focussed on the carbonised spot. Hopefully, she'd hit the thing. Fortunately she hadn't.

'It's me!' a voice shouted, sounding more than a little shaky. She'd barely missed him.

'It's me and Artoo.'

'Artoo Detoo!' Threepio clambered out of the cockpit, moved to greet his squat counterpart.

'Artoo, it's good to ...' Threepio paused, then continued in a different tone. 'What do you think you're doing, making me wait like this? When I think of the anguish you've caused me. ...'

'Luke, are you all right?'

He began climbing up the damaged side of the

fighter and sat down next to the open cockpit. 'Yes. I touched down behind you. I was afraid Artoo and I might miss you.'

'I was afraid you . . .' She stopped, looked down, unable to meet his gaze. 'I apologise, Luke. I made a mistake in trying to land here.'

Luke also looked away, embarrassed. 'Nobody could have foreseen the atmospheric disturbance that forced us down, Leia.'

She looked into the jungle. 'I managed to plot the location of that homing beacon before my instruments went out completely.' She pointed slightly behind them and to her left.

'It's back that way. Once we reach the station we can locate whoever's in charge and arrange for passage off this world.'

'If there's a station,' Luke pointed out mildly, 'or anyone in charge of it.'

'It occurred to me that it might be a fully automated station,' she confessed, 'but I don't know what else we can do.'

'Agreed,' said Luke with a slow sigh. 'We've got nothing to gain by sitting here. I used to believe in miracles. I don't, anymore. We can get eaten just as quickly here as we can on the trail.'

The Princess looked downcast. 'You've encountered carnivorous life, then?'

'No, hardly any life at all, actually. The only animal of any size I confronted,' he went on with a slight grin, 'took one look at me and ran off like a spooked Bantha.' He turned, moved to enter the cockpit. 'Let's get started while it's still light. I'll give you a hand making up a pack.'

Carefully he lowered himself in next to her. As he unlatched her seat he became conscious of the confined space they were working in. Awkwardly pressed up against him, the Princess seemed to take no notice of their proximity. In the dampness, though, her body heat was near palpable to Luke and he had to force himself to keep his attention on what he was doing.

Raising herself from the cockpit, the Princess stood on the nose of the fighter and reached down to him. 'Hand it up, Luke.'

He lifted the burgeoning pack. 'Too heavy?' he asked as he handed it to her. She slid it on to her back, slipped both arms through the straps and adjusted the weight before tightening them.

'The burden of public office was a lot heavier,' she shot back. 'Let's get moving.'

Briskly scrambling over the side, she let herself drop to the ground, planted her feet, took two steps in the direction of the distant beacon . . . and began to sink.

'Luke . . . Threepio . . .'

'Take it easy, Princess.' Edging carefully over the same side, he walked out on the intact wing facing her.

'Luke!' Already she was up to her knees in grey muck. If anything, she was beginning to sink faster.

Trying to anchor himself with his left hand, Luke reached out with his right from the wing edge. 'Lean towards me. Artoo, you lock on to the ship. Threepio, give me your hand.'

She did as she was told, the motion generating squelching sounds from the bog. Her hand flailed for him, smacking the soft ground many centimetres from his.

Rising, he scrambled back to the cockpit and retrieved his walking stick, then returned hurriedly to his prone position on the wing and extended it. 'Lean towards me,' he urged her again. 'Threepio, you and Artoo hold tight or I'll go in with her.'

'Don't worry sir,' Threepio assured him. Artoo added a whistle.

She was up to her waist now. On the first try she missed the pole. The second time her fingers locked around it and were joined by her other hand.

Luke wrapped both hands around his end of the

stick and sat up on the wing, leaning back. His feet slid and scraped on the smooth metal. 'Artoo, Threepio ... pull!'

Having secured a firm grip on her, the earth was reluctant to yield its prize. Every muscle in his body taut, Luke struggled to heave and to conjure the Force simultaneously. He tried to put all of his weight behind his arms, behind his desperate pull.

A tired sucking noise sounded, and the Princess lurched forward. Luke allowed his exhausted arms a brief respite and hyperventilated while he had the chance.

'You can play toy engine later,' the Princess admonished him. 'Pull *now.*'

Momentary anger gave him enough energy to pull her the rest of the way clear. Reaching down, he gave her a hand up and then they were both sitting on the edge of the wing.

Covered from the ribs down in a packing of green-grey mud and pieces of what looked like dried straw, the Princess appeared decidedly unregal. She pushed futilely at the mud, which was drying rapidly to the consistency of thin concrete. She said nothing, and Luke knew anything he might venture would not be terribly well received.

'Come on,' he suggested simply. Taking up his walking stick, he moved to the back side of the wing. Leaning over, he probed at the ground, which displayed no inclination to eat his stick. But still he kept one hand on the wing edge when he stepped off. His feet sank, but only half a centimetre into the spongy loam. Yet the earth here looked no different from the quickclay that had almost taken the Princess.

She dropped down easily beside him and soon they were travelling through intermittent patches of half-familiar vegetation. Branches and bushes blocked tired legs and occasional thorns tore hopefully at them, but Luke's assumption that the ground beneath the taller growths was the firmest held true with gratifying consistency. Even the weighty 'droids didn't sink into the muck.

From time to time as they hiked along, the Princess would dab or push disgustedly at her lower body, which was now solidly caked with the gook she'd slid into. She remained unusually quiet. Luke couldn't tell whether her silence was due to a desire to conserve her strength or embarrassment at her present situation. He tended to think the former. To his knowledge, being embarrassed was not something she was subject to.

Frequently they would pause, turn circles, and then match up pointer alignment on their tracomps to insure they were still marching towards the beacon site.

'Even if it is an automatic station,' he remarked several days later, in an effort to cheer her, 'somebody put it down here and so they have to maintain it. However infrequently. I saw some pretty big ruins near the place we set down. Perhaps natives are still living in them or they might be empty, but the beacon *could* be for the use of a xenoarchaeological research post.'

'That's possible,' she admitted brightly. 'Yes . . . that would also explain why the beacon's not listed. A small scientific outpost could be temporary!'

'And recent,' Luke added, excited by the plausibility of his own supposition. Just talking about such a possibility made him, made them both feel better. 'If that's the case, then even an automated station that's only used on occasion ought to contain an emergency shelter and survival provisions. Heck, there might even be a subspace planetary relay for contacting Circarpous IV when the scientific team is operating here.'

'A cry for help would be a poor way for me to announce my presence,' the Princess observed, brushing at her dark hair. 'Not,' she added quickly, 'that I'm going to be particular. I'll settle for arriving in a medical cocoon.'

They walked on in silence for a while before another

question entered Luke's mind. 'I still wonder, Princess, what caused our instruments to go crazy. That enormous volume of rising free energy we passed through . . . bolts jumping from sky to ship and ship back to sky again . . . I've never seen anything like that before.'

'Nor have I, sir,' commented Threepio. 'I thought I might go mad.'

'Neither have I,' admitted the Princess thoughtfully. 'And I've never read of a natural phenomenon like it. Several colonised gas giants have bigger storms, but never with so much colour. And big thunderheads are always involved. We were above the thick cloud layer when it happened. Still,' she hesitated, 'the whole thing was almost familiar, somehow.' Artoo beeped his agreement.

'You'd think whoever established that homing beacon in this area would also have put a message in the transmission warning ships away from the danger.'

'Yes,' the Princess agreed. 'Hard to imagine a scientific expedition, or any other kind, being that negligent. The omission, it's almost criminal.' She shook her head slowly. 'That effect . . . I can almost remember something like it.' A diffident smile, 'My head's still full of the conference.'

It should be, Luke thought, full of one thing only – making it to that homing beacon and hoping there was more there than just a pile of machinery. What he said was, 'I understand, Princess.'

Not the Force, but a more ancient, more highly developed sense in man half convinced him they were being watched. He found himself turning rapidly to scan the trees and mist behind them and at each side. Nothing looked back at him, but the feeling refused to go away.

Once she spotted him peering hard at a dank copse. 'Nervous?' It was part question, part challenge.

'You bet I'm nervous,' he shot back. 'I'm nervous and frightened and I wish to hell we were on Circarpous right now. *Anywhere* on Circarpous, instead of trudging through this swamp on foot.'

Turning serious, the Princess told him, 'One learns to accept whatever events life has in store with the best possible spirits.' She stared straight ahead.

'That's just what I'm doing,' Luke confessed, 'accepting them in the best possible spirits – nervousness and fear.'

'Well, you needn't look at me as if this is all *my* fault.'

'Did I imply that? Did I say that?' Luke countered, a touch more tightly than he intended. She glanced sharply at him and he cursed his inability to conceal his feelings. He would have been, he decided, a rotten card player. Or politician.

'No, but you as much as . . .' she began hotly.

'Princess,' he interrupted softly, 'we still have a long way to go according to your plotted location. Just because something full of teeth and claws hasn't pounced on us from every tree doesn't mean such creatures don't thrive here. One thing we haven't got is time to fight between ourselves. Besides, responsibility is a dead issue now. It's been superseded by survival. Survive we will, if the Force is with us.'

There was no reply. That in itself was encouraging. They trudged on, Luke stealing admiring glances at her when she wasn't looking. Dishevelled and caked with mud from the waist down, she was still beautiful. He knew she was upset, not at him, but at the possibility they might miss the scheduled conference with the Circarpousian underground.

There's no night so dark as a night filled with fog, and every night on Mimban was like that. They made a bed for themselves between the parted roots of a great tree. While the Princess started a fire, Luke and the 'droids constructed a rain shelter by stretching the two survival capes between both massive roots.

They huddled together for warmth and watched the

night try to slip around the edges of the fire. It crackled reassuringly despite the mist as the night sounds chorused around them. They were no different from day sounds, but anything that wears the cloak of night, especially on an alien world, partakes of the night's mystery and terror.

'Don't worry, sir,' said Threepio. 'Artoo and I will keep watch. We don't require sleep, and there's nothing out there that can ingest us.' Something sounding like a broken pipe gurgled stentorianly in the darkness and Threepio started. Artoo gave a derisive beep, and the two 'droids moved out into the darkness.

'Very funny,' Threepio admonished his companion. 'I hope one of the local carnivores chokes on you and breaks every one of your external sensors.'

Artoo whistled back, sounding unimpressed.

The Princess pressed close against Luke. He tried to comfort her without appearing anxious, but as the darkness closed to a stygian blackness around them and the night sounds turned to sepulchral moans and hootings, his arm instinctively went around her shoulders. She didn't object. It made him feel good to sit there like that, leaning against her and trying to ignore the damp ground beneath.

Something called out with an abyssal shrillness, startling Luke from his sleep. Nothing moved beyond the dying fire. With his free hand he tossed several shards of wood on to the embers and watched the fire blaze again.

Then he happened to glance down at his companion's face. It was not the face of a Princess and a Senator or of a leader of the Rebel Alliance, but instead that of a chilled child. Moistly parted in sleep, her lips seemed to beckon to him. He leaned closer, seeking refuge from the damp green and brown of the swamp in that hypnotic redness.

He hesitated, pulled back. She was an aristocrat and Rebel leader. For all he'd accomplished above Yavin, he was still only a pilot and, before that, a farmer's nephew. Peasant and Princess, he mused disgustedly.

His assignment was to protect her. He wouldn't abuse that trust, no matter what his own hopeless hopes were. He would defend her against anything that leapt out of the darkness, crawled from the slime, dropped from the gnarled branches they walked under. He would do it out of respect and admiration and possibly out of the most powerful of emotions, unrequited love.

He would even defend her from himself, he determined tiredly. In five minutes he was fast asleep. . . .

Any awkwardness was spared by the fact that he awakened first. Removing his arm from her shoulders, he nudged her gently once, twice. With the third nudge she sat straight up, eyes wide and staring with sudden wakefulness. She turned sharply to stare at him. Then the events of the past several days came flooding back to her and she relaxed a little.

'Sorry. I thought I was some place else. I was a little frightened.' She started to rummage through her survival pack, and Luke did the same with his. Threepio offered a cheery 'Good morning.'

While the cloud-masked sun rose somewhere behind them, warming the mist slightly, they shared a meagre breakfast of emergency cube concentrates.

'Whoever created these,' she grimaced in distaste, biting off a small piece of a pink square, 'must have been part machine. They didn't programme anything like taste or flavour into them.'

Luke tried not to let the awful taste he was experiencing show. 'Oh, I don't know. They're designed to keep you alive, not to taste good.'

'Want another one?' She extended a blue square with the consistency of dead sponge. Luke eyed it, half-smiling queasily.

'Not . . . right away. I'm kind of full.' She nodded knowingly, then smiled. He grinned back at her.

The long day never grew truly comfortable, but their suits and the thermal capes kept them warm enough. By late morning it had grown sufficiently hot for them to unhook the capes, fold the thin material into small rectangles, and put them away in suit pockets.

The rare breaks in the mist were never large enough to give them a view of the rising sun, though Threepio and Artoo assured them it was there. It attacked the mist persistently, raising the light level from mere dimness to a kind of enthusiastic twilight.

'We should be getting close to the beacon,' the Princess told them all around midday. Luke wondered how many hours they'd slept. Nights and days would be long on Circarpous/Mimban.

'We have to be prepared to find nothing, Princess. There might not be a beacon station.'

'I know,' she admitted quietly. 'We'll have to search, though. We can walk in an expanding spiral from the place I plotted, and hope.'

A long wall of trees and lesser growth lay ahead. They plunged into it without hesitating, trading ease of passage for secure footing.

'Pardon me, sir.'

Luke looked slightly ahead and to his right. Both robots had paused and See Threepio was leaning against something. 'What is it, Threepio?'

'Your pardon, sir, but this isn't a tree I'm pressing against,' the 'droid said, 'it's metal. I thought the matter worthy enough to bring to your notice. There is a possibility . . .' A loud beep cut him off and he glared down at Artoo. 'Talk too much? What do you mean I talk too much, you factory second!'

'Metal . . . it *is* metal!' The Princess was standing alongside the robots, waiting for Luke to make his way through the brush.

'Artoo, see if you can clear some of this undergrowth away.' The little 'droid activated a small cutting flame and used it to burn a path through the jungle. 'It's a wall . . . it's got to be,' Luke muttered as they walked parallel to the forest-scarred metal surface.

Sure enough, the metal finally ended, and they emerged from the trees into a modestly cleared roadway. It lead into a street paved with packed clay-earth. Buildings lined both sides of the glorified alley, marching resolutely into the swirling fog. Warm yellow glows shone from lights hidden behind tightly sealed windows, illuminating and outlining raised metal sidewalks canopied against the mist and rain.

'Thank the Force,' the Princess murmured.

'First,' Luke began, 'We find a place to get cleaned up. Then . . .' He took a step foward. A hand caught his shoulder, held him back. He eyed Leia curiously. 'What's the matter?'

'Think a minute, Luke,' she urged him softly. 'This is more than just a simple homing beacon site. Much more.' Cautiously, she leaned around the corner of the metal wall, peered down the street. Figures were strolling along the metal walkways now. Others crossed the mist-slicked street. 'It's too substantial for a scientific post, too.'

Luke turned his own attention to the shrouded streets, took in the figures, the crude shape of the structures. 'You're right. It's a big installation. Maybe some company from Circarpous . . .'

'No.' She gestured sharply. 'Look there.'

Two figures were swaying down the centre of the street. They wore armour instead of loose clothing, formed armour of white and black. Armour that was all too familiar.

Both men carried their helmets casually. One dropped his, bent to retrieve it, kicked it accidentally up the street. His companion chided him. Cursing, the clumsy Imperial picked up his helmet, and the two continued on their meandering path.

Luke's eyes had grown as wide as Leia's. 'Imperial

stormtroopers, here. Without the Circarpousians' knowledge, or we'd have heard of it from the underground there.'

She was nodding excitedly. 'If the Circarpousians find out, they'll quit the Empire faster than a bureaucrat can quote forms!'

'And who's going to inform them about the violation?' Luke wanted to know.

'Why, we . . .' The Princess stopped, looked sombre. 'We have two reasons to need help now, Luke.'

'Shsssh,' he whispered. They drew back further into the darkness. A large cluster of men and women appeared around the near corner. They were chatting softly among themselves, but it wasn't their inaudible conversation that intrigued Luke and Leia. They wore unusual clothing, coveralls of some black, reflective material which tucked into matching high boots.

The coveralls rose to end in a cap that fitted over the wearer's head. Some members of the group had their hoods up and fastened, others wore them folded flat against their upper back. Various types of equipment Luke didn't recognise hung and swayed from wide belts.

Evidently the Princess knew what they were. 'Miners,' she informed him, watching as the group moved off down one metal walkway. 'They're wearing mining suits. The Empire's digging something valuable out of this planet, and the Circarpousians don't know a thing about it.'

'How can you be so sure?' Luke inquired.

The Princess sounded positive. 'They'd have their own installation here, and no troops. The Empire obviously doesn't want anyone to know about this.' Artoo whistled soft agreement.

Further conversation was made impossible when the air was suddenly filled with a distant, violent howling. It sounded like a parade of demons tramping along just beneath the surface.

The sound continued for several minutes, then ceased. Realisation transformed the Princess' expression.

'Energy mining!' she explained breathlessly to Luke. 'They're using some big generators here.' A thoughtful pause, then, 'That might account for the atmospheric disturbance which forced us down. I *knew* I'd read about that effect somewhere. A ship has to be specially insulated to drop down through an area where an energy drill is working. By-products, including excess charges, are shunted away skyward.

'But the fallout materials – if this world supports a native race, it's illegal, that kind of mining.'

'Since when,' observed Luke bitterly, 'did legalities ever matter to the Empire?'

'You're right, of course.'

'We can't stand here forever,' he went on. 'First thing we have to do is obtain some substantial food. Those concentrates can keep you alive for only so long without some protein to work with. And,' he added, glancing at her muddy exterior, 'we've got to get cleaned up. We can't attract any attention. Since Yavin and the Death Star we're both well known to Imperial enforcement officials: we'd be taken on sight.'

He studied her pilot's suit, then his own. 'We can't go strolling around town in these. I think we'd better work on stealing a change of clothing.'

'Steal?' the Princess objected, drawing herself up. 'From a possibly honest shopkeeper? If you think for a minute that a former Princess of the royal house of Alderaan, a Senator, is going to resort to—'

'I'll steal them,' Luke said curtly. He leaned around the metal corner. The mist-shrouded street was momentarily deserted and he beckoned for her to follow.

They hugged the walls of the buildings, trying to pass quickly before any lit windows or open doors, slipping furtively from shadow to shadow. Luke hastily examined each storefront in passing. Finally he halted and indicated the sign above a doorway.

'Miner's supplies,' he whispered. 'This is the one we want.' While the Princess watched the walkways, he tried to peer through one dark window. 'Maybe it's a holiday,' he guessed hopefully.

'More likely the only establishments open this time of night sell nothing but intoxicants,' the Princess pointed out prosaically. 'What now?' She looked uncomfortable.

By way of reply Luke led her around the back. The rear entrance he'd hoped for was there. But it was secured, as he'd feared. To complicate matters there was a broad open lane behind the building, from which the jungle and bog had been shunted away. If anyone happened to come walking past, they'd have nowhere to hide.

'Wonderful,' the Princess observed as Luke tried the locked portal. 'How do we get in?' She was indicating the seamless metal door which, no doubt, was locked and controlled from the inside. The back of the building was devoid of windows, possibly to foil intentions such as theirs.

Luke removed the lightsabre from his waist, very slowly adjusting the controls set in the handle.

'What are you going to do, Luke?'

'I don't know how big this town is, but a noisy break-in would attract too much attention. So I'm trying not to be noisy.'

Watching with interest, the Princess took a couple of steps back, looking nervously up and down the alleyway. Any second she expected to see a squad of angry troopers racing around a corner towards her, alerted by some hidden alarm they had unknowingly triggered.

Only jungle sounds reached her, however, as Luke activated his sabre. Instead of the metre-plus shaft of white energy, the pommel put forth a short, needle-thin spoke. With concentratation worthy of a master craftsman, Luke stepped forward and moved the energy beam along the slight space visible between door and frame. A third of the way down the door a distinct click sounded and the door slid obediently aside. Readjusting his sabre, Luke flicked it off and replaced it at his waist.

'Go ahead,' she told him. 'The 'droids and I will keep watch.'

He nodded and vanished inside.

Luke's principal objective was conveniently located close to the back of the store. He spent several minutes scrounging through the racks before he found what he wanted. Taking the well-used clothing, he hurried to the back entrance and tossed the booty to the Princess. Then he stepped just outside the door, reached back in and touched the *Close* stud. He pulled his arm clear as the door slid shut behind him. With luck it might be several weeks before the storekeeper discovered his loss.

Well pleased with himself, Luke steppped down to the ground and began unsnapping his flight suit. He was partly undressed when he paused and noticed the Princess standing and staring at him.

'Come on. We have to hurry.'

She put hands on seal-curve hips, cocked her head to one side and stared meaningfully at him.

'Oh,' he murmured, half-smiling. He turned away and continued undressing. Feeling that nothing had changed behind him, he sneaked a glance, saw the Princess still eyeing him uncomfortably. 'What's wrong, Princess?'

She sounded embarrassed. 'Luke, I like you, and we've known each other for a while, but I'm not sure I can trust you . . . now.'

He grinned. 'You know it won't make any difference if the stormtroopers find us here in our flight suits.' He gestured. 'You can change in the bush.'

Turning away from her, he continued changing his own attire. She looked back at the nearby jungle. Tiny yellow points of light, the eyes of unknown creatures, winked on and off in the bushes. Strange, discomfiting sounds hissed and bleated at her. She sighed, started to slip out of her own flight suit, then paused.

'Well, what are you two staring at?'

'Oh . . . sorry, I . . .' An insistent whistle. 'Yes, you're right, Artoo.' Both 'droids turned away from the Princess.

Shortly, Luke was able to turn and study her approvingly. Her simple, worn suit was a bit snug, but otherwise looked quite natural on her.

'Well?' she asked, obviously not enthralled with her new wardrobe. 'What are *you* staring at?'

'I think maybe something in a print . . .' he began. He had to react quickly to duck the boot she threw at him. It clattered off the metal door.

'Sorry,' he told her, sounding like he meant it as he picked up the boot. Bending over his old suit he began transferring various items from it and from his backpack to the belt pouches of the miner's uniform.

He flipped one small case open carefully and went rapidly through its contents before snapping it shut and slipping it into a pocket. 'I've got enough Imperial currency to last us a while. You?'

She glanced away from him. 'What would a representative of the Alliance be doing with common currency on a diplomatic mission?'

Luke sighed. 'We'll make do, I suppose. How would you like something to eat besides a concentrate?'

She faced him, visibly more cheerful. 'I could eat half a Chou-shou, Luke. Are you sure we ought to though?'

'We have to mingle sometime. As long as we don't look or act like total strangers, no one should bother us.' They started back towards the main street, after burying their packs and flight suits in a syrupy bog.

They were halfway there when the increasing light caused Luke to stop.

'What's the matter?' the Princess asked, worried.

'Two things,' Luke insisted, eyeing her. 'First of all, there's your walk.'

'And what's wrong with my walk?'

'Nothing. That's the trouble.'

Her brows drew together in puzzlement. 'I don't follow you, Luke.'

He explained slowly. 'You're walking like ... like a Princess. Not like a working woman. Slump your shoulders, take some of the confidence and distance out of your stride. Stagger a little. You've got to walk like a tired mineral-grubber, not like one of the Imperial family. And then there's the second thing....'

Reaching out, he tousled her neat hair-do violently.

'Hey!' she objected, struggling. When he stepped back, her hair formed a nebulous maze of undisciplined strands around her head and face, the intricate double-bun she'd worn now completely obliterated.

'That's better,' he observed, 'but there's still something not right.' After a moment, he reached down, picked up a handful of moist earth, then stepped towards her.

'Oh no,' she warned him, putting up both hands defensively and moving backward. 'I've been living in sludge for days. I'm not letting you smear that gunk on me!'

'Have it your way, Leia.' He dropped the dirt and it hit the ground with a loud splat. '*You* do it.'

The Princess hesitated. Then, using spit and hands and a minimum of dirt, she succeded in wiping every trace of make-up from her face and dirtying it as little as possible.

'How's this?' she asked guardedly.

Luke nodded approvingly. 'Much better. You look like someone who's been out in the desert too long without water.'

'Thanks,' she muttered. 'I'm beginning to feel like it, too.'

'It's necessary. I just want to see us get off this world alive.'

'We won't if we don't find that food you mentioned.' He had to hurry to catch up with her as she headed towards the street. . . .

□ III

THEY conversed in whispers as they made their way down the metal walkway towards the better-lit buildings. More and more miners and other figures began to appear, materialising out of the mists.

'The town's beginning to come alive,' Leia murmured. 'They probably run three alternating shifts at the mine. Looks like one is just letting out.'

'I don't know,' Luke confessed, 'but you've got to do something about your walk. Slouch some more.'

She nodded and made an effort to comply. Luke tried not to stare at passing faces, afraid one might be staring back at them.

'You're still too tense. Relax. There, that's better.'

They stopped before a reasonably quiet, fairly well maintained structure that advertised itself as a tavern.

'It *looks* peaceful enough.' He turned. 'Threepio, you and Artoo wait out here. No sense asking for trouble. Find a dark corner somewhere and stay quiet until we come back.'

'You don't have to urge me, Master Luke,' the tall golden 'droid exclaimed fervently. 'Come on, Artoo.' Both 'droids headed for a narrow passageway between the tavern and its neighbouring building.

'What do you think, Princess? Should we take a chance?'

'I'm starving . . . we've wasted enough time.' She put a hand over the door switch. Immediately the double doors slid apart.

Lights and noise and talk in overwhelming quantities assailed them instantly. Having exposed themselves, they had no choice but to enter, as casually as they could manage.

Low booths filled with hectic humanity honeycombed the tavern interior. The miasma of narcotic incense and other smokes nearly asphyxiated Luke, and he had to struggle not to cough.

'What's wrong?' The Princess looked worried, though unaffected by the decadent atmosphere. 'People are looking at you.'

'It's . . . the air,' he explained, fighting to breathe normally. 'There's something in it. A whole bunch of something.'

The Princess chuckled. 'Too much for you, fighter pilot?'

Luke wasn't ashamed to admit it. When he could spare the wind for talk again, he told her, 'Basically, I'm a country boy, Leia. I haven't had too much exposure to sophisticated entertainments.'

She sniffed the air appraisingly. 'I wouldn't call these scents sophisticated. Thick, yes, but not sophisticated.'

Somewhere near the centre of the human whirlpool they miraculously came upon an empty table. The Princess concentrated intently on the tabletop when the human waiter approached them. She needn't have worried. He didn't give them a glance.

'Your pleasure?' he inquired simply, distantly. The man smoked something on the job, Luke noted.

'What's best tonight?' he asked the man, striving to sound like someone who'd just spent ten hours in the bowels of the earth.

'Kommerken steak, flank cut; and ootoowergs . . . usual supplements.'

'For two,' Luke told him, keeping conversation to a minimum.

That appeared to suit the attendant fine. 'Got it,' he replied with equal perfunctoriness, and waded off into the mob.

'He didn't ask any questions,' the Princess murmured excitedly, looking back up at Luke.

'No. This might be easier than I thought.' He was beginning to feel something like hope.

Then his expression darkened.

'What is it, Luke?' He gestured, and she turned to look towards the bar.

A large, hulking miner was being feebly assailed by something human-sized, skinny, and covered completely with light green fur. It had wide, nocturnal eyes and a crest of higher, darker fur running from the crown of its head down the middle of its back. A simply worked skin of some unknown animal was wrapped about its pelvic region and several jangling necklaces adorned with primitive decorations swung from the neck.

Presently the creature began making mewing, begging noises in a high, rippling voice. The alien singsong was coated with an unmistakable hint of desperation.

'Vease, sir,' it begged, 'smav drink? Vickerman, vickerman?'

The big miner met this pitiful request by putting out a broad foot and kicking the native in the face. Luke winced and looked away. The Princess glanced at him.

'What's wrong, Luke?'

'I can't stand to see anything abused like that,' he muttered. 'Human or animal or alien.' He faced her curiously. 'How can you watch it?'

'I saw my whole world, several million people, destroyed,' she responded with chilling matter-of-factness. 'Nothing mankind does surprises me any more, except that anyone could still be surprised by it.' She turned her clinical gaze back to the scene at the bar.

'Bootop!' the miner bellowed at the aborigine, while his companions chortled among themselves. 'Bootop, yes?'

Its head twitching in what seemed to be an unnatural action, the whining, pleading alien stared up at the man, wiping the blood from its face. 'Vickerman, vickerman?'

'Yeah, vickerman,' the miner admitted, tiring of the game a little. 'Bootop.'

Without further prompting the native dropped on its belly. An unexpectedly long, snake-like tongue darted out and began to lick the grime and mud from the man's boots.

'I'm going to be sick,' Luke whispered, barely audible. The Princess merely shrugged.

'We have our devils and our angels, Luke. You have to be ready to handle both.'

When she looked back to the bar the native had finished its demeaning task and was holding up cupped hands anxiously. 'Tend vickerman, now, now?'

'Yeah, sure,' the miner said. Reaching on to the bar he picked up an oddly formed bottle and touched a button on its side. Part of the bottle's upper section filled with a dark liquid. It stopped filling with a click.

Turning to face the expectant native, the miner tilted the bottle over, spilling the thick red liquor on to the floor instead of in the cupped hands. While the men and women at the bar enjoyed their final laugh at the poor creature's expense, it dropped to a prone position and that amazing tongue flicked in and out like a frog's, to lap up the liquor before it retreated into cracks and depressions in the floor.

Unable to watch further, Luke let his curious gaze wander around the large, smoke-filled chamber. Now he saw more of the green-furred bipeds moving about. Many were begging with an air of frantic hopefulness, others engaged in performing some menial task.

'I don't recognise this race.'

'Neither do I,' the Princess admitted. 'They must be native to this world. The Empire isn't noted for the gentleness with which it treats non-allied aborigines.'

Luke was about to comment, but she made a quieting gesture. The attendant had arrived with their food.

The meat had a peculiar colour, the vegetables more so. But everything was hot and of good flavour. Three spigots emerged flower-like from the centre of their table. Filling his glass from one, he sampled the contents expectantly. 'Not bad.'

Meanwhile the Princess tasted her meat gingerly. Her mouth wrinkled as she chewed, swallowed. 'Not what I'd order if I had a choice . . .'

'We don't,' Luke pointed out.

'No . . . we don't. We . . .' She stopped, staring, and Luke turned to look behind him.

The attendant was still standing there, watching her. As soon as he noticed her looking back at him, he turned and walked away.

'You think he suspects?' she murmured worriedly.

'How could he? Your clothes are right, even I wouldn't recognise you.'

Partly reassured, Leia bent over her plate and resumed eating.

'Look, over there,' she said. Luke turned, glanced furtively in the indicated direction.

The attendant was talking with a tall, urbane man dressed in the uniform of an Imperial civil servant.

'They do suspect!' she whispered tightly. She started to stand. 'I've had enough, Luke. Let's get out of here.'

'We can't rush off, especially if we're being watched,' he countered. 'Don't panic, Princess.'

'I said I'm leaving, Luke.' Nervous, she started to turn and leave.

Without realising what he was doing, he reached out, slapped her hard across the face, and as heads turned in their direction said loudly, 'No favours for you until *I'm* finished eating!'

One hand went to her burning cheek. Wide-eyed and voiceless, the Princess slowly sat back down. Luke frantically attacked his steak as the uniformed Imperial sauntered over to them, backed by the attendant at a discreet distance.

'If there's some trouble . . .' he began.

'No, no trouble,' Luke assured him, forcing a smile. The man didn't leave. 'Can I help you, maybe?'

'Not you. It's clear what you are, miner.' The bureaucrat's oily gaze shifted to Leia. 'I'm more curious about your companion here.' Leia didn't look up at him.

'Why?' Luke wondered cheerfully. 'What's the problem?'

'Well, she dresses a little like a miner,' the man said, 'but as Elarles here,' and he indicated the attendant, 'noted, her hands would seem to indicate some other profession.'

With a start, Luke also noticed the Princess' hands: soft, pale, uncalloused, clearly the hands of anyone but a manual worker. Luke's years on his uncle's farm had equipped his body, including his hands, to play the role of simple miner, but Princess Organa had probably spent her time handling only booktapes, never an excavator or pitter.

He thought furiously. 'No, she's . . . uh, I bought her.' Leia twitched, stared at him a moment before returning resolutely to her food. 'Yes, she's a servant of mine. Spent all my earnings on her.' He tried to sound indifferent, shrugged as he returned to his eating. 'She's not much, of course.' Her shoulders shook. 'But she was the best I could afford. And she's kind of amusing to have around, though she tends to get out of line at times and I have to slap her down.'

The bureaucrat nodded understandingly, smiled for the first time. 'I sympathise, young man. Sorry to interrupt your meal.'

'No bother,' Luke called as the man returned to his own table.

The Princess glared up at him. 'You enjoyed that, didn't you?'

'No, of course not. I had to do it, to save us.'

She rubbed her cheek. 'And that servant-girl story?'

'It was the first logical thing I could think of,' he insisted. 'Besides, it explains you as well as anything could.' He sounded pleased. 'No one will question you once the word gets around.'

'Gets around?' She rose. 'If you think, Luke Skywalker, that I'm going to act as your servant until—'

'Hey, honey . . . you okay?' a new voice inquired. Luke looked at the old woman who'd appeared next to the Princess. Placing a firm hand on the Princess's shoulder, she exerted a gentle but unyielding pressure. Still slightly stunned, the Princess sat down slowly.

Luke eyed the woman warily as she pulled a chair up to their table. 'We haven't met. And I don't remember inviting you to join us. So if you'll just leave my servant and me alone.'

'Oh, I wouldn't bother you two, boy,' the woman insisted in a tone suggesting subtly that she knew something they didn't. She jerked her head towards the Princess.

'Ain't surprised we haven't met before. You two are strangers here, ain't you?'

That statement seemed to snap the Princess out of her paralysis. She gave the old woman a startled stare, then looked away . . . anywhere but at those knowing, accusing eyes.

'What makes you say a ridiculous thing like that?' Luke stammered.

She leaned conspiratorially close. 'Old Halla has a pretty good eye for faces. You're not residents of this town and I ain't seen you in none of the other four. Sick and decrepit as this world is, I know all the sickies and decrepits inhabiting it. You're new to me.'

'We . . . we came in on the last ship,' Luke alibied blindly.

She grinned at him, unimpressed. 'Did you now? Tryin' to fool old Halla, ain't you? No, don't look so frightened, boy and girl. Your face is turnin' white as the inside of a trooper's belly. So you're strangers ... That's good, good. I need strangers. I need you to help me.'

The Princess swerved to stare wonderingly at her. '*You* want us to help *you*?'

'Surprised, ain't you?' Halla cackled.

'Help you do what?' Luke queried in confusion.

'Just help,' she said, casually cryptic. 'You help me, I help you. And I know you need help, because there are no strangers on this world, and yet you're here. Want to know how I know you're strangers?' She leaned over the table again and wagged a knowing finger at Luke.

'Because, young man, the Force is strong within you.'

Luke smiled sickly at her. 'The Force is a superstition, a myth people swear by. It's used to frighten children.'

'Is that so?' Halla sat back and folded her arms in satisfaction. 'Well then, boy, the superstition is strong in you. Much stronger than in anyone else I've met on this forsaken scoop of mud.'

Abruptly, Luke was peering closer at her. 'What is it, Luke?' the Princess asked, seeing the expression that had come over his face. He ignored her.

'You said your name was Halla.' The woman nodded slowly, once. 'You have a little of the Force about you, too.'

'More than a little, sapling,' she argued indignantly. 'I am a master of the Force, a master!'

Luke said nothing. 'You want proof, then?' she went on. 'Watch!'

Concentrating hard on a spice shaker in the middle of the table, under one of the spigots, she made it quiver slightly. It bounced once against the table, twice, and moved several centimetres to its left. Sitting back, Halla took a deep breath and wiped the sweat from her brow.

'There, you see? *A little of the Force,* indeed!'

'I'm convinced,' Luke confessed, with a curious look towards the curious Princess, a look that said he was anything but impressed by such parlour tricks. 'You do have a lot of the Force about you.'

'I can do other things when I want to, too,' Halla announced proudly. 'Two manipulators of the Force ... we're destined to join hands, eh?'

'I'm not so sure ...' the Princess began.

'Don't worry about me, little pretty,' Halla instructed her. She reached out to touch the Princess's hand. Leia drew hers away uncertainly. Halla studied her, smiled, grabbed the wrist hard.

'You think I'm crazy, don't you? You think old Halla's crazy.'

The Princess shook her head. 'No ... I didn't say that. I never said that.'

'Eh, but you thought it, didn't you?' When Leia didn't reply, Halla shrugged. If she was offended, she didn't show it. 'No matter, no matter.' She let go of the Princess's wrist and Leia drew it away slowly, rubbing it with her other hand.

'Why do you want to help us?' Luke inquired firmly. 'Assuming just for the sake of discussion that we need any help and that your guesses are right.'

'Just for the sake of discussion, boy,' she mimicked him, 'I'll get to that. Tell me what you need from me.'

'Now look, old woman,' Luke began threateningly.

She wasn't intimidated. 'It won't work with me, swaddle-clothes. You don't want it widely advertised that you're strangers here, do you?' Her voice rose slightly with the last, and Luke made shushing motions at her, glancing around to see if anyone had overheard.

'Okay. Since you know we're strangers, you know what we need. We have to get off this planet.' The Princess gave him a warning look, but he shook it off.

'No, relax. She does have the Force about her.' He

turned back to face the oldster. 'Who are you, anyway?'

'Just old Halla,' the woman declared blankly. 'And you just want to get off Mimban. You didn't pick me a simple one, did you?' She frowned slyly. 'Say, how did you two get here, anyways? You can't convince me you came on the regular supply ship.'

'Regular supply ship?' Leia exclaimed. 'You mean Circarpous knows about this installation?"

'Now, woman, did I say where the transport was from?' Halla snorted derisively. 'The Circarpousians . . . those provincials! This place is right in their backyard and they don't know about it. No, the Imperial government operates the mine and the towns direct.'

'We suspected as much,' Luke admitted.

'They monitor space out for many planetary diameters,' Halla went on. 'The Circarpousians have a pretty good colony going on Ten. If a ship passes anywhere close by, they shut down everything. The mine, the landing beacon, everything.'

'I think I see why they didn't detect us,' Luke ventured. Leia put out a restraining hand, looked at him warningly. He shook her off. 'Either we trust Halla or we don't. She already suspects enough to turn us over to the local enforcers anytime she wants to.'

He looked openly at the old woman. 'We were travelling from Circarpous X to Four on business.'

'You were coming from the Rebel base on Fourteen, you mean,' Halla corrected him smugly. 'So much for trust.' When Luke choked on his reply, she waved it away. 'Never mind, boy. The only government I recognise is my own. If I wanted to sell out the Rebels, do you think that base'd still be there?'

Luke forced himself to relax, smiled at her. 'We were travelling in a pair of single-seat fighters. If the instrumentation here is standard, it's not calibrated to recognise anything that small. That must be why there's been no alarm raised. We got down undetected.'

'Where are your two ships?' Halla asked with concern. 'If they're nearby, they might be found soon.'

Luke made an indifferent gesture in a generally northeast direction. 'Out there, somewhere, several days' walking. That's if the muck that passes for ground here hasn't swallowed them up by now.'

Halla gave a gratified snort. 'Good! People don't stray very far from the towns. Not likely they'll be discovered. How did you manage to land without the field and beacon?'

'Land!' the Princess snapped. 'That's funny. We ran into some kind of field-distortion effect, produced by the energy mining, I'll bet. It wiped out our on-board instrumentation. I'd expect a ship needs special shielding to pass through an atmosphere affected by that kind of waste energy. It's a damn good thing we did, though, or we would have set down right on the Imperials' field,' she finished.

'You see, Halla,' Luke explained. 'You have to help us arrange off-world passage.'

'Next to impossible, boy. Think of something else. You're here illegal, without proper identification. The moment anyone asks you to produce it and you can't, they'll dump you in the local lock-tight for questioning. The local head is a mind-ugly-ug named Grammel.' She looked at each of them in turn, solemn. 'A good man to avoid.'

'All right,' Luke agreed easily, 'then if we can't leave through normal channels, you'll have to help us steal a ship.'

For the first time since she'd joined them, Halla sat speechless. 'Anything else you'd like, boy?' she finally wondered. 'Grammel's cloak of office, or maybe the Emperor's Dualities? Steal a ship? You've got to be out of your mind, boy.'

'We're in sound company, then,' the Princess observed with satisfaction.

Halla turned on her. 'I've had just about enough of you, little pretty. I'm not sure I need *your* help.'

'Do you have any idea who I am?' the Princess started to tell her. She caught herself just in time. 'Not that it matters. What does matter is that you can't do it, can you?'

Halla started to object but the Princess cut her off challengingly. '*Can* you?'

'It's not that I can't, little pretty,' Halla said carefully. 'It's that the risks involved to make it worthwhile . . .' She went quiet, finally looked up reluctantly at Luke. 'All right, boy and lady. I'll help you steal your ship.'

Luke looked excitedly over at the Princess, who continued to watch Halla. 'On that one condition.'

The Princess nodded knowingly. 'What condition?' she inquired formally.

'You help me first.'

'I don't see that we have much choice,' Luke essayed. 'What do you need us to help you with?'

'To find something,' Halla began. 'With your knowledge of the Force combined with mine, boy, it should be simple. But it's something I can't do alone, and something I can't trust anybody else with. I know I can trust you, because if you try to cross me, I'll sell you to Grammel.'

'Sensible,' the Princess noted easily. 'You say the task will be simple. What are we supposed to find?'

Halla looked around the table with seriocomic intensity before turning back to them. 'I don't suppose either of you children have ever heard of the Kaiburr crystal?'

'Right so far,' Leia admitted, unimpressed.

'Your ignorance ain't surprising,' Halla explained. 'Only a few people familiar with the exploration of Mimban have heard of it, Circarpousian xeno-archaeologists first heard about it on their one and only exploration expedition to this planet. They eventually decided it was a myth, a local tall story concocted by the natives in an attempt to coax more liquor from them. Mostly they forgot about it. But it was in the Imperial records when the mining outfit set up their hole here.

'According to the myth, the crystal is located in the temple of Pomojema. It's a minor local deity, say the greenies I've talked with.'

'All sounds plausible,' Luke was willing to concede. 'Where's the temple?'

'A long haul from here, again according to the native information I've been able to piece together,' Halla went on. 'This world is rotten with temples. And remember, this Pomojema's a third-rate god. So nobody's been too interested in finding his templehouse.'

'Temples, god, crystals,' the Princess murmured. 'Okay, suppose this legendary place does exist,' she hypothesised, jabbing an accusing finger at Halla. 'This Kaiburr crystal, just what is it supposed to be . . . a big gemstone of some kind?'

'Of some kind,' Halla confessed with that sly smile of hers. 'Interested in spite of yourself, ain't you?' The Princess looked away.

'We're interested in anything that brings us closer to getting off here,' Luke admitted. 'I have to say this story of the crystal sounds intriguing on its own. What kind of gem is it?'

'Pfagh! I could care less what kind of necklace it could make for some spoiled noblewoman, boy.' She eyed the Princess meaningfully before continuing. 'I'm more interested in a certain property it's supposed to have.'

'More stories,' the Princess murmured. 'How can you be so absolutely convinced, Halla? So certain that the xenoarchaeologists weren't right and that it's all a native tale?'

'Because,' Halla returned triumphantly, 'I have proof!' Reaching into her suit top, she extricated a packet of insulating material and unrolled it on the table. It contained a tiny metal box. Using the nail of her right-hand little finger she turned the minature combination lock several times. With an infinitesimal pop the tiny lid flipped open.

Luke peered close for a good look. The Princess did the same.

What they saw was a splinter of something that looked like red glass and glowed softly. The colour was deeper, richer than red, corundum. It had a vitreous lustre resembling crystallised honey.

'Well,' Halla asked them after a long moment, 'now are you convinced I'm telling the truth?'

Still sceptical, the Princess sat back and looked askance at Halla. 'A small fragment of radiant glass or plastic, or an ordinary silicate treated to glow. You expect me to accept that as proof?'

'This is a piece of the Kaiburr crystal itself!' Halla insisted offended by her disbelief.

'Sure it is,' the Princess agreed, nodding. 'Where did you get it?'

'From a greenie, in exchange for a bottle of tipples.'

Leia gave her a strained look. 'So you're trying to tell us that one of the primitive, superstitious locals would part with a shard of some half-legendary gem, from one of his own temples, for a lousy bottle of liquor?'

'It wasn't *his* ancestor's temple or god,' Halla countered with mild contempt. 'Even if it was, it wouldn't matter. Look at the pitiful things.' She gestured, and they saw the degraded, crawling beggars pleading with patrons for a chance to perform the most servile acts in return for a sip of alcohol.

'They'll do anything short of killing themselves for a drink. Perform the most menial jobs for days for a tenth of a bottle.'

'Maybe you're right,' Leia had to admit uncomfortably. 'Just maybe this could be a piece of what you claim it to be from where you say it came from. I still don't see why you have this drive to go hunting for it, especially if you insist its jewel potential doesn't interest you.'

'Still can't see, can you?' Halla murmured. She turned sharply to face Luke. 'Touch it, boy.'

Luke hesitated, his gaze moving from the Princess to Halla and back again. Halla removed it from the box and extended it towards him in a cupped hand.

'See, it's not hot,' she told him. 'Go on, touch it and believe. Are you afraid?' Luke continued to hesitate.

'I'll touch it,' the Princess volunteered, extending a finger. But Halla pulled it of her reach.

'No. This isn't for you. Touching it would prove nothing to you.' She reached out towards Luke again. 'Go on, boy. It won't hurt you.'

Licking his lower lip, Luke cautiously probed for the splinter with a finger. Touched it.

It felt exactly like what it resembled, a piece of glowing heatless glass. But the sensations that coursed through him did not come from his finger, were not carried by the nerves in his skin. He quickly drew back his arm as if he'd contacted a live current.

'Luke, what is it?' the Princess exclaimed, suddenly concerned. She stared accusingly at Halla. 'You've hurt him!'

'No, little pretty mouth, I haven't hurt him. He has been startled and shocked and surprised, much as I was when I first contacted the crystal.'

Leia faced Luke. 'What did you feel?'

'I ... didn't *feel* anything,' he informed her softly, now utterly convinced of the old woman's sincerity. 'I experienced it. This,' and he indicated the fragment of red mineral, 'increases one's perception of the Force. It magnifies and clarifies ... in proportion to its size and density, I think.' He gazed hard at Halla. 'Anyone in possession of the entire crystal, if it's much larger than this fragment, would have such a lock on the Force that he could do almost anything, anything at all.'

'My thought also, boy,' Halla agreed. She replaced the fragment in its box and snapped the lid shut, then re-rolled it in the soft material. She handed it to Luke. 'To show you I mean what I say, you keep it. Go, take it.' Luke did so, then slipped it into a pocket.

'And now, I think,' she went on, 'you have no choice but to help me, and without delay.'

'Who says so?' the Princess grumbled.

'No one says so, little pretty. Facts say so. By touching the fragment, Luke here set up a tiny but perceptible stirring in the Force. I felt it. It might have affected sensitives halfway across the galaxy. There are Force-sensitives in the Imperial government who might feel such a stirring.

'However,' she continued with a shrug, 'as I said, the sensation might have gone no farther than myself. But can you take that chance, Luke? If you're both with the Alliance, as I'm pretty sure by now you are, then the Imperials should be real interested in Luke here. From what I hear, they don't like to think of there being anyone on the Rebel side capable of handling the Force.

'Besides, boy, you know what kind of damage a Force master could do with the entire crystal in his hands. Can you take a chance on the Empire finding it first?' She looked almost apologetic. 'Sorry, but I had to do something to shove you both past the no-return point. Couldn't risk having my first really secure helpers back out on me, could I?'

'She's right, Leia,' Luke told his companion. 'We can't take the chance of having the crystal fall into Imperial hands.'

'If you're right, Luke . . .'

'Besides, Leia we have no choice. We need Halla to help us get off-planet, and she won't do that until we find the crystal anyway.' He eyed her hopefully. 'All right?'

'My, my, what's this? A miner asking permission from his servant girl?' Neither of them could meet her shrewd gaze. 'Take it easy, children. I won't give you away, whoever you are.' She glanced around. 'This isn't the most private place to do business. Now, if you're finished with your supper, we'd do well to talk elsewhere.'

Luke nodded. 'It's about time we reassured Artoo and Threepio.'

'Just a minute.' Halla put out a restraining hand. 'I thought there were only the two of you.'

Luke grinned. 'Two 'droids I acquired . . . inherited, you might say.'

'Oh, that's all right, then. Never could afford a personal 'droid myself.'

While paying their bill, Luke sneaked a glance in the direction of the Imperial civil servant. The man evidenced no further interest in them, didn't even look in their direction. The servant-girl story had apparently convinced him.

Once outside with the double metal door panels shut behind them, Leia kicked Luke sharply in the shins. He went staggering, tumbled off the narrow walkway into the mud-filled trench which separated walkway from more solid street. When he recovered his senses, he gazed at her in surprise.

'Now you look more like a miner,' she grinned at him. 'That's for slapping me inside. No hard feelings?'

Luke shook some of the mud from his hands, wiped at his chest, then smiled at her. 'No hard feelings, Leia.' He reached up, extended a hand. The Princess leaned forward, her left hand gripping a supporting post, her right extended to help Luke.

Her caution didn't matter. Luke yanked hard, and she plunged messily into the trench beside him. He sat there, grinning, as she turned around, looked down at herself in distress.

'Look at me! Look what you've done to me!'

'Made you look a little more like a servant girl,' he replied easily. 'Can't be too careful here, you know.'

'Well, in that case . . .' Luke ducked the first handful of gook she heaved in his direction, caught part of the second and grappled with her.

Halla was watching, amused, until several large men came out of the tavern behind her. They paused, their attention also drawn by the wrestling match in the mud. They were all just drunk enough to be dangerous and the longer they watched, the quieter they became.

Much too quiet to suit Halla . . .

□ IV

'FOR our souls and health,' she muttered hastily to the two combatants, 'stop it, you two!'

Encased in mud, neither Luke nor the Princess heard Halla's anxiously whispered warning.

One of the men leaned to his right, spat something out between his beard and commented, 'Servant's not supposed to fight back, boys.'

'Doesn't seem proper somehow,' his companion agreed.

'Besides,' the first man added, 'fightin' in public's against the town decrees, ain't it?'

'That's right,' another man concurred. 'Maybe we can straighten 'em out before the night troop takes 'em in. Be doin' 'em a good turn.' He called down to Luke. 'Hang in there, young fella. We won't let her hurt you.'

Grinning and chuckling among themselves, the five stepped down off the walkway. Finding herself providently ignored by all concerned, Halla slipped back into the shadows.

'Is there anything we can do, madam?' a voice said into her ear. She jumped. Threepio jumped.

'You've no right scaring me like that, you refugee from a scrap shop!'

'I apologise, but my master and the lady . . .'

'Oh. Are you Threepio?' The 'droid nodded slightly. 'And this must be Artoo.' A beep sounded from a dim shape nearby. 'We can't do anything yet, I'm afraid.' She peered back out into the street. 'Maybe those bulk-boys are just teasing.'

Two of the men pulled Leia off Luke. That provided

them with a good glimpse of her for the first time. Their initial amusement abruptly shifted as less pleasant emotions surfaced.

'Well now,' murmured a barrel-chested individual with a Manchu moustache, 'This is no 'droid servant, that's for sure.'

Leila became aware of the miners' stares. Several buckles and straps on the tight-fitting clothes had come undone while she'd been wrestling with Luke. Despite the coating of mud over them, their exposed areas were drawing an uncomfortable amount of attention. She felt as if something was crawling all over her under her clothing.

Ignoring the mud and trying to draw the loose ends of her attire together, she drew herself up regally, announced with shaky dignity, 'Thank you very much. This is a private matter. Now, if you'll all be so kind as to leave us to settle our differences.'

'*Thank you very much, this is a private matter,*' one of the men echoed in a mincing tone. The others guffawed. The one with the beard leered down at her.

'You're not a registered citizen, lady-love.' He indicated her shoulder. 'No name tag, nothing. Fighting in a public street's against the law. Mine law says we got to apprehend anyone breaking the law when and where we can. C'mere and lemme apprehend you.' He reached out a massive paw.

Backing up a quick step, the Princess continued to glare at them, but her confidence was seeping away like snow on a stove.

'I can't tell you who I am, but if any of you put a hand on me, you'll answer for it.'

Barrel-chest moved closer. There was no humour in his voice and he did not smile at her. 'Little mudhen, I'll put more than a hand on you. . . .'

A slim form interposed itself between the Princess and her would-be apprehender. 'Look, this is a private argument and we can finish it ourselves, friend.'

'I ain't your friend, sonny,' the man said evenly, putting out a hand and shoving Luke backward. 'Stay out of this. Your argument ain't important any more.'

The Princess let out a startled exclamation. One of the other men had slipped up behind her and had grabbed her around the chest with his left arm. Luke stepped over quickly, brought the edge of his palm down hard on the other's wrist. Letting out a hurt yelp, the miner stepped back, holding his wrist.

It had grown deadly silent on the street. All eyes were focused on Luke now, not on the Princess. The only sounds in the mist came from the distant jungle.

'Sonny boy wants to play,' snickered the man whose wrist Luke had clipped. 'Resistin' public apprehension.' He flicked his right forearm. There was a clicking sound and a double-bladed stiletto slid out from under his coverall sleeve. The flat of the blades lay flush against the back of his fist. Faded light from the shielded tavern windows reflected ominously off both blades as the man started moving in a low crouch towards Luke.

The Princess said nothing, just stared. So did Halla, Threepio, and Artoo from the safety of the shadows.

'Come on, sonny,' the man urged, gesturing with his unarmed hand for Luke to approach. Then he flicked the weapon, and twin blades flashed out of his empty sleeve. He kicked his right leg, then his left. Double blades protruded from each boot sole. 'Come on, let's dance. I'll make it last.'

Trying to watch all eight blades at once, Luke tried to distract his attacker. 'The lady and I were discussing something. We don't need any outside involvement.'

'Too late, sonny,' the man grinned. 'You and I are involved, now.' His companions were watching and chuckling, occasionally nudging one another. They were obviously enjoying every second of the action.

Jumping forward, the knife-wielder swung at Luke with his left hand, followed up the miss as Luke moved back with a spinning side kick, then swung around in an arc, reaching with his right hand. The double blades made *whooshing* sounds in the thick, damp night air.

'We don't want any trouble,' Luke declared, his hand moving reluctantly to the pommel of his lightsabre.

'In a couple of minutes you won't have to worry about it,' his assailant assured him. He dived with a yell towards Luke, who dodged both kicks and arm swings agilely.

'Look out, Luke!' the Princess shouted ... too late. One of the other men had come up behind Luke and now pinned both arms to his sides. The knife-wielder was approaching leisurely, the smile gone from his face, making entwining motions with his fists. The blades gleamed like his eyes.

'Fancy dancer, ain't you, boy? I'm tired of chasing you.'

'Do him slow, Jake,' one of the onlookers advised. 'Wise mouth kid.'

'I said,' Luke began, keeping his eyes on those nearing, weaving blades even as his right hand moved to his waist again, 'we don't want any trouble.' He pushed the stud on the hilt of the sabre.

Activated, the backward-pointing, meter-long beam of blue energy materialized, straight through the right thigh of the man who was holding him. Howling, the man let go of Luke and dropped to the ground, clutching at his leg.

Knife-wielder froze for a moment, then started forward. With the sabre, Luke described an intricate series of interweaving arcs and circles in the near darkness that caused his attacker to hesitate. A steady moaning came from the man on the ground.

Luke lunged at the knife artist, just enough to make him retreat. 'All of you, now ... clear off.'

Instead of clearing off, the grim-faced quartet exposed more blades and other hand weapons. They began manoeuvring to encircle Luke, staying just out of range of that darting, lethal beam of light.

Leia evened up the odds by leaping on the back of the man nearest her and clawing at his face. The three remaining men continued to probe at Luke with their own weapons, testing his speed and reflexes with professional acumen, talking among themselves and comparing notes on Luke's abilities while planning the best way to take him. If they were waiting for their fourth companion to join them, they'd be disappointed. He had his hands full with the Princess, who was cursing them at the top of her lungs.

Halla was looking on anxiously when movement further up the street drew her attention from the fight. A knot of efficient figures clad in black and white armour was moving at a fast trot towards the tavern. From the approaching Imperials she looked back to the stalemated battle.

One man lunged at Luke from behind. Luke jumped above the charged prod the man was wielding and swung downward simultaneously. Off came a hand, cut and cauterised neatly at the wrist, to land in the mud and lie there smoking slightly. The man fell backward, speechless, staring at his carbonised stump.

The troopers were close now. Halla left her hiding place and, gesturing for Artoo and Threepio to follow, slunk off down the accessway between the buildings, vanishing into the night. After a second's pause to see they could do no good by getting themselves captured, the two 'droids followed.

Both remaining assailants continued to stalk Luke, more cautiously now. Having despatched her single opponent with judicious pressure in the right place, the Princess was looking to take on another when something sun-bright and loud exploded in their midst, stunning everyone. They all turned, blinking against the lingering glare, to see a number of energy rifles focussed on them.

'Put up your weapons,' the sergeant in charge ordered them sharply, the angular markings on his armoured sleeve showing triple in the dim light. Matching marks crossed his helmet. 'You are remanded to custody, in the name of the Emperor, for fighting with weaponry in a public place.'

As soon as the miners had retracted or otherwise holstered their various weapons, Luke shut off his sabre. Two troopers came around and collected the small arsenal. The Princess noticed her one victim recovering consciousness and kicked him soundly.

'You there, stop that!' the sergeant ordered.

'Sorry,' she replied sweetly.

They were marched through the town under armed convoy. Luke took the opportunity to study the surrounding structures. Few showed much difference from those they'd already encountered. In a town like this, interchangeability was an economic necessity, he reflected.

Those inhabitants who encountered them pressed close to the walls of the buildings and whispered among themselves, pointing from time to time at the unlucky miscreants. The spectators obviously had some idea what was in store for them.

Luke wished he did, too.

'Where do you suppose they're taking us?' he murmured to the Princess.

'To the local jail, where else?'

Luke nodded forward. 'If that's it, I'm impressed.'

They were approaching a massive, forbidding ziggurat of ancient Mimbanian architecture. It was constructed of grey and black stone, exactly like the ruins Luke had spotted when searching for the Princess's ship. The edifice towered, despite its roughly tapering shape, over the more recent, simpler structures of the mining town.

'Not your average lockup,' he commented softly as they strode under the thick stone arch over the entrance. Boldly, he queried the trooper next to him. 'What is this place?'

The helmeted soldier turned to him with, 'Prisoners and violators of the law are to provide answers, not questions.'

Surprisingly, as they moved down a stone corridor lined with modern tubing and electronic componentry, the trooper volunteered some information. 'This is one of the old temples built by the natives of this world.'

Luke's surprise was genuine. 'You mean, those pitiful wretches who beg for drinks?'

Unexpectedly, the man laughed. 'Good, you've got a sense of humour. You'll need it. Greenies, building *this?* You must spend all your time in the mines. Not me.' The trooper swelled with self-importance. 'I'm always trying to improve myself. As you know,' he began, 'there are several semi-intelligent races on this world, besides the greenies. Some are more degenerate than the others. Whatever race built these places,' and he gestured with his rifle at the stone roof arching overhead, 'has long since died out. At least, insofar as the Imperial survey has been able to determine.' They turned another corner and Luke marvelled at the size of the structure.

'This one's been converted to house the mine offices and Imperial headquarters for Mimban.' He shook his head. 'You miners, you don't know much of anything except your own work.'

'That's true,' Luke admitted, feeling no remorse at damning all miners. They hadn't been particularly hospitable to him since he'd landed in their company. 'We're from another town,' he added for good measure.

The trooper's brief venture into camaraderie vanished and he replied coldly. 'That may or may not be. You chronic brawlers lie a lot. Just because the Empire tolerates a limited amount of disorder here as a safety valve for you people is no reason to abuse the privilege. You make it tough on all your fellows.' He pointed ahead, to the trooper who was hefting the satchel of confiscated weapons.

'When killing devices are involved, it becomes more than a question of worker discipline. Charges will be brought. Too bad for you. I hope you get what you deserve.'

'Thanks,' said Luke dryly.

One of the miners grumbled, 'Not our fault. Sabre-man and woman led us on.'

'Shut up, you,' ordered the sergeant. 'You'll have your own chance to tell your side of it to Captain-Supervisor Grammel.'

That caused both Luke and Leia to start violently. Grammel was the man Halla had warned them about.

'Perhaps he'll be generous,' the sergeant went on philosophically. 'Good workers are difficult to get here. He may leave you most of your fingers.'

'I wish we'd asked Halla more about this Grammel,' Luke murmured.

'Yes, Halla.' The Princess sounded discouraged. 'She didn't break her back trying to save us, did she?'

'What could she do,' Luke countered, 'against Imperials?'

'You're right, I guess. But I would've thought she'd try something.' Leia shrugged. 'I suppose I can't blame her for saving herself.'

'At least Threepio and Artoo got away,' Luke added softly.

'Hey, any more chatter back there and I'll take off some digits myself,' the sergeant warned.

'How would you like to bury yourself under four feet of mud for about an hour?' the Princess snapped.

'I wouldn't,' admitted the sergeant calmly. 'How would you like your pretty tongue burnt out with a low-power blaster?'

Leia subsided. They were in enough trouble. She'd gain nothing by provoking them more. She concentrated her stare on the middle of the sergeant's back, trying to drive him insane. The sergeant showed no hint of being affected. Probably solid bone under the helmet, she mused.

They turned a last corner and entered a large chamber. After the spartan grey stone inside and out, the sybaritic furnishings here came as a shock. Real and artificial fur was used lavishly. Many of the creature comforts Luke would have associated with a far more developed world than Mimban were present. They were not flaunted, however, which indicated that the inhabitant of this chamber regarded them as his natural accoutrements.

Across the chamber a single man sat behind an unimposing, functional desk. 'Bring them over, sergeant.' His bored voice was broken and gravelly. Luke thought he must have suffered some damage to his vocal cords.

At a gesture from the sergeant, the seven prisoners – including one with a limp and a crudely bandaged leg – were herded across the room to stand close by the desk.

The most impressive thing about Grammel, Luke thought, was the reaction to him by the miners. All of their bluster and swagger had disappeared. They stood staring at the floor, the walls, each other – anywhere but at the man behind the desk. Feet shuffled uneasily.

Without seeming to stare, Luke tried to see the personage who inspired such respectful subservience from hardened men like the five miners. Grammel had his head buried in his hands and leaned his elbows on the desk as he surveyed them.

Grammel added no colour to his surroundings. His face was egg-shell pale, and the image of the Imperial officer was tarnished further when he stood to reveal a modest paunch curving gently from beneath his sternum like a frozen waterfall of suet, to crash and tumble somewhere below the waistline in a jumble of uniform.

The silver and gray uniform itself was spotless and neat, however, as if in an attempt to camouflage the belly beneath. Above the tight, high collar the neck jumped out to a square jaw bordered by a drooping moustache. The line of that facial hair matched well the dour expression the Captain-Supervisor wore – habitually, Luke guessed. Tiny, penetrating eyes peered out from beneath brows like a granite ridge, over-topped by uneasy black and grey hair.

This was a face that rarely laughed, Luke decided, and then for the wrong reasons.

Grammel began examining each of the uneasy group in turn. Luke borrowed a hint from the miners and tried to concentrate solely on a stain on the furred floor.

'So these are the disturbers, who break the peace to fight with killing weapons,' he observed disapprovingly. Once more that voice grated on Luke's ears, like a piece of a rusty machinery long overdue for lubrication. Full of grimy squeaks and groans, it suited Grammel perfectly.

Stepping forward smartly, the sergeant reported, 'Yes, Captain-Supervisor. Permission to take the two wounded to the infirmary.'

'Granted,' said Grammel. He did not quite smile, but his permanent frown faded enough for his lips to straighten slightly. "For a time, they will be better off than those who remain here.'

Under guard, the handless miner and the one with the limp were taken from the room. Grammel resumed his examination of the remaining people. When he reached Luke and the Princess, his mouth twitched as if someone had jabbed him with a pin.

'You two I don't recognise. Who are you?' He came around from behind the desk, stood nose to nose with Luke. 'You, boy! What are you?'

'Just a contract miner, Captain-Supervisor,' Luke stammered, trying to sound appropriately terrified. It wasn't a difficult task. Nor did he mind a little verbal grovelling if his life hung in the balance.

Grammel moved to stare down at the Princess. Now he smiled gingerly, as if the effort hurt him. 'And you, my dear? You're a miner too, I suppose.'

'No.' Leia didn't look at him. She nodded briefly towards Luke. 'I'm his . . . servant.'

'That's right,' Luke said quickly. 'She's only my—'

'I can hear, boy,' Grammel murmured. He stared at her, ran a finger down one cheek. 'Pretty woman . . .' She twitched out of his grip. 'Spirited, too.' He looked at Luke. 'I congratulate you on your taste, boy.'

'Thank you, sir.' Leia glared at him, but what else could he have said?

'Your manners are probably matched only by your incompetence,' the Princess told him.

Grammel merely nodded with satisfaction. 'Manners,' he repeated. 'Incompetence. Odd way for a servant to speak.' He barked at the sergeant, standing stiffly at attention nearby: 'What identification did you find on these two?'

'Identification, Captain-Supervisor? We assumed that it was standard, sir.'

'You haven't checked their identification, Sergeant?' Grammel inquired slowly.

Succeeding only in giving the impression of a man sweating beneath his armour, the officer explained lamely, 'No, sir. We just assumed.'

'Never assume, Sergeant. The universe is full of dead people who lived by assumption.' He turned politely to Luke and Leia. 'Your identification now, please?'

Luke made a pretence of searching his clothing, tried to look stunned when the nonexistent identification didn't materialise. The Princess fought to imitate him.

'We must have lost it during the fight,' he declared. and then hurriedly tried to change the subject. 'These five – three now – attacked us without provocation and—'

'It's a lie!' one of the miners objected strenuously. He looked to Grammel for sympathy, found none.

'You,' Grammel told the man very quietly, 'shut up.' The man complied with alacrity.

A trooper entered the chamber, called out ingratiatingly, 'Captain-Supervisor?'

Grammel appeared irritated at the interruption. 'Yes, what is it?'

The trooper approached the desk, whispered something in Grammel's ear. Grammel looked surprised. 'Yes, I'll see him.' He walked towards the door.

A small cloaked figure entered and engaged Grammel in conversation. Luke couldn't make out more than an occasional word. Leaning over, he whispered to the Princess, 'I don't like this, Leia.'

She whispered back tightly, 'You have this wonderfully evocative way about you, Luke, of reducing the most excruciatingly uncomfortable circumstances to the merely mundane.'

Luke looked hurt. The Captain-Supervisor concluded his conversation with the stunted figure, which promptly bowed and scurried from the room. Idly Luke wondered if the thing under the cloak was human or maybe one of the natives. His speculation was interrupted by Grammel's return.

'You miners started the fight,' he stated in a no-nonsense tone, pointedly excluding Luke and Leia from that category.

'Oh, but Captain-Supervisor,' the largest of the three began obsequiously, 'we were provoked. We were trying only to uphold the town law about fighting.'

'By breaking it,' Grammel countered, 'and by attacking this young lady?'

'It wasn't anything serious,' the man ventured. 'We were only goin' to have a little fun, first.'

'Your *fun* will cost each of you a half time-period's

pay,' Grammel declared. 'I'm going to be lenient with you.' The three men hardly dared appear hopeful. 'The mine laws here are lax and permit you considerable leeway in terms of relaxation.' Now he glowered at them.

'However, assault with intent to murder is not the Empire's idea of productive leisure. Whatever,' he added as an afterthought, 'I may think personally.'

Emboldened, one of the miners decided to push his luck. Stepping forward, he announced, 'Captain-Supervisor Grammel, I appeal the judgment.'

Grammel eyed the man the way a botanist would a new species of weed. 'You have that right. On what grounds?'

'Shortness ... shortness of trial and informality of circumstances,' the man finally got out.

'Very well. Since I am the Imperial law here, I will consider your appeal myself.' Grammel paused a moment, then said easily, 'Your appeal is rejected.'

'Then I appeal to the Imperial Department of Resources representative in charge of mining operations,' the man riposted. 'I want to see the judgment reviewed in another fashion.'

'Certainly,' Grammel agreed. He walked over to the wall behind his desk. Taking a long thin bar of plastic from its place there, he pressed the switch at one end as he came back around the desk. 'The conversation has been recorded,' he informed them all.

He depressed another switch and the bar showed a moving line of words across its waxy surface. When the record had finished, he raised and abruptly thrust one end of the unyielding plastic into the argumentative miner's left eye.

Blood and pulp squirted in all directions as the man collapsed, screaming, to the floor. One of his terrified companions bent over him, tried to staunch the flow of blood from the ruined socket. It ran in a steady stream down the man's face and coverall front.

'You three are dismissed,' Grammel told them perfunctorily, as if nothing unusual had happened. 'Sergeant?'

'Captain-Supervisor?'

'Take these three into the rear holding cells. Their two companions can join them as soon as they're well enough. Let them sit and think for a while. Record their names and identification codes so that they may more easily pay their fines. Unless,' he finished conversationally, tapping the recorder rod in one palm, 'someone else would like to appeal my judgment?'

As the two miners half-carried, half-dragged their unconscious companion to the exit, under guard, Grammel gestured at them with the rod. 'He still has his eye, you know. It's recorded permanently on this. Bring him back when he recovers and I'll let him see it again.'

The sergeant saw the guards and miners out, then returned to stand watch beside the door.

'I dislike these administrative details,' Grammel said amiably to Luke and the Princess. 'But this a largely unknown, unexplored world and I have little time to waste. Sometimes my decisions must be fast and harsh.

'Only the degree of the ability to devise more sophisticated debasements for themselves separates the human animals that work here from the natives. This kind of inventiveness has been a persistent and lamentable quality of mankind's for millennia. Realising that as you must, I'm sure you two will be more sensible than those lower types who just left us.' He sat back on the edge of the desk, commenced tapping his lower leg with the red-tipped rod. Luke watched it nervously.

'I told you, Captain-Supervisor,' he reiterated, 'We must have lost our identification in the fight. It must have fallen in the mud. If you'll just let us go back there I'm sure we can find it. Unless,' he added with seeming concern, 'Someone came by after the fight and stole it.'

'Oh, I don't think any of our hard-working citizens would do that,' Grammel commented, turning away. He looked sharply back over his shoulder. 'In fact, I don't think it's lying there, either. I don't think you two had any identification to lose.

'From what I've been told, you both are more than strangers to this town. You're strangers to the mine, to the Imperial presence here, to this very world. How you arrived undetected and unauthorised and in one piece I can't imagine.' He gritted his teeth and added dangerously, 'I *will* find out, however. I always find out what I want to know.'

'That's funny,' noted the Princess, 'because you strike me as having a particularly limited capacity for learning.'

Her remark didn't faze Grammel. If anything, the Princess's studied insults appeared to please him. 'A little while ago, young lady, you called me incompetent. Now you belittle me intellectually. I am no intellectual, but I am also neither incompetent nor uneducated. I got that way by learning how to get answers to my questions.

'But your first comment was correct, about my manners.' He drew back his left foot and kicked her in the left thigh with the point of his boot. Moaning in pain, the Princess grabbed her side below the hip and sank forward to her knees. Her right hand stopped her fall while the other continued holding the bruised place. Luke raged inside but resolutely stared straight ahead. This was not the place or time to die.

'However, I *am* straightforward,' Grammel continued, gazing down at her. Using his leg again, he kicked her right arm out from under her. She fell forward, then rolled over and sat up, still holding her left leg. The Captain-Supervisor kicked out sharply, catching the base of the spine but not hard enough to paralyse her. She wailed as both hands went to the small of her back and she fell over on her side, where she lay moaning.

Grammel drew back his leg again. Unable to stand by any longer, Luke stepped between them, said rapidly, 'If I told you the truth, Captain-Supervisor, you wouldn't believe me.'

That offer was intriguing enough to cause Grammel to forget the Princess for the moment. 'I'm always willing to listen, young man.'

Luke took a disconsolate breath, looked downcast. 'We're escaped criminals from Circarpous,' he confessed painfully. 'We're wanted there for extortion and blackmail.' He indicated the prone form of the Princess.

'The girl's my partner and lure. We ... made the mistake of compromising some people who turned out to be more important than we thought. We're not very important criminals, but we managed to get some very important people mad at us.' He stopped.

'Go on,' urged Grammel noncommittally.

'Circarpous still maintains the death penalty for many crimes,' Luke continued. 'It's a hectic, private-enterprise-style world.'

'I know all about Circarpous,' the Captain-Supervisor snapped impatiently.

Luke hastened to go on with his story. 'We stole a small lifeship. We'd heard about the small colonies on Twelve and Ten.'

'So you tried to flee there,' Grammel interjected. 'Logical enough.'

'In hopes of finding a way to gain passage out-system,' Luke finished rapidly. His enthusiasm was honest, because Grammel, at least so far, hadn't rejected the story out of hand. 'We even,' he added for good measure, 'went so far as to consider joining the Rebels if that would help us escape prosecution.'

'You'd both make pretty pitiful traitors,' Grammel

observed. 'The rebels would have sneered at you. They don't enrol criminals in their ranks. Odd, since they're all technically the worst sort of criminals. Anyone can see by looking at you that you'd never be accepted by them.' Fortunately, the Princess was in too much pain to snicker, Luke knew.

'I happen to think that your story, young man, though plausible, is a cleverly crafted falsehood.' Luke went cold inside. 'But . . . it *could* be true. If that's the case, if you are what you claim to be, we might even manage to bend the laws a little for you. I admire ingenuity in others.

'We might even find something for you to do here on Mimban. The Empire has many malcontents working in the mines. You've already encountered five of them.

'Of course,' he concluded, 'I could always return you to Circarpous for prosecution there.'

'Oh no, Captain-Supervisor!' Luke cried, dropping to his knees and clutching desperately at Grammel's trouser legs. 'Please don't do that. They'll have us executed. Please, we'll work till we drop, but don't send us back there!' He was sobbing openly now.

'Get off my boots,' Grammel ordered disgustedly. As Luke backed away obediently the Captain-Supervisor bent to brush at his pants where Luke had touched him.

Wiping tears conjured with difficulty away from his eyes, Luke tried not to appear too hopeful as he regarded Grammel. The Princess, meanwhile, had shifted to a sitting position. She was still rubbing the small of her back with one hand, carefully avoiding Grammel's gaze.

'As I stated, everything you've told me is possible and unlikely,' the Captain-Supervisor went on. He eyed Luke in a funny way. 'There is one thing which does interest me, however. It would be a sign of your good faith if you were honest with me about it.'

'I don't understand, Captain-Supervisor,' Luke admitted blankly.

'I am told,' Grammel continued, 'that you have in your possession a small gemstone. . . .'

Luke froze.

□ V

'GREAT Captain-Supervisor,' he finally managed to say, 'I'm not sure what you mean.'

'Please,' Grammel requested, showing a hint of genuine emotion for the first time, 'don't toy with me. You were observed conversing with a *local person*,' the last words uttered with obvious distaste, 'whose presence here is barely tolerated by the Imperial law. She remains always just the safe side of illegality. Despite personal feelings, deporting her illegally and unnecessarily would irritate certain segments of the populace who find her amusing. Besides, it would be expensive.

'You were seen showing her a small glowing red stone. Something you acquired during your illegal sojourning on Circarpous, perhaps?'

Luke's thoughts were in turmoil. Unquestionably some informant of Grammel's, probably the tiny cloaked figure the Captain-Supervisor had talked with some minutes ago, had seen the shard of Kaiburr crystal that Halla had presented to them. But the spy hadn't seen Halla bring it out and show it to Luke.

So Grammel and his spy were assuming that the stone was something Luke had brought with him and was showing to Halla! Which was fine for the old woman, he thought. She shouldn't be drawn into this now.

For an awful moment Luke thought that Grammel might be a Force-sensitive with the knowledge and ability to operate the crystal, or at least to sense its special property. But a hasty reaching out revealed only the usual vapid vacuum associated with normal humans hovering about Grammel's mind. He couldn't suspect anything about the fragment's real importance. Nevertheless, Luke balked at turning over the precious splinter to a servant of the Empire.

Grammel wasn't one to waste time. 'Come on, young man. You seem like a sensible sort. Surely it can't be worth additional inconvenience to you?'

'Really,' Luke insisted, stalling frantically, 'I don't know what you're talking about.'

'Oh, if you will press me,' Grammel responded, not particularly displeased. He turned his attention to the Princess, who continued to sit on the floor nursing her bruises. 'The young lady is something more than a business associate, maybe? She means something to you?'

Luke shrugged elaborately. 'She means nothing to me.'

'Fine,' said the Captain-Supervisor. 'Then you won't mind what's going to happen next.'

He gestured to the sergeant. The armour-clad soldier walked over and reached down for the Princess. Leia reached up to grab his hand, slipped a leg under his, and pulled and kicked simultaneously. As the trooper went crashing to the floor, she was rushing for the doorway, calling for Luke to follow.

No matter how she tried the door key and switch, it wouldn't open for her.

'You're wasting your time, my dear,' Grammel advised her. 'You should have gone for his weapon. The door is keyed to me personally, to certain close members of my staff, and to troopers who have the proper resonator built into their armour. You don't qualify at any level, I'm afraid.'

Angry now, the sergeant was back on his feet, moving towards her with open arms. She started to run past him, stumbled, and went sprawling to the floor. Grammel loomed over her, his right hand forming into a fist.

'No,' Luke exclaimed at the absolute last possible moment. Grammel's hand paused in midair as he glanced back at him.

'That's much better,' he advised Luke. 'Better to be sensible than obstinate. I'd find the stone anyway of course, but you'd find the finding unpleasant.'

Luke unsnapped a pocket, reaching in. 'You can't!' a voice objected. He turned to see the Princess staring up at him. Evidently she'd come to believe at least part of Halla's story. Or maybe, he corrected himself, she was simply playing out her part of the petty thief reluctant to part with hard-won goods.

'We've no choice.' As long as Grammel didn't ask for names, he saw no point in volunteering any, faked or otherwise. Unwrapping the small box, he handed it to the expectant administrator.

Grammel eyed it, asked a question Luke hadn't prepared for. 'What's the combination?'

For a second, Luke panicked. If he confessed that he didn't know the combination, his whole carefully fabricated lie would disintegrate here and now. So he took the only gamble he could.

'It's open.'

Both he and Leia held their breath as Grammel touched the tiny catch. There was an audible click. Luke had never bothered to rescramble the combination after Halla had given him the box.

Captain-Supervisor Grammel stared fascinated at the fragment of glowing crimson. 'Very pretty. What is it?'

'I don't know,' Luke lied. 'I have no idea what kind of gem it is.' Grammel looked sternly at him. 'It's true . . . I'm no gemologist or chemist.' There, that much was easily said.

'Is the glow natural,' Grammel inquired, 'or the result of external excitation?' He moved the gem around in the box with a probing finger.

'I've no idea. It's glowed ever since we've had it, so

I'd hazard a guess that it's a natural property of the stone.'

The Captain-Supervisor smiled at him in a way he didn't like. 'If you know so little about it, why did you steal it?'

'I didn't say we stole it.' Grammel snickered derisively and Luke, playing the part willingly, assumed a defensive attitude. 'All right, so we stole it. It was pretty and I'd never seen anything like it. Anything pretty and rare is likely to be valuable.'

'You told me your field of expertise was extortion, not burglary,' Grammel countered.

'The thing intrigued me and I had the chance to swipe it, so I did,' Luke responded with a touch of belligerent bravado.

Apparently that was the right approach. 'Sensible,' Grammel conceded. He turned his gaze back to the splinter. 'I don't recognize it either. As a gem it's not very impressive ... not faceted or even trimmed for cutting. But you're right about it being unusual. The radiant property alone is enough to mark it as that.' Abruptly, he stopped turning it over and over with his fingers, moved his hand away.

'It's not harmful, is it?'

'Not so far,' Luke conceded, affecting an attitude of sudden concern. Let Grammel sweat a little!

'You haven't suffered any ill effects since it's been in your possession?'

'Not until we were brought here.' That almost produced laughter from the administrator.

'I think,' he went on slowly, putting the box on his desk and moving away from it, 'that I'll have it analysed professionally before I come to any conclusions about it.' He looked amiably at Luke.

'It's been confiscated, of course. You may consider it your fine for being involved in the fight.'

'We were were the ones assaulted,' Luke argued, for appearance's sake.

'Are you disputing my judgment?' Grammel asked dangerously.

'No, Captain-Supervisor!'

'That's good. I can see that you're an intelligent young man. Pity your companion works her mouth to the exclusion of her brain.' Leia glared at him, but for once had the sense not to say anything.

'I believe we can work something out. Meanwhile, it remains that you two are here on this world illegally, in defiance of a great deal of Imperial effort to keep this installation a secret. So you will be detained until I can verify your story.'

Luke started to speak but Grammel waved him to silence. 'No, don't bother with names. I'd expect you to offer me an alias anyway. We'll take retinal prints, natural portraits and other suitable information. I have contacts on Circarpous, both legal and not so.

'If they send me back information that you two are known petty criminals on that world, and judging from your story you ought to be known, then what you've told me will be substantiated and we'll adjust relationships accordingly – and not necessarily to to your detriment.

'If it turns out that no one unearths any information on you, or information that conflicts with what you've said, then I'll have to assume that everything you've told me is pure fabrication. In that unfortunate event I'll be forced to resort to indelicate methods of obtaining the truth.' Luke would have preferred any kind of smile to the empty, inhuman expression Grammel wore as he said that.

'But there's no reason why we can't be pleasant about things until then. Sergeant!'

'Captain-Supervisor!' the noncom acknowledged, stepping over smartly.

'See these two escorted to the restraining area.'

'Which cell, sir?'

'The maximum-security holding pen,' Grammel replied, his face unreadable.

The sergeant hesitated. 'But, sir, that cell's already occupied. Its occupants are dangerous ... they've already put three men in the infirmary.'

'No matter,' Grammel insisted indifferently. 'I'm sure these two can handle themselves. Besides, prisoners don't fight other prisoners. Not too often, anyway.'

'What are you talking about?' the Princess demanded to know, climbing to her feet. 'What are you caging us with?'

'You'll find out,' Grammel assured her pleasantly. Several troops entered the room and boxed themselves around Luke and Leia. 'Please try to keep yourselves alive until I can check on your story. I'd be distressed if it developed that you've been telling me the truth and couldn't survive the company of your cell companions long enough to be released.'

'We've *been* honest with you!' Luke insisted, sounding desperate.

'Sergeant?'

The noncom led the two prisoners to the exit. Grammel ignored Luke's entreaties to know what they were being sent to.

When they were gone and the chamber was quiet again, the Captain-Supervisor spent several minutes gazing at the glowing fragment of crystal. Then he touched a switch behind his desk. Another door opened and a small cloaked figure entered the room for the second time.

'That's the thing you saw, Bot?' said Grammel, gesturing at the open box sitting on the desk. A nod from the hooded shape. 'You know what it is?' A negative shake this time.

'Neither do I,' Grammel confessed. 'I think the youth underestimates its strangeness. I've never seen or heard of anything remotely like it. Have you?' Another sideways shake of the hooded skull.

Grammel glanced at the closed doorway where Luke and Leia had been taken out. 'Those two *could* be what the boy said they were. I don't know. I have the feeling his story is a little too neat, too convenient. Almost as if he were gauging his responses to what I wanted to hear. I can't decide whether he's an inefficient crook or a supernally smooth liar.

'Something else. He sounded almost confident that he and the girl could make contact with Rebels on the Ten or Twelve. None of our agents have been able to do that.'

A husk of a sentence from the cloaked figure and Grammel nodded.

'I know that the Rebels have ways of separating true traitors from our people, but the boy's confidence still troubles me. It seems misplaced in a petty criminal. And the girl had more spirit than her type normally displays. I'm puzzled, Bot. But I think . . . I think there might be something important in all this. I just don't have the facts available to glue it all together with . . . yet. It might mean much to us both.' The figure nodded vigorously, pleased.

Grammel reached a decision. 'I'm going to have to contact higher authority. I don't like the idea of sharing anything like this, but I don't see a way around it.' He jerked his head contemptuously towards the door. 'In any event, we'll cut the truth out of them before anyone of importance can get here.'

Leaving the desk, he walked to the wall behind and touched a small switch. A section of wall vanished, leaving revealed behind it a blank screen of golden hue. Grammel adjusted another control. A panel awash with dials and studs slid out of the wall beneath the reflective screen. Further adjustment, and then he spoke into a protruding vo-pickup.

'I must have deep-space communication of the First Priority with Governor Bin Essada, on the territorial administrative world of Gyndine.' He glanced back at the cloaked form for reassurance and was rewarded with a nod.

'Call is being processed,' a computer voice declared flatly. Visual static appeared for a moment, then the screen cleared with gratifying speed. By Imperial distances Gyndine was not very far away.

The portrait that appeared on the screen was an overweight, swarthy individual whose most outstanding feature was a series of chins falling in steps to the upper part of his shirt. Curly black hair, touched with white at the sides and dyed orange in a spiral pattern on top, crowned the face like seaweed on some water-worn boulder. Dark eyes squinted perpetually, their pink pupils ever sensitive to light. 'I have work to do,' Governor Essada grunted in a porcine contralto. 'Who calls and what for?'

With that smug, powerful visage looming over him on the screen, much of Grammel's customary assurance melted away. His own words came out sounding shaky and subservient.

'It is only I, Governor, a humble servant of the Emperor, Captain-Supervisor Grammel.'

'I don't know any Captain-Supervisor Grammel,' the voice said.'

'I am in charge of the secret mining colony on Circarpous V, sir,' explained Grammel hopefully.

Essada paused momentarily, looking up from the tape he was inspecting. 'I am familiar with the Imperial operations in that system,' he replied guardedly. 'What business do you have that requires First Priority with me?' The huge bulk leaned forward. 'It had better be important, Captain-Supervisor Grammel. I know you now.'

'Yes, sir.' Grammel bowed his head repeatedly to the screen. 'It's a matter involving two strangers who somehow set down here secretly. Two strangers and a peculiar bit of crystal they had in their possession. The people aren't important, but as you, sir, are widely famed as an expert on unusual radiation, I thought perhaps—'

'Don't waste my time with flattery, Grammel,' Essada warned. 'Since the Emperor dissolved the Senate, we regional governors have been overwhelmed with work.'

'I understand, sir,' Grammel said hastily, rushing to gather up the tiny box containing the stone. He held it so that the vis-pickup in the room could see it. 'Here it is.'

Essada peered at it. 'Strange . . . I've never seen anything like that, Grammel. The radiation is generated from within?'

'Yes, sir, I'm certain.'

'I'm not,' the Governor replied, 'but I admit it looks to be so. Tell me more about the people who had it.'

Grammel shrugged. 'They're nothing, probably just a couple of petty thieves who stole it, sir.'

'A couple of petty thieves penetrated and landed in secret on Circarpous V?' said the Governor disbelievingly.

'I think so, sir. A boy and a young woman . . .'

'Young woman,' Essada repeated. 'We've heard rumours from Circarpous IV, about an important meeting that the underground leaders there were preparing for . . . a young woman, you say? Would she be dark-haired, fiery-tempered, perhaps even a touch sarcastic?'

'The very person, sir,' a startled Grammel stammered.

'You have identified them?'

'No, sir. We've only just imprisoned them. They've been jailed together with—'

'Chaos take your details, Grammel!' Essada shouted. 'Give me visual representation of both of these people.'

'That is easily done,' a relieved Grammel replied. He took the plastic recorder rod from the desk, held it up uncertainly before the screen. 'This has not yet been transferred, sir. Do you think you can make out the rod imagery?'

'I can make out many things, Grammel, down to the shallow depths of your own soul. Place it close to your vis-pickup.'

The administrator adjusted the requisite switch and placed the long glassy tube close to the screen panel. He touched the retrieval stud and two-dimensional portraits appeared within the rod's substance. A pause, and then he shifted the rod to show full-length views of both subjects.

'It may be her, by the Force, it just may be,' Governor Essada muttered, now excited. 'The youth I don't know, but he may also be important. I am pleased.'

'Important, sir? You know of them?'

'I hope to have part credit for their capture and eventual execution – hers, at least.' Essada looked sharply at the bewildered officer. 'They must not be harmed or injured until proper authority arrives for them, Grammel.'

'It shall be as you say, sir,' a bemused Captain-Supervisor conceded. 'But I don't understand. Who are they, and how do they come to the notice of someone such as—'

'I require only service from you, Grammel. Not questions.'

'Yes, sir,' the administrator barked stiffly.

Essada took a lighter tack. 'You did well to contact me directly, though not for the reasons you thought. Once those two are in Imperial hands, you will become Colonel-Supervisor Grammel.'

'Governor!' Grammel lost his poise completely. 'Sir, you are too generous. I don't know what to say. . . .'

'Say nothing,' Essada suggested. 'It makes you more tolerable. Keep them alive, Grammel. Whether you go to hell or glory is dependent on how well you carry out these orders. Beyond keeping them alive and healthy you have my permission to restrain them as you please.'

'Yes, sir. Sir, may I . . .'

But Governor Essada had already all but forgotten Grammel.

'One particular party should find this information of particular notice. It will be well for me, yes.' Abruptly, he noticed that communications were still open.

'Alive, Grammel. Remember that.'

'But, sir, can't you tell . . .?'

The screen went blank.

The Captain-Supervisor stood motionless before the dark rectangle for several long, thoughtful moments. Then he repositioned screen and control panel and turned to the cloaked figure which was crawling out from behind the concealing bulk of a free-formed chair across the room.

'We appear to have stumbled on to something far more important than either of us dreamed, Bot. "Colonel-Supervisor"!' He gazed down at the crystal in his hand, all thoughts of its possible lethal nature pushed aside by the vision of the glittering future ahead of him. 'We must take care.'

The cloaked figure nodded energetically. . . .

□ VI

'TAKE it easy,' Luke complained, shrugging his arm free of the trooper who was escorting them down the long, narrow stone hallway. As they paced, Luke took the opportunity to study the damp, dripping walls. Some of them showed dark moss. Clearly, the omnipresent moisture of Mimban penetrated the old walls here.

'You'd think the Imperial government could have invested some credit in modern quarters,' he murmured.

'Why,' the sub-officer ahead of them wanted to know, 'when the primitives of this world left us such useful structures?'

'A temple, a place of worship, and it's been turned into offices and a prison,' the Princess declared angrily.

'The Empire does what is necessary,' the sub-officer observed in a phlegmatic manner which would have gratified his superiors. 'I am told this mining is an expensive venture. The Empire is smart enough to save where it is able,' he concluded with pride.

'That probably extends to your pay and retirement benefits,' the Princess ventured maliciously.

'That's enough talk from the prisoners,' the disgruntled sub-officer decided aloud, unhappy with the turn the conversation had taken. They rounded a sharp corner. A network of intersecting diagonal bars formed an unbreakable mesh at the end of the corridor.

'Here's your new home,' the sub-officer informed them. 'Inside you can muse about what the Empire has in store for your future.' As the sub-officer passed a palm over the wall on his immediate right, an unbarred ellipsoid appeared in the centre of the metal grille.

'Move,' the trooper next to Luke ordered, prodding him with his rifle.

'I was told we were going to have company,' Luke ventured, walking towards the empty space with great reluctance. This provoked considerable merriment among the assembled troopers.

'You'll find it soon enough,' the sub-officer chuckled, 'or it'll find you.'

Once both prisoners stood inside the cell, the sub-officer passed his hand over the photoplate again and the dematerialised bars reappeared with a solid *clank*.

'Company, he says,' one of the retreating troopers echoed, as they walked back up the corridor. They continued laughing among themselves.

'For some reason I'm not amused,' Luke muttered. Each of the angled bars was as big around as his forearm. He flicked one with a nail and it rang like a bell. 'Solid, not tubular,' he announced. 'This cell was designed to hold more than ordinary people. I wonder what—'

The Princess gasped, pointed to a far corner and began backing towards the nearest wall. Two massive hairy mounds lay clustered near the back of the cell, under the single window. The fur moved up and down, indicating it was surrounding something alive.

'Easy . . . easy,' Luke instructed, backing close to her and putting both hands on her shoulders. She leaned into him. 'We don't know who they are yet.'

'We don't know *what* they are,' the Princess whispered fearfully. 'I think they're waking up.'

One of the huge shapes stood, stretched and let out a grunt like a volcano clearing its throat. It turned and caught sight of them.

Luke's eyes bugged. He started towards the figure. The Princess put out a hand to hold him back, but he shook it off.

'Are you out of your mind, Luke? They'll tear you to pieces.'

He continued walking towards the waiting figure. It stood little taller than he did, but was built much more massively. Its hair-covered arms reached to the cell floor, the hands dragging on the stone. A long snout protruded from the centre of the face, obscuring any mouth. Two huge black eyes stared expectantly at him.

'Luke, don't do this ... come back here.'

A querulous growl-rumble sounding like an angry underground spring came from the figure Luke was nearing. The Princess became quiet, pressed worriedly back against the cold stone wall as she slid towards the farthest corner.

Luke eyed the massive creature warily. They had to make friends fast, or he and Leia wouldn't have to worry about getting off Mimban except in fragments. He reached out, touched an arm in a certain way. His eyes never left the jet-black orbs staring into his own.

With startling speed, the creature took a backward hop, chittered something. It was several times Luke's weight. Dim light from the sealed illuminators in the cell ceiling shone on cable-like shoulder muscles above those double-length arms.

A pair of plate-sized hands reached out for Luke. He responded by uttering something in low tones. Shaking its head, its snout swinging, the creature hesitated, then rumbled again. Luke spoke louder gibberish at it.

Reaching out, the beast grabbed Luke with both hands and lifted him off the ground over its head, as if preparing to dash him against the stone floor. The Princess screamed. The creature brought Luke close to its body, closer ... and planted a wet kiss on each of Luke's cheeks before setting him gently back on the floor.

The Princess stared in disbelief at Luke's affectionate assailant. 'Why didn't it tear your head off? You . . .' she gazed at Luke admiringly, 'you *talked* to it.'

'Yes,' Luke admitted modestly. 'I used to study a lot about certain worlds, back on my uncle's farm on Tatooine. It was my only escape, and educational as well. This,' and he indicated the creature resting a massive long arm on his head and shaking him in a friendly fashion, 'is a Yuzzem.'

'I've heard of them, but this is the first time I've seen one.'

'They're temperamental,' Luke told her, 'so I thought it would be better to try and make the first greeting ourselves, using what little language I learned.' He jabbered at the creature, which chittered back. 'It might've killed me somewhere else, but all prisoners are allies, it seems.'

The Yuzzem turned, staggered backwards and bumped into the wall. It leaned over and began shaking its still somnolent companion. The second Yuzzem rolled over awake and swung angrily at the first. The massive hand missed, connecting instead with the wall hard enough to leave an impression in the rock. Rolling to a sitting position, it started chittering to its waker, holding its head with one hand.

'Why,' Leia exclaimed as the realisation struck her, 'they're both drunk!' The second Yuzzem finally managed to get to its feet. It growled at her. 'No offence,' she added quickly.

'The one I talked to is called, as near as I can translate it, Hin. That's Kee leaning against the wall, wishing to be someplace else.' He jabbered at Hin, listening to the reply.

'I think he said that they've been working for the Imperial government's operation here, got fed up about a week ago and started breaking things. They've been locked in here ever since.'

'I didn't know the Imperials were hiring nonhumans.'

'Apparently these two didn't have any choice,' Luke explained, listening to Hin. 'They don't like the Imperials any more than we do. I've been trying to convince them that all humans aren't like the Imperials. I'm pretty sure I'm succeeding.'

'I hope so,' Leia said, eyeing the massively muscled, long-armed creatures.

'Both Hin and Kee are young, about our age, and not very experienced in Imperial affairs. They signed themselves into – well, I guess you couldn't quite call it slavery, but indentured servitude is too polite a term.

'When they protested, finally, some mine official waved a lot of documents at them and made jokes. So they took their equipment and started trying to fill in the mine instead of emptying it out.

'According to Hin, the only reason Grammel didn't have them shot immediately was because each of them does the work of any three men and because they were both intoxicated out of their minds. Apparently Yuzzem,' he added unnecessarily, 'have long hangovers. Hin believes the Imperials will give them another chance. But he's not so sure he wants one.

'They're in here because the regular cells won't hold them. Come say hello.' The Princess hesitated and Luke walked over to her and whispered, 'It's okay. I think we could count on them. But better not tell them who we are.'

She nodded, walking over and reached out with a hand. It vanished into a hairy paw. Hin chittered at her. 'The same, I'm sure,' she said, gaining confidence rapidly. Kee howled and both humans looked to the other Yuzzem who babbled at Luke.

'Says someone's been using a mining drill on his head for the past week.'

Leia began walking away from him, towards the single window. It showed a panorama of mist-obscured lights from the town and was blacked by the same configuration of thick, diagonally placed bars.

'I know someone I'd like to take a drill to,' she muttered disconsolately.

'You mean Halla,' Luke declared. 'She couldn't and can't do a thing for us. If I were in her situation I'd probably be running, too.'

Looking over at him, she smiled dazzlingly. 'You know that's not true, Luke. You're too loyal and responsible for your own good.' Her gaze turned back to the mist-shrouded roofs of the distant town.

'If we hadn't lost control of ourselves back in front of the tavern, we wouldn't have attracted the attention of those miners. We wouldn't be here now. It's my fault.'

He put a reassuring hand on her shoulder. 'Come on, Leia ... Princess. This mess was nobody's fault. Besides, it's fun losing control once in a while.'

She smiled again, thankfully. 'You know, Luke, the Rebellion is lucky to have you. You're a good man.'

'Yeah.' He turned away. 'Lucky for the Rebellion.'

There was a chattering from across the cell. Leia eyed Luke questioningly. 'Kee says someone's coming,' he translated.

Together with the two Yuzzem, they turned their attention to the corridor. Footsteps approached rapidly. Several stormtroopers appeared, an anxious Grammel leading them. He seemed to relax a little on catching sight of his prisoners.

'You're both unharmed?' Luke nodded. 'Good,' he declared, visibly relieved. His gaze travelled to the Yuzzem and back again to Luke. 'I see you're sharing your cell agreeably ... so far. I'm pleased. I was afraid I'd have to move you, but if the Yuzzem can tolerate your presence then I think you should stay. You'll be more secure in here. It develops that someone else has expressed an interest in your case.'

Luke looked blankly at the Princess, who stared back with equal lack of comprehension.

'Yeah, one of the enforcers back on Circarpous, I'll bet,' Luke essayed boldly.

'Not exactly.' Another of those enigmatic half-smiles that sent chills down Luke's spine. 'An Imperial representative is coming here to question you personally. That's enough for me. I know when to stand aside. So I'm not going to contact our sources on Circarpous until he tells me to.'

'Oh,' was all Luke could find to say. He was at once pleased and concerned – pleased, because their little tale of being escaped criminals from Circarpous was apparently going to avoid scrutiny for a little while longer; concerned, because he couldn't imagine anything Grammel might have told someone that would intrigue an Imperial representative. Where might they have slipped and revealed something?

'Why would an Imperial representative be so interested in us?' he asked, fishing for information.

'That's what I'd like to know,' Grammel replied. He walked to stand next to the bars. 'I don't suppose you'd care to tell me?'

'I don't know what you mean,' Luke responded, stepping back from the bars.

'I could make you tell me,' Grammel growled, 'but I've been ordered to . . .' he had to force himself away from the bars, 'to leave you strictly alone. Don't let that make you confident. I am of the impression that this representative – and he is a very important one – will have his own plans for you, and that they will be more unpleasant than anything I in my simple way could devise.'

'You or some Imperial officer,' Luke shrugged, affecting the casual attitude of the street-wise, 'it's all the same to us, so long as we don't get sent back to Circarpous. Wish I knew why all the fuss over us, though.'

Grammel shook his head slowly. 'You impress me, the two of you. I really wish you'd tell me who you are, and what this is all about.' He reached into a pocket and pulled out the little box containing the splinter of Kaiburr crystal.

'But I don't suppose that you will,' he concluded with a sigh, replacing the box in the pocket. 'As my hands are now tied, I can't force it from you the way I'd like to. I must admit that whatever Governor Essada sees in you two escapes me utterly.'

'An Imperial Governor . . .' Leia had slumped, was backing away and breathing unevenly, both hands going to her face. Sweat beaded on her forehead.

Grammel was studying her intently. 'Yes . . . why should that bother you so?' He glanced sharply at Luke. 'What's going on here?'

Ignoring him, Luke moved to comfort the Princess. 'Take it easy, Leia, it might not mean anything.'

'Imperial Governors don't take an interest in common thieves, Luke,' she whispered tightly. Something was clutching at her throat. 'I'll be interrogated again . . . like that time . . . that time.' She broke away, pressing herself up against the back wall of the cell.

That time back on the Death Star. Small black worms crawled through her brain. Another Governor's demands, those of the now-dead Grand Moff Tarkin, the machine drifting into her holding cell. The remorseless black machine, illegal, concocted by twisted Imperial scientists in defiance of every code, legal and moral. It drifted over to her, moved down, metal limbs preparing to perform efficiently, emotionlessly, in response to inhuman programming.

Screaming, screaming, screaming never to stop she was . . .

Something hit her hard. She blinked, turned to see Luke looking at her, worried. She slid down to sit up against the wall. Hin had ambled over. The massive black-eyed Yuzzem bent solicitously over her. One long arm went to touch her curiously, the long flexible snout sniffing at her.

'She'll be okay, Hin,' Luke told the alien in its own language as he helped Leia wipe away cold tears.

'Just the Empire's reputation for cruelty,' he called

back to Grammel. The explanation sounded lame even to his own ears.

Grammel pressed up against the bars again. 'She's been through questioning before. She knows something,' he insisted excitedly. 'Who is she? Who are you two? Tell me!' He pounded on the bars with a fist. 'Tell me!' Then his tone turned sly-soft.

'Maybe I can intercede on your behalf with whomever the Imperial representative is. I want everything I can get out of this, you hear me? You two will be my ticket off this lost world. I want off and I want the promotion Essada promised me, and I want more if I can get it! Tell me who you are, what you know. I'll bargain with you. Give me something to use, some information to trade with so I won't meet your inquisitor unarmed!'

Luke gave Grammel a pitying look.

'Who are you!' Grammel screamed furiously, furious at his own helplessness to do anything but beg, an action he was unaccustomed to. 'Why are you so important to him? Tell me, or I'll have the woman dismembered before your eyes in spite of what Essada ordered! Tell me, tell me, tell me . . . *unk*!'

An enormous paw had shot through the bars and had Grammel by the throat . . . almost. With a desperate effort the Captain-Supervisor barely managed to pull free. Another paw reached after the first. An alert trooper had dropped to one knee and fired his rifle. Even though it was set for stun, the bolt which caught Kee in the side sent the Yuzzem tumbling across the floor. A scorched black streak showed on the thick fur. Kee rolled over, holding the burnt place, panting softly and staring through the bars. Hin moved to his injured companion and checked the wound, also glaring frighteningly out at Grammel. Then he moved to the bars.

Grammel stood just out of the long reach, not smiling, as Hin lunged for his throat. A huge hand flailed at the air centimetres away while the Captain-Supervisor massaged his neck. The Yuzzem grabbed the bars, pulled in opposite directions, straining, straining.

Looking on with academic interest, Grammel reassured the sub-officer standing next to him. 'There's no more danger, Puddra. They can't break those bars. Not a dozen Yuzzem could.'

Despite this confidence it seemed that Hin, with a supreme effort, actually did bend one bar slightly. Then he gave up, gasping deeply. Holding the bars and shaking with rage, he gave Grammel a stare of naked hatred.

Grammel sighed a little in spite of himself. 'See, I told you,' he confided to the sub-officer.

'You're all right, Captain-Supervisor?' the man inquired from behind his armour.

'Fine now, Puddra,' he assured the subordinate. He made a show of wrinkling his nose. 'Except for the smell, of course.' He spoke easily to Luke: 'You two must be special. Anyone who can stand the odour of a Yuzzem ...' He made a face, shook his head in mock astonishment. 'To exist in that stink for more than a few minutes requires *some* special quality.' Hin obliged by howling madly at the Captain-Supervisor. 'Go ahead and rage,' Grammel told Hin pleasantly. 'As soon as I can convince the mine director that you two aren't worth the risk of rehabilitation for work, I'll disassemble you personally. After having you thoroughly deodorised, of course.' He turned to leave.

As he did so, Hin made a strange sound. It was followed by a forceful *phut* from the long snout. The huge blob of spit struck Grammel on the back of the neck, just above the high collar. Wiping it away, the Captain-Supervisor growled viciously back over his shoulder.

'You grinning travesty of a man. Soon, very soon, I promise.' He gestured sharply to the troops, and they disappeared in a body up the corridor.

Hin left the bars and walked back to check on the

Princess. She had fainted and Luke was supporting her with one arm. A grumble and Luke commented knowingly.

'Yes, he's a prince, our jailer, isn't he?'

By way of reply, Hin picked up a piece of gravel from the floor. Rolling it between two long fingers, he pulverised it effortlessly and let the dust trickle back to the ground.

'I hope you can do that to him someday, Hin,' Luke agreed, eyeing the Yuzzem. 'Right now, though I'm afraid our chances of getting out of here, let alone of getting to the Captain-Supervisor, aren't very good.'

A moan, and the Princess reached out towards Luke. He caught her hands and she opened her eyes in surprise. An uncertain glance, then she saw the huge eyed Hin staring at her curiously.

'I'm sorry, Luke.' He helped her to her feet. 'The thought of going through an Imperial interrogation again . . . I lost control.'

'That's understandable. You won't go through another session. I'll see to that.'

She smiled at him. Why discourage such confidence with mere facts?

Luke had moved to the single window and was testing the bars with exploratory pulls. 'They're just as solid as they look,' he grunted. 'No way out here.'

'The Yuzzem probably already tried that,' she pointed out reasonably.

A small section of stone wall slid aside and she jumped. A reassuring rush to the wall from both Yuzzem caused Luke to relax. Several bowls and dishes of something steaming were slipped into the cell on smooth metal trays before the stone panel slid back into place.

Hin and Kee left no doubt as to the contents of the dishes. They grabbed one apiece and started wolfing down the contents.

'I don't think much of Yuzzem table manners,' Luke observed. 'I think if we want something to eat, we'd better hurry or they won't leave us a thing.'

Exchanging glances, they studied the contents of the two remaining trays. Luke sniffed at the contents of one bowl, shrugged, and tried a spoonful.

'Some kind of stew,' he decided. 'Not bad for prison fare.'

'Remember,' Leia said, 'Grammel's under instructions to keep us healthy. Until the Imperial Governor's representative arrives.'

Luke paused between mouthfuls to venture hopefully, 'At least if we do get a chance to escape, we'll be able to do it on a full stomach.'

Luke finished his meal, rose and walked over to the bars forming their cell. He stared down the corridor at the distant spot on the stone wall where the cell entry control was emplaced. Leia eyed him quietly.

If only they could cover the recessed photosensitive switch with something, he mused. His gaze travelled around the cell. The trays on which their food had appeared were smooth, unmalleable metal. No way to attach them to one another. The result wouldn't be nearly long enough to reach the far-off switch anyway. And it was, self-evidently, well out of the extended reach of the two Yuzzem.

'We've got to get a hand or something over that switch,' he muttered in frustration.

'Or something, Luke boy.'

Everyone started at the unexpected voice, especially the excitable Yuzzem. Hin rushed towards the window but Luke, fortunately, got there before him.

'No . . . it's a friend, Hin.' The Yuzzem gibbered and clacked at him, but finally moved away. Luke rushed to the opening himself, grabbed the bars and stood on tiptoe to look out. A wrinkled, smiling face stared brightly back at him.

'Halla!' he almost shouted. 'You didn't forget us

after all!' He tried to see past her. 'What about Threepio and Artoo Detoo?'

'Your 'droids are fine, boy. As for me, I never forget a partner. Besides, I need you two. So don't go emotional on me. It's the crystal I'm after. Her grin faded and she stared hard at him. 'Did you tell that maggot Grammel anything about me?'

'No,' Luke assured her. There was a cough and he noticed the Princess staring at him. 'Well, not exactly,' he corrected himself. 'He thinks *we* were trying to sell the crystal fragment to *you*.'

Halla chuckled. 'So that's why I wasn't brought in for questioning. Grammel always did see things through the wrong end. He's taken the fragment, I guess.'

'I'm sorry,' Luke looked downcast. 'We couldn't do anything about it.'

'Never mind, boy. We'll have the whole crystal soon. Soon's we get you out.'

'How? You've got something to blow the wall?'

'Now, that would be a waste of time, boy. What would you do, run away from here?' She paused realisation striking. 'Say, I'll bet you can't see down out of this window, can you?'

'No, only in a straight line,' Luke admitted.

'Boy, I'm standing on a ledge about ten centimetres wide, over a forty-metre-deep trench. There's a barrier on the other side that would detect any energy weapons or explosives anyone tried to carry over here. Or did you think I was pressing this close to the wall because I like the way your breath smells?'

'Halla, you're crazy! What if you slip?'

'I'll make a small splash, Luke boy. As for the first, since everyone seems so sure I'm crazy, I don't see any harm in acting like it. Only a crazy old woman would come sliding out on this little bitty ledge here. That means you couldn't negotiate it. No, boy. The only way out of here is back the way you came.'

A loud, exuberant grunting sounded behind Luke. Hin came over, put a hand on Luke's shoulder and eyed Halla imploringly. Then he and Luke engaged in a rapid exchange of grunts. Hin walked back into the cell and commenced a low dialogue with Kee while Halla looked on uncertainly.

'What was that all about?' she asked Luke. 'I don't understand that monkey talk.'

'Hin told me,' Luke translated for her, 'that if you can get us out of the cell, Kee and he will take care of getting us out of the building.'

'You think they can?' Halla wondered, licking her lips.

Luke looked confident. 'I wouldn't want to bet against a pair of desperate Yuzzem. There's something else. If we help them escape, they'll help us in the hunt for the crystal.'

'A help they'd be,' Halla admitted readily. 'And I can see why they'd throw in with us. Once they break jail, they've no hope of leniency from Grammel.'

'How are you going to get us out of here?'

Halla adjusted her precarious stance above the sheer drop, then said proudly, 'I told you I was a master of the Force. Stand aside, young man.'

Not knowing what to expect, Luke did as he was told. The Princess folded her arms and looked sceptical and anxious simultaneously.

Halla's eyes closed and she appeared to enter some kind of trance. Luke felt the stirring, knew that she was manipulating the Force in a way he could never manage well. Not necessarily in a superior fashion, just . . . different. His greatest concern was that in her altered condition she might lose her grip on the temple's exterior. But she remained in place as if frozen there, her brow contorted as she strained.

He heard a gasp, and he spun around to look where the Princess was pointing. One of the metal food trays had risen, drifting lazily in the air of the cell. It began moving towards the bars. Luke looked back at Halla. It was a simple parlour trick, but one he could never have duplicated. Levitation was not a skill he had mastered very well. But it seemed to be the one thing Halla could do. He remembered the spice shaker on the tavern table, and held his breath.

Sweating, her face twisted with the effort, Halla moved the tray. It thumped against the bars. Luke winced, thinking it might be too wide to squeeze through any of the openings. But the tray turned, angled to match the bars, and slipped through with a slight scraping sound. Fluttering, it continued drifting up the corridor.

Halla was hardly breathing now, her entire being thrown into the tremendous effort she was making. Luke watched as the tray dipped, rose to its former height, dipped again before continuing on up the corridor.

'Boy,' came an echo of the old woman's voice, 'you got to help me.' Her eyes were still closed.

'I can't, Halla,' he told her tightly. 'I'm no good at this.'

'Got to, boy. Can't hold it myself much longer.' Even as she finished the tray dipped, striking the ground with a clang before rising once again.

Luke shut his own eyes and tried to concentrate only on the tray, ignoring the cell, the Princess, everything but the floating flat plane of formed metal. A familiar voice seemed to remind him of something.

'Don't try so hard, Luke,' the voice said. 'Remember how I taught you. Relax, relax, let the Force work through you. Don't try to force the Force.'

Letting other thoughts leak into his mind, pleasant thoughts, Luke strove to comply. A general sense of well-being flowed through him and he smiled. The tray lifted firmly to its former height and continued on the hallway at a rapid pace.

The Princess switched her gaze constantly from Luke

to Halla and back. Striking the corridor wall, the tray commenced bumping along it. It finally reached the recessed control, turned itself flat to the wall and covered the depression. A very faint click sounded. An open ellipsoid appeared in the middle of the cell bars.

Halla let out a long, slow sigh and wavered, almost falling. She caught herself as the tray plunged towards the floor. Hin and Kee gasped, as did the Princess.

Luke leaned forward, his brow lifting sharply. Something caught the tray barely a centimetre above the hard stone floor and lowered it gently, and silently, the rest of the way.

First through the gap were the two Yuzzem. The Princess followed immediately behind. Once clear, she turned and called to Luke. 'What are you waiting for . . . come on!'

But Luke was back at the window. 'Are you all right, old woman?'

'I will be,' Halla quipped, her face still showing the strain, 'if you don't call me that too often. Couldn't have done it without your help, boy. Your control is good.'

'Not as good as your guidance,' he responded gently. 'You showed me the way. I've been lucky. I've had good teachers.'

She reached through the bars and patted his hand. 'You're kind, Luke boy. There's a big landspeeder garage and maintenance yard nearby. You turn right as you exit this mausoleum and pass some prefab administrative co-ops. Continue on until you hit a small adjusted stream. Turn right again, follow the stream. You'll pass a few more, larger buildings.

'Eventually you'll reach the depot. The garage is the big structure on the immediate left. I'll meet you there with your 'droids.'

'What happens when we get there?'

'Happens? Why boy, we've got to steal a landspeeder or crawlhigh. Or do you think we're going to walk to the crystal? Not on this planet! See you there.'

'Right,' Luke acknowledged.

'Hurry up, Luke!' the Princess was calling to him, expecting a flood of troops at any moment. When he didn't reply, she rushed back into the cell, grabbed one arm and pulled. He came willingly, still glancing back towards the window Halla had already abandoned.

A loud commotion sounded ahead and Luke made worried noises.

'What's wrong?' the Princess asked, trying to see around corners in front of them.

'It's the Yuzzem.'

'Sounds like they're having fun,' she demurred, after an especially violent crashing echoed down the corridor.

'We ought to be trying to sneak out of here quietly.'

'A subtle Yuzzem. You might as well wish for a squadron of Y-wings,' she snorted derisively. She picked up the tray and passed it over the cell lock, then slipped it back inside the bars.

'That should give them something to think about,' she announced with satisfaction. 'Let them think we dematerialised the bars. It won't bother Grammel, but it might make some of his troops uneasy. I want anyone trailing me to be as nervous as possible.'

Together, they started up the corridor.

Hin and Kee were waiting around the second corner. The first Yuzzem was standing over the limp forms of three troopers. He was using a 'droid to beat a fourth soldier to pulp. The 'droid he was holding by one leg was coming apart at roughly the same rate as the man.

Kee had a long armful of weapons apparently taken from the decommissioned troopers. Luke caught a pistol tossed to him, as did Leia, while the two aliens armed themselves.

Kee promptly assumed a listening pose, turned and dashed towards a far doorway. 'No, not now!' Luke protested. Reaching out, he came away with two handfuls of brown hair. This did not seem to affect the big alien in the least.

'I was afraid of this,' he groaned. It took only seconds for Kee to flatten the door and burst inside. They followed.

The large room was a communications centre, possibly the central one for the whole temple complex. Kee was rushing about, firing wildly with a rifle held in one massive hand while using the other to demolish both instrumentation and operators with casual indifference as to whether the target was inorganic or protesting.

Luke charged in behind, yelling in Yuzz: 'We've got to get out of here, Kee! Listen to me!'

No use. The creature was beyond reason. Luke left the room. As he did so an energy bolt smashed into the wall just above him. Dropping to one knee, he whirled and fired his pistol, dropping an Imperial trooper charging towards them down a secondary corridor. Leia caught another in the midsection and the remaining pair dived for cover, firing as they did.

'Regulars are beginning to show up, Luke!' she shouted. 'We can't stay . . . we've got to get out.'

'I can see that,' Luke shot back nervously. He pressed back against the wall, pushed and shoved at Hin to get his attention. 'Come on, Hin use your head instead of your back for a change!'

The big Yuzzem growled dangerously at him. Luke didn't let that intimidate him. 'I know this whole place stinks. I'd like to blow it to hell and gone myself, but we're just a little outnumbered.'

Hin bared sharp canines and grabbed Luke by the neck. Luke stared resolutely at his furry visage. Abruptly, the hand moved away and Hin nodded slowly, giving out with an apologetic grunt.

'Okay then,' Luke sighed. 'Go get Kee.' Another bolt broke stone above them and he turned to return the fire. The hallway was starting to fill with Imperial troops. Luke retreated up the hall, calling 'Come on, Leia!' Under his covering fire, she ran to join him. Then the two of them covered the alien's retreat.

As Kee emerged from the communications room, a tremendous explosion shattered the door frame behind him. Smoke and flame gushed from the ruined portal, singeing the Yuzzem's back fur, but that helped screen them from the massing troops.

Hin had a surprise for Luke and handed it to him expectantly. 'My lightsabre! Where'd you find it?' The Yuzzem explained that the soldier who'd appropriated it wouldn't need it anymore.

Luke refastened the heirloom at his belt as the four of them ran for the front of the building, leaving confusion and blood in equal amounts behind them. . . .

VII

GRAMMEL rushed into the corridor, several troops at his heels. The Captain-Supervisor finished buckling on his pants and screamed at the assembled mass of troops.

'What the double moons is happening here?'

'Get down, get down, sir!' one of the sub-officers yelled frantically to him.

'What for, you idiot!' Grammel roared. 'Can't you see they're interested in escaping, not in killing you?' Pulling a pistol from its holster, he grabbed at the sergeant next to him. 'Get in there,' he instructed the noncom as he gestured towards the communications room with the pistol, 'and tell them to secure every exit. No one goes in or out of the complex until I give my personal okay.'

'Yes, Captain-Supervisor!' As the sergeant rushed from the room, Grammel led the by now enormous body of armed troops up the smoking hallway.

Very soon the sergeant exited from the room, shouted after them that communications were out and everyone inside was dead or dying. But Grammel was already out of earshot. The sergeant rushed after him.

Luke threw up a warning hand and the four would-be escapees slowed to a halt. 'There's the exit,' he informed them, pointing around the corner.

Ahead lay double transparent doors leading to the now-attractive damp ground outside. An unarmoured soldier sat scribbling at a desk to one side of the doorway.

'They haven't heard the alarm here yet,' Luke muttered.

'That won't last long,' the Princess declared knowingly. 'He's not alone.' She indicated the two guards flanking the exit. Each was armed with assorted devices in addition to a brace of heavy rifles.

Luke leaned against the wall, thinking furiously. It was a long way across an open floor to the doorway.

'We could cover the Yuzzem,' the Princess suggested. 'If they can take out the man at the desk before he can sound an alarm . . .'

'No,' Luke objected. 'Too risky. If the two guards are good shots Hin and Kee will both be killed. Maybe if you and I put our weapons down and fake one of us being in trouble . . .

'Well,' Luke went on thoughtfully, 'we could make some noise here, maybe draw one or both of them away from the alarm switches . . .'

Hin and Kee listened a minute longer to the two humans chattering, then exchanged glances. Hin grunted and Kee nodded in reply.

An ear-splitting shriek made both Luke and Leia jump. Waving their gangly arms and brandishing their rifles like toys, the two Yuzzem went charging around the corner like a hirsute avalanche.

The tactic was unrefined, but it worked. All three guards became momentarily paralysed by the sight of the two giants bearing down on them. At the desk the uniformed trooper shakily hit two studs . . . neither of them the right one.

Hin was on the first guard before he could raise his heavy weapon. It went off, blasted a gaping hole in the floor. Without bothering to remove the man's armour, Hin proceeded to dismember him.

Kee picked up the entire desk and communications console and brought it down on the terrified trooper behind it. The other guard had finally unlimbered his heavy weapon. He was taking aim on the nearest rampaging Yuzzem.

'Kee, look out!' Luke yelled, even as he and Leia

were charging around the corner and across the alcove. A bolt of energy ionised the air above the Yuzzem and then exploded against the far wall. Luke dropped the guard with one burst from his pistol.

By then the Princess had reached the double doors and was trying the manual release frantically. 'It's no good, Luke! It's got to be activated remotely. From that, probably.' She pointed to the demolished desk.

Luke looked around, started fumbling at the body of the soldier he'd shot. There were several smooth, hand-sized canisters attached to the man's waist and he carefully removed them.

Taking action of his own, Hin yanked the helmet off the man he had killed. Placing it over his fist, he began punching at the transparent doors. Despite the Yuzzem's enormous strength, the fragile-looking material refused to crack.

'That won't work, Hin,' Luke finally informed him, hurrying up alongside. 'Security material ... you'd never break through. Get behind the corner. You too, Princess.'

She didn't argue with him. Together with the two Yuzzem she rushed to take cover around the bend from which they'd attacked.

Luke twisted the dial set on top of the canister, flipped the small cylinder over and adjusted a matching dial set on the bottom. After placing it at the junction of the double doors, he ran to join his companions. Several seconds passed.

The blast gave the feeling that lightning had struck just behind them. Green fire flared around the corner and faded instantly to acrid smoke. When they peered around the wall, they saw that both doors and a portion of the building's foundation had vanished.

'They've improved those things,' Luke observed professionally. The Princess didn't wait for the smoke to dissipate. She was already picking her way towards freedom through the steaming rubble. Hin and Kee followed close behind.

A shot passed over Luke's head and he ducked, hesitating. Leia had reached the gaping hole where the doorway had been. She paused, looked back and waved anxiously. 'Come on, Luke!'

But Luke was busy. Kneeling on the floor while bolts continued to strike around him, he activated the remaining three canisters he'd taken. One energy bolt struck dangerously close, making him blink. Rapidly, he rolled each canister down the hallway, then rose and ran madly after his companions.

Grammel and the mass of troops behind him pulled up short as the canisters came rolling and bouncing innocently towards them. The corridor cleared with inhuman speed.

Luke passed through the blown doorway, counting out loud to himself. When he got to six, he threw himself to the ground and placed both arms over his face. Three titanic explosions erupted inside the temple, sending shards of both modern metal and ancient stone *whoo-whooing* over his head.

When the debris finally stopped falling, he scrambled to his feet and ran on. Leia and the Yuzzem left their concealing trees and rushed to meet him.

'Nothing broken,' Luke assured them in response to the unvoiced question. He brushed mud and plastic splinters from his coveralls. 'I feel filthy all over, though.'

'Funny,' said the Princess tightly, 'that's the feeling I got whenever Grammel looked at me.' She gestured behind him. 'They won't be chasing us for a couple of minutes, anyway.'

Luke turned. The entire entrance of the temple had collapsed. Smoke and flames were issuing from cracks in the wall and roof. Sirens and alarms were beginning to sound from the town.

Moving at a fast trot, with the Yuzzem hurrying to

keep pace with the two humans, they rushed off in the direction specified by Halla. Eventually they encountered the stream, hurried on alongside it. Before too long they reached the maintenance yard, which was larger and more imposing than Luke had expected. It was dark out now. The vast, silent open space was littered with huge sections of mining machinery and portable transporters, some lying about in assorted stages of breakdown.

'I don't see anything,' Luke whispered.

Beside him, the Princess's suspicions were returning. 'Do you think she left without waiting for us?'

Luke shot her a look of irritation. 'She risked her life to get us out of that cell.'

'Even certifiable heroes can panic,' was the Princess's cool rejoinder.

'I will panic,' came a voice, startling them all, 'if we don't get out of here and fast!' Halla emerged from the shadows cloaking the vast assembly shed on their left. Two figures, one humanoid, the other not, trailed her.

'Threepio . . . Artoo!'

'Master Luke!' Threepio called. 'We were worried you wouldn't get free. Oh.'

Threepio was staring at the squat, snouty shapes standing behind Luke and the Princess.

'Don't worry. These are Hin and Kee, a couple of Yuzzem. They're with us.' Artoo beeped querulously. 'I know they look ferocious, Artoo, but they helped us escape.' A pleased whistling.

Halla was looking admiringly at Luke. 'What did you do, boy?' A faint explosion sounded by way of footnote to her comment, from the general direction of the temple headquarters. 'Sounds like the mine itself's going up.'

'I just tried to delay our pursuit a little while,' he explained modestly. Another explosion made them all wince reflectively. A pillar of yellow flame lit the night sky, piercing the mist. 'I might've overdone it a little.'

Halla led them inside the open shed, directing them between a long line of massive shapes to an open vehicle mounted on bloated, multiple wheels. They climbed in. Halla positioned herself behind the controls. 'At first I didn't know how I was going to start this beast,' she told them. 'Your little friend took care of that. Artoo, get us going.'

The stubby Detoo unit trundled forward. Extending an arm, it positioned a tool part of itself into a coded, locked slot. The engine rumbled to life immediately.

'Occasionally,' Threepio was forced to concede, 'he's useful for something.'

'Are you sure you can drive something this size?' the Princess inquired.

'No, but I can drive anything smaller, and I learn fast.' Halla touched something with a finger and the crawler leaped forward with startling acceleration for so bulky a vehicle. They exploded out the shed entrance, nearly running over several mechanics who were walking towards them to investigate the noise the engine had made. They scattered, one man throwing his helmetcap after them in disgust and frustration. Others ran to notify their superiors.

Halla put the wheel hard over. They smashed through a wire fence. In seconds the graded ground gave way to bog and jungle. She headed the swamp crawler over the soft bog and through the trees and bushes with reckless disregard for whether or not they might be travelling over solid earth or bottomless peat.

After barrelling for half an hour through total darkness broken only by the crawler's multiple fog lamps, Luke finally put a restraining hand on Halla's arm. 'I think we can slow down now,' he said, with a glance back the way they'd come. At least, he thought it was the way they'd come. Halla had made so many frantic turns and swerves during their wild flight he couldn't be sure any more.

'Yes, slow down,' the Princess urged, 'Luke may not

have left anyone capable of organising immediate pursuit.'

Halla brushed a strand of grey hair clear of her eyes and brought the crawler to a gradual idle. Using a flex-lamp set on her side of the crawler's open cab, she hunted through the mist until it settled on a high clump of vegetation. After driving the crawler into it she switched off the engine, leaving only the internal cab lights on.

'There!' she exclaimed tiredly, leaning back in the driver's chair. 'Even if they're right behind us, which I'd bet against, they'll have a time finding us here.'

The cab lights gleamed eerily in the gentle swirling mist.

A querulous chittering sounded behind them. 'Kee wonders if we have anything to eat,' Luke asked. A second grunt. 'Hin wonders, too.'

'Never heard of a Yuzzem that wasn't always hungry,' Halla replied. She turned in the chair and pointed towards the rear of the vehicle. 'There's a big storage locker back there. It's full of rations.' She permitted herself a smug grin. 'I checked through the yard pretty thorough before settling on this particular mud-mauler. Engines are full-charged and we can run on them for weeks. Plenty of food and equipment on board. Water's never a problem on Mimban, so long as you take care to kill the things that live in it before you drink.'

'I'm impressed,' the Princess admitted. 'How did someone like you – not authorised, I mean – manage to set up the theft of a fully equipped, expensive vehicle like this crawler?'

'You sure are strangers here,' Halla commented. 'Nothing's put under guard here if it's larger than a personal handcase. There's nowhere to run off to with anything big. The only way off-planet is under Imperial supervision and they check everything that comes down and especially anything going off.

Anyone could make off with a crawler like this one or a truck. But just try and steal one drill bit! No, any thief has only one place to run to, and that's back to one of the five mine towns . . . and Grammel.'

The Princess nodded. 'I'm hungry myself. Luke?'

'In a minute.' While she moved to excavate something for them to eat, Luke turned to Halla.

'How far do you estimate we have to go before we reach the temple where the crystal's supposed to be?'

'According to what the native told me . . . Oh, here, it makes more sense if you can see it.' She reached inside the top of her suit and brought out a small slip-case. It bulged with papers. Hunting through it, she finally selected one and unfolded it before Luke.

He studied the drawing in the dim light of the crawler's console illumination. 'I can't make anything of it.'

'I'm no artist,' she grumbled, 'and the native wasn't either.'

'No, you're not.' Luke stared at this enigmatic old woman in the mist. 'What are you, Halla?'

She broke into a wide, toothy smile. 'I'm ambitious, boy. That's enough for you to know.' Picking up the map, she checked some instrumentation on the console, then pointed into the darkness.

'A week to ten days' travel, local time, in the crawler.'

'That's all?' Luke exclaimed in surprise. 'So close to the mine? I'd think a ship coming down would be able to spot it easily.'

'Even if it could, through this soup,' Halla told him, it wouldn't inspire a rush to the site. There are probably a hundred temples in the immediate vicinity of the mine towns, and more scattered through the jungle nearby. Why bother with it? Also, a thousand men could march within five metres of a temple here and miss it entirely.'

'I see.' Luke sat back, considering. 'What kind of place is it? Is it anything like the temple building that Grammel's people used for a headquarters?'

'That, nobody knows, not even the natives. No human's ever seen the temple of Pomojema. Remember, the natives who built the temples had thousands of gods and deities. Each had its own sanctuary.

'According to the records I managed to get a look at – they're not classified or anything – this Pomojema was a minor god, but one who was supposed to be able to give his priests the ability to perform miraculous feats. Healing the sick and stuff like that. Of course, half the Mimbanian gods were supposed to be capable of miracles. Nobody wants his neighbour's god to have a bigger reputation than his own. But with this Pomojema, those legends could hold some truth. The Kaiburr crystal could be the basis for those stories.'

'If Grammel's Essada gets hold of it,' Luke muttered disconsolately, 'it'll become a force for destruction, not healing.'

Halla frowned. 'Essada? Who's this Essada?' Her gaze went from Luke back to the Princess. 'Is there something you two aren't telling me?'

'Governor Essada,' the Princess told her, shifting uncomfortably at the mention of the name.

'A Governor? An Imperial Governor?' Halla was becoming visibly upset. Luke nodded. 'An Imperial Governor's after you two?' Another nod.

She spun in her seat, started the crawler's engine. 'This expedition is cancelled, boy! Off! I've heard rumours of what the Governors can order done to ordinary citizens. I don't want any part of it.'

'Stop it, Halla! Stop it! Luke was wrestling with her for the controls. His greater strength finally prevailed and he shut the engine back down. 'Artoo, don't start up again unless I give permission.' A response beep sounded.

Halla gave up, slumping tiredly. 'Leave it alone, boy. I'm an old woman, but I've still got some life left in me. I don't want to throw it away. Not even for a chance at the crystal.'

'Halla, we have to find the crystal, and we have to do it before Grammel can catch us or this Governor or his representatives arrive on Mimban.'

'Grammel,' she muttered knowingly. 'He must have recognised the significance of the splinter he took from you. He must have contacted this Essada.'

'He did,' admitted Luke, 'but I'm not so sure he understands the worth of the crystal, or this Essada either. We can't take that chance. We have to find it first, because if we're captured, they'll learn about it from us . . . no matter how hard we try to keep it a secret.'

'That's so,' she admitted.

'And if we can't escape with it,' Luke continued remorselessly, 'we have to destroy it. It must not be allowed to come into Imperial possession.'

'Seven years, boy, seven years,' Halla muttered. 'I can't promise you that if we do find it, I'll be ready to break it into dust.'

'All right,' Luke agreed. 'Let's say we won't worry about that now. All that's important is finding it before Grammel finds us.'

'A week to ten days,' she told him. 'If the terrain doesn't get too bad and we don't run into trouble with the locals.'

'What locals?' The Princess wasn't impressed. 'You don't mean those pitiful things we saw crawling and begging for a drink back in the town?'

'Some of the native races of Mimban haven't been ruined by contact with human beings,' Halla told them. 'They're not all as degraded as the greenies. Some of them can, and will, fight. Keep in mind how little of this world has actually been explored. Nobody really has much idea what's out there,' she waved towards the night, 'beyond the immediate perimeter of the mine towns. Not the archaeologists, not the anthropologists . . . no one.

'There are enough discoveries right by the towns to keep the small scientific station here plenty occupied, girl. They don't have the time or the need to go tramping off into this muck looking for specimens. Not when the specimens wander into town.

'We'll be going places no one's had reason to go before, and we'll likely encounter things no one's met up with before. This is a thriving, healthy world. We're a nice dollop of meat. I've seen visuals of some of the carnivores of Mimban. Their described methods of eating aren't any prettier than they are.'

She turned back to Luke. 'Look under the seat, boy.' Luke did so, found a compartment holding two blaster rifles and four pistols. 'They're all charged,' she informed him, 'which is more than you can say for the ones you broke out with.'

Luke removed the two rifles and passed them to the Yuzzem who would be able to handle the bulky weapons easily. Then he handed a pistol to Leia, gave one to Halla, and kept the third for himself. The remaining one he left inside the compartment.

Hin began sighting along the rifle experimentally. On this model, the trigger guard was set close to the trigger itself. Too close for a thick Yuzzem finger. Hin used both hands, applied pressure in a certain way. After the guard snapped off, he tossed it over the side and thumbed the trigger with satisfaction.

Luke speculatively aimed his own pistol at a nearby bush. A touch of the firing stud and a brief flare of intense light dissolved the bush. Pleased with the new weapon, he slipped on the safety and attached it to his belt.

There was one more thing he had to do. Taking the pistol he had brought with him, he flipped open its butt end. Switching the terminal control from *Charge* to

Draw, he attached it to the matching terminals in the haft of his lightsabre.

Leaning back, he regarded the mist silently as his father's ancient weapon sucked power . . .

□ VIII

AFTER replacing the marrow, the doctor had heat-sealed the bone, then folded muscle, flesh and skin around it to reform. An epidermal flush concluded the operation and assured that the new skin would take and not fall off in fragments and flakes in the near future.

While powerful, the local anaesthetic the doctor had used was beginning to wear off. Captain-Supervisor Grammel still had no sensation in his right arm, but he could see it. He used his left hand to lift the rebuilt limb towards the light and turned it over for a look at the obverse side.

Experimentally he tried flexing his fingers. They reacted only slightly, but they reacted.

'There is no permanent nerve damage,' the doctor informed him as Grammel slid out of the infirmary surgery booth. Grammel continued to study his arm. 'The nerves were easy to lay back in and the bone sealed smooth. Your arm is as good as new. It will feel and act like it in about five days. Only one thing.' The Captain-Supervisor looked at her. 'You'll never sweat from that arm again.' As the doctor continued putting away her instruments, she continued conversationally, 'If more than your forearm had been equally destroyed – let's suppose the entire upper half of your right side – then we'd have had to equip you with at least one series of artificial perspirators. But with radical reconstruction restricted to your right forearm, your body will compensate for the lost area easily enough.'

With an exploratory hand she reached out and

touched the right side of Grammel's face. 'How is your hearing on this side?'

'Adequate,' Grammel replied curtly. 'You're an efficient mechanic, Doctor. I'll see that you're suitably rewarded.'

'There is a way to do that.'

'What would you like?'

She slipped out of her stained robe and returned to arranging her instruments neatly within the proper cabinets. She was an old woman and her eyesight and hearing were not what they once were. Certainly not as good as Captain-Supervisor Grammel's, even allowing for the new timpanium she'd installed in the rebuilt ear.

An unlucky woman, she'd permitted her modest talents to be used by the Empire. Such was often the case with people who no longer cared much about living or dying. She hadn't cared since a particular young man had perished in a fiery landspeeder crash some forty years ago. The Empire had stepped in and given her, if not exactly a reason to live, something useful to do in lieu of dying.

She squinted up at him. 'Don't execute those six troops. The ones from the rear restraint detachment.'

'That's a surprising request for a reward,' Grammel mused. 'No,' he added sombrely, seeing the expression on her face, 'I suppose it's not. Not coming from you. I have to refuse.'

He ran a hand over the dark suture that ran from the upper part of his partly shaved skull down by his rebuilt ear to disappear like a fishing line into his lower jaw. There was an organic suspension implanted along that line. It would hold his jaw in place and allow it to function normally until that side of his face knitted properly. When the healing process was complete, the suture would be absorbed into his body.

'They're incompetent,' he finished.

'Unlucky,' the doctor countered firmly. She was

about the only person on Mimban who dared argue with the Captain-Supervisor. Healers can usually afford to be independent. Those who might be tempted to fight with them never know when they might have need of their services. To Grammel, a little dissension was cheap insurance against an accidental slip of the bone welder.

Turning from her, he studied himself in a mirror. 'Six fools. They allowed the prisoners to escape.'

As usual, the doctor couldn't begin to read Grammel's thoughts. It was entirely possible he was admiring the scar running parallel to her suture. Most men would have been appalled by it. Grammel's aesthetics, however, differed from those of most men.

'Two Yuzzem,' the doctor reminded him, 'with human aid are a difficult combination to fight. Especially if outside help was involved.'

Grammel turned to her. 'That is what has been troubling me. They must have had such help. The escape was too clean, too neat, for it to be otherwise. Especially for a pair of strangers. You still have not given me a legitimate reason for cancelling the execution of the six guards.'

'Two of them are permanently maimed,' she told him, 'and the others all scarred in various ways beyond my ability to repair. Your resources here are far from limitless, Captain-Supervisor. If you intend to search the region around all the towns you're going to need every walking man you have. Besides, compassion makes men work harder than fear.'

'You're a romantic, Doctor,' Grammel countered. 'Despite which, your evaluation of my resources is quite accurate.' He turned to exit the room.

'Then you'll countermand those execution orders?' she called after him.

'I have no choice,' he admitted. 'One cannot argue with figures.' The door closed silently behind him.

The doctor turned back to her white sanctuary, gratified. Her task was to save lives. Whenever she could do that in a situation in which Grammel was involved, she felt a true sense of accomplishment....

Days passed, became four, then five, six.

On the morning of the seventh day, Luke slid into the seat alongside Halla. The old woman insisted on taking her turn behind the controls and neither Luke nor Leia could talk her out of it.

'You said seven days,' Luke finally ventured evenly.

'To ten,' she admitted amiably, continuing to keep her attention on the ground ahead of them. She fought to give the impression that age had honed instead of weakened her ability to penetrate the mist.

Great trees with down-curving branches hung close by them. Halla negotiated a winding path around the thick boles.

Leia was resting on one of the cushioned, water-repellent seats behind them, gnawing on an oblong piece of fruit she'd found in one of the food lockers. The fruit shone in the dim daylight. It had been treated with some kind of slick preservative that gave it a honey-like glaze.

'You sure we're going in the right direction?'

'Oh, there's no mistaking that, girl,' Halla insisted. 'But the distance could be a little uncertain. The greenies have a way of telling you what you want to hear. Maybe the one who babbled to me felt that if he'd told me the temple of Pomojema was a month's journey off instead of a week's, I wouldn't have given him his methanol roll.'

'Maybe,' the Princess suggested, 'he told you there was a temple because he thought the same way. Maybe there is no such temple.'

'We do have the piece of crystal as proof,' Luke pointed out. 'At least, we did.' He looked downcast.

'There now, Luke boy,' Halla comforted him. 'As you

said, there was nothing you could have done about that.'

'Are you sure about the crystal's properties, Luke?' the Princess asked uncertainly.

Luke nodded slowly. 'I couldn't have made a mistake, Leia. That stirring inside me when I touched it ... I've only felt that before in the presence of Obi-wan Kenobi.' He stared off into the damp greenery. 'It's strange, like waves breaking inside your head, through your whole body.'

'Okay, the crystal gets first priority then.' She turned to face Halla. 'But afterwards, we have to get off this planet. The Alliance will give you whatever reward you wish, Halla, if you help us.'

'Oh, you can count on that,' she said. 'I'll do my best for you two.' She noticed a beep from Artoo and added, 'Excuse me ... you four. But I want nothin' to do with the Rebels. I'm no outlaw.'

'We're not outlaws either!' an outraged Leia exclaimed. 'We're revolutionaries and reformers.'

'Political outlaws, then,' Halla shot back.

'The Empire is staffed by outlaws.'

The old woman grinned back at Leia, her expression wizened by years. 'I'm no philosopher, girl, and I lost any martyr complex I might've had forty years ago.'

'Come on, you two,' Luke brought in uncomfortably.

'Do you think she's right, Luke?' the Princess asked quietly.

'Leia, I ...'

'Well, boy?' Halla watched him expectantly.

He was saved the necessity of a response as an abrupt lurch threw everyone towards the left side of the crawler. Halla responded swiftly by throwing all six wheels into reverse. Leaning over the side, Luke had a bad moment when he saw the forward balloon wheel sinking into something with the consistency of watered porridge.

But the crawler was well designed. Multiwheel drive and the powerful engine pulled them clear. Halla leaned over the wheel for a minute, then studied the terrain ahead. A paler plot of ground lay between patches of the treacherous sludge. Running forward once more, the crawler pushed on over firmer ground.

'You have to be alert every second on Mimban,' Halla declared. 'This is a crazy world, where the ground itself is your most uncertain enemy.' As if in response, the ground trembled beneath them. Luke frowned, peered over the side.

'Just how stable is this region?' the Princess inquired uneasily.

'First you want me to be a philosopher, now a seismologist,' quipped Halla. 'Stable? You know as much as I, child. There are no volcanoes hereabouts, but—'

She froze, barely retaining enough sensation to bring the crawler to a halt.

'I knew that *quake* wasn't the right word,' Luke stated.

The firm, winding path they were travelling had risen abruptly in front of them, turned back on itself, and was now staring at them quizzically.

'Force preserve us!' Halla yelped, even as she spun the crawler on its central global wheel and sent them racing at high speed back the way they'd come.

The ground continued to turn and come after them.

Pale cream in colour, with streaks of brown, the colossus possessed nothing resembling a normal eye. Instead, the blunt end which was curling back towards them boasted a score of haphazardly spaced dull, black spots like the eyes of a spider.

A ragged tear below the black orbs was the only other recognisable feature. It split now, revealing jet-black teeth set in concentric circles lining an endless gullet.

Both Yuzzem were chattering madly and firing at the great hulk, with as little accuracy as effect. The rifles left thin black streaks on the anaemic-looking flesh, but didn't penetrate deeply enough to cause any real destruction. Luke had his own pistol out and working, as did the Princess. Their bolts glanced harmlessly off back or sides, or the bottom body plates. Threepio and Artoo hung on desperately.

'Wandrella!' Halla was yelling. 'It's a wandrella! We're finished.'

The great blunt head was still winding ponderously back towards them. They were travelling on firm ground now and not on the monster's back. But the swamp crawler was built for sturdiness and stability, not speed.

Branches and whole trees snapped off as the probing head curled after them, followed by the great train of the wandrella's gargantuan body. Thick sucking sounds issued from beneath the huge body plates as the creature humped along after them. It travelled slowly, but each time it moved it covered metres. And it moved in an inexorable straight line, whereas the crawler had to dodge trees and pools of bottomless ooze. It drew so close that Luke and the others gathered desperately in the front of the crawler.

'Aim for the eye-spots!' he ordered.

Everyone took his advice, and this time their shots seemed more effective. Several bolts struck a couple of black circles, searing them badly. A dull rumble boiled up out of the creature's depths, a lingering, moaning thunder. It was part confusion, part barely realised pain.

By now it was clear that the wandrella's nervous system was either too primitive to be instantly neutralised by energy fire, or too evenly distributed throughout its mass and thus devoid of any vital centre.

Ten metres of its front end lifted up, dropped like a great white tree falling in slow motion. Halla tried to dodge, and the crawler struck a thick, rotting stump. The first wheel climbed over with a jolt, sending them tumbling to the floor of the crawler cab, but the second did not. They were hung, the stump pinning them between first and second axle, as that nightmare torso plunged down on them.

Opening wide, the black maw bit and clamped tight around the rear of the crawler. Its grip was devastatingly firm for so rubbery-looking a creature. No one had to give the order to abandon the vehicle. That was understood instantaneously.

Kee was last off, lingering for a final shot down the partly opened throat. He barely leapt clear as the crawler rose into the air. Only his extra-long arms enabled him to retreat safely.

Then they were sprinting for a hiding place, but there weren't any. No mountains to climb, no caves in hillsides here, and they had to be cautious or seemingly solid ground would devour them as efficiently as the worm behind them.

Crumpling noises reached them. Looking back over a shoulder as they ran, Luke saw the wandrella chewing the swamp crawler as if it were some choice morsel plucked from a tree. The analogy was not lost on him. If any of them had tried climbing a tree for protection, the same fate would befall them as the unlucky crawler.

Their only chance was to find *some* kind of hiding place, secret themselves out of sight, and pray that the hulking threat's sense of smell did not match its size.

Possibly the creature belonged to so primitive a species that it would regard prey as out of sight, out of mind. If it could no longer see them, hopefully the dull-witted monstrosity would interpret that to mean they no longer existed.

'This way!' Luke abruptly decided, turning and running to his left. Leia followed. Slightly ahead and sandwiched between the two Yuzzem, Halla didn't hear him. She and the two big aliens continued on the way they were headed.

Several minutes passed before a tired Halla slowed and did think to glance behind her. When she did, she saw only the phosphorescent convoy of white worm sliding through the mist well behind them.

She came to a stop, admonishing the two Yuzzem to do likewise. 'It's gone off in a different direction,' she exclaimed. Hin, panting like an engine, nodded affirmation. The trio squinted into the fog around them.

'Luke boy, child,' she called, 'you can come out now. It's given up on us.' Mist-sounds and peeps from the underbrush responded blankly. 'Come on, Luke boy,' she added, beginning to feel a little nervous, 'don't be fooling old Halla like this.'

Trying to help, Kee let out a stentorian bellow. Halla had to jump to clap a hand over his mouth, then put her own hand over her own mouth and shook her head, pointing to the last bit of wandrella disappearing into the growth not far enough away. Kee nodded realisation, called again more softly through his snout for their missing companions. Artoo was whistling mournfully.

'Luke,' Halla called again, worried. Together, the three began searching the surrounding brush. When several minutes of this failed to turn up any sign of the Princess or Luke, Halla gathered up the two Yuzzem and glanced back the way they'd come.

'I don't think it got them . . . not yet, anyhow. They were right behind us.' She turned, and they started to retrace their steps in the hope that Luke and Leia had somehow managed to elude the beast.

'They may be hiding under a tree somewhere,' ventured Threepio hopefully.

Neither assumption was correct. Luke and the Princess hadn't been devoured, but neither had they lost their lumpish pursuer. As they had deserted the crawler, the wandrella noted the movement unemotionally. Once the mangled swamp vehicle proved itself unappetising, the leviathan had turned after smaller and, it was hoped, more nutritious prey.

But mysteriously, its food had split into two parts. In primitive wandrella reasoning, the nearer was tastier. Ignoring Halla and the others, it swerved to follow Luke and Leia.

'It's still behind us,' Luke told her, breathing with difficulty. A massive circle lined with black dots was humping through bog and brush after them. Leia stumbled over a gnarled root and Luke fought to help her up.

'I . . . don't know how much longer I can . . . keep this up, Luke.'

'Neither do I,' he confessed tiredly, his frantic gaze hunting for somewhere, anywhere, to conceal themselves.

'What about a tree?'

'Already thought of that,' he informed her, as they stumbled on. 'That thing could pull us out of the biggest tree here, or push it down.'

'It's getting closer,' she exclaimed, with a backwards glance. Her voice was starting to crack.

Luke squinted, saw what appeared to be a regular line of rocks. 'Over there,' he urged.

They staggered up to what turned out to be, not a natural formation, but an artificial construct. Each stone was shaped in a hexagonal pattern and fitted to its neighbours without any visible cement or putty. A peculiar tripod of wood and plaited vines decorated with paint or dyes was arranged above the circular wall.

'Looks like some kind of ceremonial cistern,' the Princess decided as they stumbled the last few metres towards it. 'Maybe it holds water for a dry season.' She looked back. The merciless pale horror continued remorselessly towards them.

Luke started to put a foot over the wall, got a glimpse beyond it at the same time and recoiled in terror. The stone wall surrounded a pit a good nine or ten metres in circumference. Though the sunlight here was far from bright, filtered as it was through mist and rain, it was sufficient to indicate that the empty gulf yawning beneath him was of frightening depth.

The Princess got a look at it too and sucked in her breath. 'Luke, we can't ...' But he was running around the edge of the abyss, calling to her.

'Over here, Leia!' She hurried around the side, came up to him.

'Luke, we can't stay ...' He shook his head and pointed to something inside the wall. Leaning over, she saw the cause of his excitement.

They were standing at a place where the wall had been cut away. A gateway covered with indecipherable alien scrawl framed the stoneless section. Attached to small stone pillars were two vines. They descended into the darkness, intertwining to form a strange spiral ladder.

'Luke, I don't know ...' she began.

He dropped to the ground, grabbed one of the vines and tugged on it with all his strength. The vine didn't give. Behind them, the wandrella had approached to within fifteen metres. It opened its toothy maw. A low, lymph-curling ululation issued from within.

That made up Luke's mind. 'We haven't got a choice,' he insisted.

'Down there, Luke?' The Princess shook her head. 'We can't. We don't know what ...'

'I'd rather die in a dark hole,' he said tightly, staring hard at her, 'than be some monster's breakfast.' Then he started down the vine ladder. 'Come on,' he urged her, yelling upward. 'It'll hold both of us!' He continued his descent.

A last look at the quivering mouth hunched towards her and the Princess swung both legs over the side of the pit and started down into nothingness. It was not quite black as night, but dark enough so that Luke had to feel for each succeeding rung. Once he moved too quickly and almost fell. With his right leg he felt around for the next rung.

There was no next rung.

He'd reached the bottom of the ladder.

'Hold it!' he shouted softly up to Leia. The slight echo of the pit gave his voice a sepulchral quality. Above, he could barely make out her frightened face as she turned to look down at him.

'What is it . . . what's the matter?'

'End of the line.' Beyond his feet he could only see unending blackness. It seemed as if they'd descended no distance at all. But as his eyes adjusted to the light, he thought he saw something a couple of steps above and to his right.

Climbing, he soon made contact with the Princess's feet. After calming her, he reached out and stepped off to one side. The ledge he'd spotted was barely a metre wide, but another of the tough vines had been attached to the wall above it, running parallel to the ledge about waist-high. Carefully, Luke hooked one arm over the vine. 'There's a ledge, Leia,' he explained, reaching out a hand for her. She stepped over, grabbed the vine with both hands and examined the rock underfoot.

'Someone cut this out of the pit wall,' she observed positively. 'I wonder who, and for what purpose?'

'I wish I knew,' Luke admitted. 'Too bad Halla's not here. I bet she could tell us.'

A loud, reverberant scraping sound from overhead killed further conversation. Pressing tight against the pit wall, they turned wide eyes upward. The sound wasn't repeated.

Luke felt the warmth of the body next to him and lowered his gaze. Framed in the faint light from above, the Princess looked more radiant, more beautiful than ever. 'Leia,' he began, 'I . . .'

More scraping, louder, ominously so. Several rocks

and pieces of wall fell from above and shot past them. They tried to bury themselves in the unyielding stone, tried to merge with the dampness dripping down its sides.

A loud *thunk* sounded far below. It was one of the fallen stones finally hitting something. Luke wasn't sure it was bottom.

Breathless, they stayed huddled together, eyes fixed on the circle of misty sunlight above. With infinite slowness, something slid into view. At the first it looked like a sooty cloud obscuring the sun. Small sounds came from the Princess's throat. Luke was completely paralysed.

The massive worm-head eclipsed the opening. It swung back and forth like a horizontal pendulum, moving from side to side, searching with senses unimaginable.

Looking around desperately, Luke spied what might have been an opening in the pit wall. It was at the far end of the ledge.

'Follow me,' he instructed the Princess. When she didn't move, he grabbed one hand and pulled. She followed him, her gaze still frozen on the monstrosity above.

The opening turned out to be large enough to hold both of them. It was tall enough so that Luke hardly had to stoop to fit inside. Both stared up and out, relieved to be off the narrow ledge.

Perhaps the creature above was sensitive to their relief. Something certainly attracted it, because the great skull abruptly ceased its weaving motion. It turned downward, facing them.

'It sees us!' the Princess breathed, gripping Luke's arm so hard it hurt. 'Oh, it sees us!'

'Maybe . . . maybe it's just looking down the pit,' Luke responded more hopeful than sanguine.

With a hunching movement that filed stone and rock from the upper edge of the chasm, the head drifted lazily down towards them. Its vast mouth was agape, framing a darkness deeper than that of the pit itself.

'It's coming down,' the Princess breathed. 'It's coming for us, Luke.'

'It can't. It can't reach us,' Luke insisted, feeling for his pistol. It wasn't there. He'd dropped it in the retreat from the crawler. His hand went around the hilt of his lightsabre.

A ponderous groaning sounded. Larger chunks of dislodged stone fell past them, went crashing and booming off the walls below.

'How long is it?' Luke wondered, indicating the worm-like creature.

'I don't know. I didn't get a good look. It seemed to go on forever,' she responded. The wandrella was less than a dozen metres above them, and still moving. There was no doubt that it saw them now. 'Can't it get a purchase on the wall? It's so slick.'

'I don't know,' he mumbled dully. His fist tightened convulsively on the hilt of the sabre.

All at once the worm-thing seemed to leap down at them. The Princess screamed, her shriek echoing madly around the walls of the pit as Luke yanked the sabre from his belt and activated it. In the plutonian confines of the well its clean blue light was small comfort.

But the wandrella was not striking at them. Over-extended even for its own incredible length, it was falling. It went rocketing past, a seemingly endless white waterfall of faintly glowing flesh. Leaning out, they saw it shrink to a dot, a pinpoint of brightness before it finally vanished into the abyssal depths. Echoes of the creature bouncing and bumping from wall to wall drifted up to them with steadily increasing faintness, dying memories of a massive death.

Luke shakily deactivated his sabre and reattached it to his belt.

At the same time, the Princess grew aware of how tightly she was clinging to him. Their proximity engendered a wash of confused emotion. It would be proper to disengage, to move away a little. Proper, but not nearly so satisfying. She was utterly drained, and the comfort she derived from leaning against him was worth any feeling of impropriety.

They stood like that for a timeless stretch. Luke slid his arm around her and she didn't resist. She didn't look yearningly up at him, either, but this was enough for him, for now at least. He was happy.

An eternity later a querulous voice bounced down the walls to them, so gently he wasn't certain he'd heard anything at all.

'Luke, boy . . . are you down there?'

They exchanged glances. Luke leaned uncertainly out of the little alcove they'd sought refuge in and stared upward. Four faces were staring back down at him from high above. Two were bewhiskered and furred. One was golden and metallic.

'Halla?' An excited chittering came back to him. Hin, unmistakably. When the hysterical hooting finally died down, Halla called to him again.

'Are you two all right, Master Luke?' Threepio called down to them.

'I think so,' he shouted back. 'It came down after us.'

'I thought you were behind me all the time,' came Halla's reply. 'I'm glad you're still alive.'

'So are we,' exclaimed the Princess, her normal self-reliance flooding back rapidly. 'We'll join you in a minute.' She started out of the rock recess.

'No, we won't,' countered Luke sombrely, putting out an arm to stop her. 'Take a look.'

Her gaze followed his pointing arm. Where the wandrella had fallen, the walls of the pit were scraped clean and chipped away as if scoured by some huge abrasive pad. The vine spiral ladder they'd climbed down was completely gone. So was more than half the ledge,

'We've no way back up,' he called out to the anxious watchers above. 'The vine ladder we came down was torn away. Can you make another one?'

Silence from above. For a few moments the faces moved out of sight. Luke found their absence worrying, but they finally returned.

'I wouldn't trust any of the vines growing near here,' Halla called down to them. 'The ladder you used must have been made from vines brought from some distance away. But there might be another way out.' Luke studied the smooth-sided interior of the pit.

'Another way? What are you talking about, Halla?'

'Where were you standing when the worm fell past you?'

'There's a small recess in the wall here, at the end of a ledge,' he informed her.

'A ledge, too,' she repeated, sounding satisfied. 'How big is the recessed place?'

'Big enough for both of us to stand in.'

'I thought so. You're in a Coway shaft, Luke boy.'

'A what?' the Princess called out, frowning.

'Coway, child,' Halla repeated. 'I told you there are, and were all kinds of races co-existing on Mimban. The Coway are related to the greenies of the towns, but they're not the least bit subservient. They live underground, which is why nobody knows a helluva lot about them. But they use the old Thrella wells for occasional access to the surface, in addition to natural sinkholes and other surface openings.'

'First Coways, now Thrella wells,' mumbled Luke, studying the emptiness below them. 'What's a Thrella well?'

'A well bored by the Thrella,' Halla replied, not unexpectedly. 'They're just called wells. Nobody knows what they were really used for, just like no one knows much about the Thrella. Maybe they built a lot of the temples, too.

'In any case, they're long gone and the Coway are

here. If you go back to your recess, you'll probably find that it opens on to a passageway.'

'If it does, we'll find it,' Luke assured her.

'The Coway don't try to conceal their surface exits,' Halla went on. 'If you can find your way out, we'll meet you there. I'm sure I can find the nearest Coway egress.'

'Sounds good,' a hopeful Luke admitted, 'except for one thing. What do we do for light? I've got an emergency luma on my belt, and I can always use the sabre, but I don't want to use up the charges.'

'Just find the passageway,' Halla told them confidently. 'You'll have plenty of light, if it *is* a Coway passage. Take my word for it, boy.'

'We'll try it,' Luke agreed. 'We'll go through and meet you.' He turned away, hesitated, then leaned back out and called upward again. 'Halla?'

A small face reappeared over the rim of the chasm.

'Yes, Luke boy?'

'What do we do if we meet any Coway?

'They're not very numerous, and they move around a lot,' Halla told him. 'It's not likely you'll run into any. If you do meet up with a couple, they'll probably be so startled they'll run from you. Remember, they're not domesticated like the greenies. They know as little about us as we do about them . . . I think. You hear lots of reports of them lingering around the towns, but they disappear if anyone goes after them. So that probably means they're shy and peaceful.'

'That's two very important probablys,' he shouted uncertainly.

'You've still got your sabre.'

Luke's hand went to the comforting haft of the weapon. 'All right. Stay there a second.' He turned to Leia. She wasn't there. 'Leia?' he said aloud. Swelling fears vanished when she reappeared seconds after his call.

'There's a tunnel back there, just like the old woman

thought,' she said cheerfully. 'I used my own luma.' She gestured with the tiny, self-contained light. 'It widens out right away.'

'Which direction?'

'Off to the east, about thirty-one-degree heading.' She indicated her suit tracomp.

'Thirty-one degrees east, Halla,' he shouted upward, relaying Leia's information.

'Okay, boy. We'll move in that direction. How are you two on rations?'

Both hurried to check their belts. The brief survey was more encouraging than Luke had hoped.

'We've got enough concentrates between us to keep going for about a week. I expect we'll find plenty of water.'

Halla's cackle rippled down the well walls. 'I expect you'll have trouble avoiding it, Luke boy. If what I know about Coway tunnels holds, we should meet up with you in a couple, three days at most. Light, food, water . . . you two kids hang on, understand? We'll find you.' A concurring series of squeaks from Hin and Kee, and then the three faces disappeared.

'Please be careful, sir,' Threepio added. Then he, too, vanished.

Luke stood a moment longer gazing upward. Despite the seeming nearness, he was not surprised to discover that he couldn't touch the sky with a fingertip.

'They're on their way,' he told Leia, turning back to her and switching on his own luma. 'We'd better be on ours. . . .'

□ IX

THEY'D been walking some ten minutes when Luke ventured thoughtfully, 'I wonder if we might not've been better off waiting in the alcove until Halla and the Yuzzem could've gone back to a town and come back with some stolen cable. Hin could pull us out of there by himself, with those arms he has.'

Leia stepped over a small pile of rough gravel. 'You think she'd consider going back to town without the crystal to face Grammel?'

'What difference would the crystal make?'

Leia eyed him fondly. 'You don't understand her, do you, Luke? Obviously she's convinced she can turn Grammel into a frog with it.'

Luke made a disparaging sound. 'Leia, she's not that irrational about the crystal.'

'You don't think so?' The Princess formed her next words carefully, gently. 'Think a moment, Luke. Halla's a very persuasive, knowledgeable old woman, but she's been on this world a long time. Years spent hunting down a myth. It's clear to me that she believes the Kaiburr has supernormal powers. Even you agree it doesn't possess any such thing.'

'I know. Okay, so maybe she's a little fanatical on the subject, but—'

'Fanatical?' The Princess sighed. 'Luke, the poor woman is sick with delusions, can't you see that? Her dreams have overwhelmed her sense of reality. But we need her, ill as she is, to get off this planet.'

'The crystal's no delusion,' Luke argued mildly. 'It's

real. If this Governor Essada and his people get to it before we do . . .'

She shuddered visibly. 'Essada. I'd almost forgotten about him.'

'Leia, why are you so afraid of an Imperial Governor?' he asked gently as they walked on. 'What could Moff Tarkin have done to you back on the Death Star before Han Solo and I rescued you?'

She turned memory-haunted eyes on him. 'Maybe I'll tell you someday, Luke. Not now. I'm not . . . I haven't forgotten enough. If I told you I might remember too much.'

'Don't you think I could take it?' he asked tightly.

She hastened to correct him. 'Oh not you, Luke, not you. It's me, my own reactions I'm worried about. Whenever I start trying to remember exactly what they did to me that time, I start to come apart.'

They walked on in silence. 'Say, don't you think it's getting brighter in here?' she finally said, with exaggerated cheerfulness.

Luke blinked, the feelings that had been running searingly through him for the past several minutes beginning to fade as he considered the import of her comment.

Yes, it did seem lighter. Almost bright, in fact.

'Switch off your luma,' he instructed her, even as he was thumbing the switch of his own.

For a brief instant it grew darker. Then their eyes compensated and it was as bright as before. The light was a faint blue-yellow, somewhat brighter than the hue of his own sabre.

When his gaze returned to the Princess he saw she was standing next to the tunnel wall. 'Over here,' she called, directing him to an especially luminous section of stone. He leaned close. It seemed as if the rock itself was pouring out the light.

'No,' she corrected when he voiced that thought, 'look closer. Here.' She dug at the stone with her nails and the light came off in her hands, setting her palm aglow. It burned coldly in her hand. After a while it started to fade out.

'Some kind of growth,' she announced, 'Lichen, a fungus . . . I don't know. I'm no botanist. This is what Halla told us we'd find if we kept on.' She brushed living light from her hand, looked on down the gradually descending cave. 'It's another world down here, but now I don't find it frightening.'

As they continued downward, the path they were travelling levelled off. The tunnel widened into a true cavern. Multi-coloured stalactites began to appear, mineral impurities turning them into painted pendants coated with the phosphorescent growths. Blunt-tipped stalagmites thrust ceilingward. They were accompanied by the ever-present music of dripping water.

A faint rumble sounded ahead and they slowed cautiously. The noise turned out to be the song of a running underground stream. It ran parallel to their path, a bubbling, unceasingly cheerful guide and companion.

They passed a hole in the cave's roof. Water poured through it and disappeared into a bottomless pond, looking for all the world like a piece of standard piping with the middle section removed.

Further on, they encountered a miniature forest of helicites. These twisted, grotesquely contorted crystals of gypsum defied gravity in their swirling projections from floor, walls and ceiling. Luke had the feeling they were walking through a gigantic clump of glass wool. Here the reflections from the glowing plant life reached blinding proportions.

In addition to the lichen-fungi, they were starting to see larger, more advanced varieties of light-generating vegetation growing from the ground and walls. Some looked like cantilevered mushrooms. They passed a tall stand of something that resembled paralysed bamboo encased in quartz. When the Princess accidentally bumped into one, they discovered another of its properties.

There was a bong. Startled, Leia jumped aside, then experimentally gave the stem a sharp rap with her knuckles. The ringing was repeated.

'Hollow, maybe,' suggested a delighted Luke.

'But are they vegetable or mineral?'

'No telling,' he admitted. He rapped another of the growths and was rewarded by a totally different ring. They exchanged smiles, and then the cave was filled with crude but sprightly tunes as the natural chimes sang under their hands. They grinned like a couple of mischievous children.

Eventually they tired of this amusement, resuming their journey as Luke broke out two concentrate cubes and handed one to the Princess. He talked while examining the path they trod.

It was unmistakably that, a pathway. 'Look at the absence of big rocks along here,' he was saying. 'This has definitely been cleared for use. I don't see any footprints, though.'

'Ground's too hard,' the Princess agreed. 'But it's an exquisite place, a fairyland. Much more attractive than the surface. If Mimban is ever settled formally, everyone should live underground, I think.' She executed a neat pirouette, evidently out of sheer pleasure, 'It's so peaceful and clean down here, I almost—'

The sentence ended in a startled scream an she started to vanish downward.

Throwing himself forward and flat, Luke stretched out a desperate arm. She caught it above the wrist. Her hand slid along his forearm until it locked in his. She hung like that, her hand in his, as she swung in emptiness. Luke felt his feet slipping as he fought to dig them into the hard ground.

'Can't hold . . . Luke,' she breathed urgently.

'Use your other hand,' he directed through clenched

teeth. She reached up and her left hand went around his forearm. The motion dragged him forward another few precious centimetres.

A large stalagmite thrust upward close by. If he was wrong and it had formed over the same crust the Princess had broken through, they'd both fall as the worm had. Every muscle and tendon in his body straining, he edged a little towards it. Releasing the precarious grip his left hand had on the ground, he threw it round the stone pillar. That arrested his forward slide, but now he was in danger of losing his hold on the Princess.

Somehow, he managed to slowly inch backward along the ground, gravel digging into his chest and belly as he used the stalagmite as a brace. Continuing to move backwards, he leaned into a sitting position, got his left leg propped against the outcropping. Now he was free to grab the Princess's wrist with his other hand.

He shoved with his left leg, his thigh muscles quivering under the strain. The Princess emerged from the hole, moving towards him. There was a faint crumbling noise and the stalagmite started to crack at the base. Shifting his right leg behind the pillar along with his left, he pushed frantically with both feet.

The Princess shot towards him. An instant later the stressed limestone gave way and the force of his shove sent Luke sliding towards the gaping blackness. Rolling away from it, the Princess caught him with a hand, her weight halting his slide. Now Luke rolled clear and came to a panting stop on her chest.

For a long moment they lay like that, suspended in time. Then their eyes met with a gaze that could have penetrated light-years.

Sitting back quickly, the Princess began brushing at her suit. Her coveralls were torn from being dragged across the jagged edge of the gap and the rubble coating the cave floor. Luke sat back, trying to knead some feeling back into his right arm.

'Maybe,' she ventured at last, 'underground wouldn't be the best place to settle on this world after all.'

Wordlessly, they climbed to their feet. With Luke testing the ground ahead, they skirted the hole that had opened in the seemingly solid floor. A glance into it revealed a pit as bottomless as the Thrella well.

Luke hesitated when a section of earth seemed to depress under his foot. He looked around, pointing to the stream that continued to swirl on its fluid way.

'The ground looks firmer over there.'

'It also looked firm where I stepped,' the Princess reminded him. Luke turned his gaze on the ceiling. Above the hole and the section of floor immediately ahead, a convex bowl showed in the roof. Above the stream and to its left the roof was filled with stalactites.

'I think we'll be okay on the other side of the water,' he decided. But when they crossed over they advanced slowly, Luke continuing to test the footing before them with a probing boot. The Princess followed behind him, her left hand locked in his right. Before long they had passed beyond the overhead bowl and the pit. Stalactites once more filled the roof from wall to wall.

Just to be certain, he unlatched his sabre. Activating it, he jabbed the lightblade into the ground ahead. There was a hissing and bubbling as stone turned molten around the blue shaft. Luke pulled it free and turned it off. Leaning over, he dropped a small pebble into the smoking hole. It hit bottom with gratifying speed.

They walked on with more confidence, but their delight in the beauties of the underground wonderland was considerably diminished.

'Let's hope we find that exit soon,' Luke commented.

But instead of turning sharply upward as they hoped, the path continued level. If anything, they seemed to be descending slightly. The tunnel continued to widen ahead of them. They turned a sharp bend, and emerged on a startling scene.

A vast underground lake lay ahead of them. Despite the phosphorescent plant light, the lake was so wide that they could not see the far shore. The water was as black as the inside of the Emperor's mind.

Their cleared path angled off to the left. It continued on to the water's edge before disappearing into it about a metre from the wall.

'I guess this explains why we haven't encountered any signs of Coways,' Luke mused. 'This portion of the trail is underwater. It must rise and fall frequently, according to the rainfall on the surface.' He followed the trail into the water, wading out until it was up to his chest before returning.

'No good. It's too deep.'

'But we have to go on, I suppose,' the Princess observed not liking the look of the glassy black surface. 'There's nothing to be gained by going back.

'Are we still moving thirty-one east?'

Luke checked his tracomp. 'A little south of that. The trail probably curves back on the opposite shore. I hope. But in a way, the lake's a good sign. Maybe it means that the ground on the other side starts to rise, because so much water collects here. I wonder how deep it is?'

'No telling,' the Princess mused. She walked into the water, bent over and felt a bit of a hidden bottom. 'It slopes downward pretty steeply.'

Luke was looking past her. On the other side of the stream they'd been following grew a small forest of water plants apparently stimulated by the steady flow of fresh nutrients here. The huge leafy pads floating on the black surface were a dull, yellow-brown colour. They were round and pointed slightly at two ends where the upturned edges met.

'You can't,' Leia commented, 'be thinking of travelling on one of *those*.'

'I'm not swimming,' Luke told her, walking towards the forest. He hopped the stream, splashing through the opposite side. Leaning over, he saw signs of broken stems just beneath the surface.

'Looks like some of the pads have already been snapped off. Probably the Coway use them.'

'Or else they broke free naturally,' the Princess grumbled, so softly that Luke didn't hear her. She moved to join him.

Tentatively, Luke stepped on to one of the flat pads. The one he was testing was two and a half metres in diameter. As he pushed down with his weight the yellow interior gave spongily. But it didn't break and his foot didn't push through.

Unsteadily he moved on to the pad. His knees sank into the surface, which held. His mouth firming, he jumped into the air and came down as hard as he could with both knees. The pad sank up to his hips in the water, then rebounded solidly.

Convinced that the pad was lake-worthy, Luke rolled to its edge and looked to see the man-thick stem which secured the pad to the lake bottom.

'I'm going to cut this one loose,' he announced.

The Princess looked sceptical. 'With what? Your sabre? I didn't know they operated under water.'

He gazed back at her solemnly. 'They'd better.'

He slipped over the side and found himself treading cold water. Then he activated the sabre and shoved it under the surface. Bubbles promptly broke the glassy water, but the hard blue light continued to gleam in the blackness, and there was no hint of malfunction.

Taking a deep breath, he slid into darkness.

Fortunately the sabre itself provided enough light to show him the stem. It took only a second or two to slice through the tough core. He noted with interest that the pad narrowed to a concave shape, instead of being flat across the bottom. That would give them at least an illusion of stability.

Then he was breaking the surface, gasping for air and wiping water from his eyes after deactivating the sabre. Once it was secured to his belt again, he put out a hand and tugged the freed pad close to shore.

He employed the sabre briefly again to cut a small hole in the rear of the pad. With a thin roll of survival cord he secured their craft to a stalagmite on shore.

'These might do for propulsion!' the Princess called to him. She was further up the shoreline and slightly uphill. Luke moved to stand beside her.

A series of transparent selenite crystals flowed from the roof to floor here. Each was taller than a man, perhaps a couple of centimetres thick. Phosphorescent growths on them gave them the look of windows in a church, and the knife-edged mineral was suffused in places with vermilion light.

'They're almost too beautiful to break,' Luke commented in admiration. 'But you're right ... they'll make good paddles.' Using the invaluable sabre once more, he cut loose four blades of the right size, shaping them with the blue beam for holding. Then they carried them down to the water and placed them carefully in the leprous lily they hoped would carry them across the lake.

'Ready to go?' he asked finally. Leia hesitated and checked her wrist chronometer.

'We've been walking for nearly sixteen hours, Luke.' She gestured at the lake. 'If we're going to try and cross that, I'd just as soon do it on a full night's sleep.'

'Or day's sleep,' Luke agreed. They had no way of telling whether it was day or night in the world above.

He found a rotting piece of one of the pad-growths marooned on shore and dragged it upslope. It would make an acceptable mattress.

'You go ahead,' he urged her, as they stretched out on the soft matter. 'I'm not quite tired yet.' She nodded and tried to find a comfortable position on the damp cellulose.

In two minutes they were both sound asleep. . . .

Luke awoke with a start, sitting up fast and flicking his eyes in all directions. He thought he'd heard something moving. But there was nothing, only the steady trickle of the stream merging with the lake, and the sound of drops falling into the lake itself from overhead.

After checking his timer he woke the Princess. She rubbed sleep from her eyes, asked, 'How long?'

'Nearly twelve hours. I guess I was exhausted, too.'

They broke out fresh concentrates and munched them hungrily. Luke brought water from the stream in a collapsible cup. They ate by the transparent brook, watching waterbugs swim anxiously back and forth.

'I never dreamed concentrates could taste so good,' the Princess observed, finishing the last of one cube and downing several swallows of water.

'My appetite will improve when we see sunlight again,' was Luke's comment. Out of excuses, he stared at the lake. 'I hope this lake's not as wide as it looks. I don't like travelling on water.'

'That's not surprising,' soothed the Princess, knowing that on the desert world of Tatooine, where Luke had been raised, an open body of water was as rare as an evergreen.

Wordlessly, they slipped on to the pad-boat. Each took up one of the long selenite blades. Luke untied the cord from the stalagmite, recoiled it and replaced it on his belt, then pushed off. They slid out on to the lake as if greased.

Luke experienced exquisite terror as they rowed out across what looked like a bottomless crater. The actual bottom could have been a mere metre beneath them, but the dark water was literally unfathomable.

Like the waterbugs in the stream, worries darted rapidly through Luke's mind. What if the lake ran on for hundreds of kilometres? Or suppose it branched in several directions? Without the visible pathway, they could easily get lost forever.

Their best chance was to hug the wall on their left, where the path had vanished into the water. It seemed unlikely that it would cut across the lake – more sensible for it to stay close to the wall, where presumably it was shallowest.

He imagined unknown terrors. Perhaps a huge subterranean waterfall drained the lake, a cataract which would send them inexorably to a lonely death on rocks that had never seen the light of day. As they travelled steadily on, such imaginary terrors lost some of their immediacy. The waterfall, for example. In the excellent acoustics of the cavern they'd heard no distant thunderous roaring.

After an hour of slow, painful paddling he discovered he no longer cared what they found at the far side of the lake, just so long as they found the far side of the lake.

His upper shoulders began aching relentlessly. He knew it must be as painful if not more so for the Princess. Yet she hadn't complained once, hadn't said a word in protest as they continued the agonisingly slow process of pushing themselves through the water. While admiring her fortitude, he wondered if the experiences they'd gone through so far on Mimban had had a mellowing effect on her. He was unable to tell, but was grateful for it nonetheless.

'Why don't you rest, Princess?' he counselled her finally. 'I'll row for awhile.'

'Don't be ridiculous,' she replied, gentle but firm yet without much enthusiasm. 'It would be silly for you to reach back and forth across this thing. I'm not that confident of its buoyancy as it is. And if you stay in one place you'll just paddle us in circles. Stay where you are and save your strength.'

Luke acceded to common sense, which might be less attractive than gallantry but more practical. They rested periodically. Half the day vanished monotonously without sight of the far shore. In the currentless black water they stopped for a midday meal of coloured cubes.

Far, far above, Luke saw that the cavern ceiling was dominated by clusters of stalactites that dwarfed any formations they'd seen thus far. Several of them must have weighed many tons. There were also long, thin ones, dozens of metres long and no thicker than a man's thumb. All were liberally coated with the luminescent lichen-fungi which filled the enormous chamber with a comforting yellow-blue glow.

As he thought back to Halla's comment on water he grinned. She'd been right about that! It was somehow magical to dip one's cup into the blackness and watch it fill, for the lake's colour was so rich and pure and solid that the blackness had to be part of the water itself.

The water was purer and fresher then any Luke had ever swallowed. As they ate and drank in silence, he reflected on how much he missed the tiny stream that had guided them this far. Its steady bubbling and gurgling had been a great comfort. Now they had to settle for the intermittent and less lively *pings* of drops falling from the stalactites overhead.

Lunch concluded, they continued on. Several hours later an uncertain Luke put a warning hand on the Princess's shoulder and motioned her to cease paddling.

'What is it?' she whispered, questioning.

Luke stared at the absolutely flat, unbroken lake surface.

'Listen.'

Leia did so, studying the water nervously in the dim light. A faint *plop-plop* sounded.

'That's just drip-water from the ceiling,' she husked.

'No,' he insisted. 'It's too erratic. Drip-water falls steadily.'

The noise ceased. 'I don't hear it anymore, Luke. It must have been drip-water.'

Luke looked worriedly at the black mirror they floated on. 'I can't hear it now, either.' Taking up his selenite paddle, he dipped it into the water and began stroking again. Occasionally he would pause for a quick look over one shoulder or the other. So far, however, nothing lay behind them except his own fears.

His nervousness communicated itself to the Princess. She was beginning to relax again, when he held up a hand.

'Stop.'

She raised her paddle clear of the water, a trifle annoyed this time.

'There it is again,' he announced tensely. 'Don't you hear it, Leia?' She didn't reply. 'Leia?' Turning, he saw that she was gazing fixedly at something in the water. Her mouth hung open, but she couldn't speak.

She could point, though. Luke reached for his lightsabre instinctively, even before he spotted the trail of fat bubbles that was arrowing rapidly towards them, as ominous and threatening as any projectile.

Moving carefully to the rear of the pad, Luke balanced himself on a knee and a leg – the activated sabre held tightly in his right hand.

The bubbles stopped and were not immediately resumed.

'Maybe . . . maybe it's gone away,' the Princess murmured tightly.

'Maybe,' Luke half-conceded.

It rose.

A pale amorphous form, shining with phosphorescence, in colour it was not unlike the great wandrella. But compared to the lake-spirit the worm-thing was a familiar creature.

There was no face, nothing recognizable in that constantly altering form. It lifted short, thick pseudopods of a whitish substance clear of the surface. They gleamed brightly in the dim cavern light. Luke thought he could see partway through the creature, and strange shapes swirling about it internally.

One pulsing white arm flailed at the fragile craft. Luke swung at it with his sabre. The blue beam passed completely through the glowing matter. While the sabre produced no visible damage, the action caused the ameoba-shape to reabsorb the limb.

Another curling tentacle swiped at Luke and this time he stabbed at it. The beam shot straight through the arm. There was no hint of blood or internal fluids of any kind. Only the lapping of water against the spongy, rocking pad and Luke's grunts as he fought frantically sounded in the chamber. For the most part the battle proceeded in hellish silence.

Each time the creature thrust at them, Luke would parry the strike with the sabre. Each time the limb would shrink back into the heaving, glowing body without suffering any visible damage.

A sweeping limb caught Luke from behind as he was cutting at another pseudopod. It swept him over the side as the Princess screamed. Somehow he kept a hand on the upcurled rim of the pad-boat. His weight caused it to tilt slightly towards him, but fortunately it was far too naturally buoyant to capsize.

Leia wrestled him halfway back aboard. Then something caught him from below and yanked him beneath the surface. The Princess barely let go in time to keep from being dragged over herself.

Anxious moments passed with no sign of Luke. Then he broke the surface not far off, spluttering and spitting. Flaring brilliantly beneath the water, his sabre swung and hacked at something unseen. It let loose long enough for him to crawl back on to the pad. The sabre arched dangerously near the Princess and his own legs as he cut at clinging pale limbs. He kept cutting until the last grasping pseudopod slunk out of sight.

Dripping wet and still choking on water, he knelt on the pad and tried to look every which way at once.

'Look!' Leia exclaimed. Luke saw the line of bubbles in the water, only now they were moving *away* from the pad-boat. Their steady *plop-plop* sounded for several minutes after the bubbles themselves vanished from sight.

Exhausted, he fell on to his back and stared at the pincushion ceiling.

'You did it, Luke. You beat it off.'

'I'm not so sure,' he panted, feeling anything but victorious. 'Maybe the thing just got tired and went away.' He studied the switched-off lightsabre in his fist. 'Or maybe it decided a sabre beam's not very palatable.' He reattached it to his belt, sat up with a groan and locked his arms about his knees. Water dripped from his hair down in front of his face.

Leia moved closer and reached out uncertainly to touch his arm. He eyed her, then coughed. She sat back. Suddenly she began screaming. Luke looked around but there was nothing in sight.

Bending over, the Princess screamed into clasped hands. The muffled wail continued for several minutes. When it ended, she looked back up at him without apology.

'I'm all right now, I think,' she said with forced steadiness. She took a deep breath. 'I just think . . . I'm ready to leave this place, Luke.' Her voice rose slightly. 'I'm ready to get out.'

'Believe me, Leia,' he replied, taking her hand in his, 'I'm in just as big a hurry as you.'

They exchanged wordless thoughts. Then each picked up a paddle and together they resumed digging black water.

Despite Luke's feeling that their translucent assailant would attack again, they weren't bothered for several hours. But then it didn't matter. The far shore of the lake finally hove into view.

Only there was something more than a naked shoreline coming towards them. 'Surely the Coway didn't build that,' Luke whispered in awe.

An ancient dock protruded from the dry ground ahead. While no boats of any kind were in sight, the long finger of metal extending out into the water left no doubt as to its function, its alien design notwithstanding.

Luke had less luck identifying the purposes of the numerous structures clustered all along the shore. Many appeared raised from stone, others had metal walls, and some were built from combinations of both materials. No matter what the composition, every one displayed signs of considerable age. Not a single edifice rose unmarred by time. Try as he might, Luke couldn't locate a single window. Openings which must have served as doors were squatly oval.

They paddled for the left-hand shore until the pad thumped bottom. Stepping out into water up to his waist, Luke extended a supportive hand for the Princess. She remained in the boat, not exactly frightened, but devoid of confidence.

'Come on,' Luke urged her, 'it's not deep here.'

'But I'd have to step in the water. I'd rather not, Luke.'

'It's all right,' he assured her, masking any impatience. 'You can make it in a few steps.'

She shook her head again. Luke sighed, waded to the edge of the pad. He extended both arms. She slipped into them and he carried her to dry land, noticing as he did so how tightly she held her eyes closed.

Finally they were sitting gratefully on the stone beam, no longer caring if their makeshift craft floated away. Behind them the city of the Thrella loomed silently.

'Okay now?' he inquired, leaning forward and looking at her face. She didn't meet his eyes.

'I'm okay. I'm sorry I was so much trouble. I'm

sorry I did so much screaming. I ... usually have better control of myself than that.'

'You've nothing to be sorry for,' he assured her firmly. 'Certainly not for screaming. As for being frightened,' he smiled gently, 'I was twice as terrified as you when that half-goblin came up out of the water at us. I was too busy to be screaming, or I'm sure I would have.'

'Oh, it wasn't the monster so much,' Leia explained disarmingly. 'That was a real, palpable threat.' She got to her feet, continued almost casually, 'It's just that I can't swim.'

Luke sat staring at her in disbelief as she wrung water from her torn coveralls. 'Why didn't you say something before we pushed off?' he finally managed to ask.

She gave him a wry smile. 'Would that have mattered, Luke? The trail vanished into the lake.' She gestured towards the unmistakable pathway that re-emerged from the water's edge nearby and wound into the subterranean city. 'We had to get across. It was an unfortunate but unavoidable situation. I didn't see any point in burdening you with my own childhood fears.' She walked towards the pathway.

'Look, it goes on through the town. I'd like to meet the people who built this place.' She glanced back at him impatiently. 'We're wasting time.'

Dumb with admiration, he climbed erect and followed her into the maze of structures. It rapidly became clear that the city was the product of an intelligence that had long since disappeared from Mimban. Everything was neatly laid out, and the metalwork showed signs of advanced techniques. The decay of the buildings was due to time, not shoddy design or construction. Given the relative paucity of natural erosion underground, the city had to be ancient indeed.

The absence of right angles as a preference for sweeping curves and arches indicated that the inhabitants of the city had been aesthetically as well as architecturally talented. Beauty of design was another luxury primitive peoples could rarely afford, generally having to gear their construction strictly to the utilitarian.

Something clattered softly behind them and Luke whirled. The mystifying oval portals stared back at him like the eye sockets of grey, bleached skulls. The Princess frowned at him.

'Thought I heard something, that's all,' he informed her, staring resolutely ahead.

They continued on through the city, but Luke's curt disclaimer belied his uneasiness. He *had* heard something. As they walked along the meandering pathway and the buildings drew closer about them, he felt a crawling sensation on his neck as if someone, or something, was staring at him. It became an almost palpable feeling. Yet every time he jerked around sharply for a look, there was nothing. Not a suggestion of movement, not a sigh, not a sound.

He was grateful when the buildings started to thin out and become less numerous. Empty doorways beckoned to him and he was tempted, very tempted, to enter one of the ruined structures to find out if its interior was as well preserved as the outside.

This was not, he reminded himself firmly, the time for playful exploration. Their first concern was to find the way out, not to go poking through this ancient metropolis. However wonderful it was.

He wondered what had caused the extinction of Mimban's advanced races, of the temple-builders and the Trella and the others. Interracial warfare, perhaps, or maybe sequential decadence ending in their being overwhelmed by aborigines like the greenies.

Rock scraped on rock. This time when he spun there was a hint of movement behind a wall of stalagmites off to their left.

'Don't tell me you didn't hear *that*.'

'Rocks fall from the roof constantly in caves,' the

Princess agreed readily. 'I know how you feel, Luke. I'm still pretty jumpy myself.'

'This wasn't my nerves,' he insisted. 'There's something following us. I saw it move.'

Ignoring the Princess's protests, he started towards the ridge of coloured spires. The sound wasn't repeated and there was no movement. Walking in a half-crouch, he reached the far end of the little wall and peered around it. There was nothing there.

'LUKE!'

Ben Kenobi would have been proud. In one smooth motion he threw up a hand to ward off the shape falling towards him, activated and drew the lightsabre at the same time. Unknowingly he performed both actions with the same arm. The hand he threw up defensively held the sabre.

The creature was quickly cut in half.

Luke ran back to rejoin the Princess. She was pointing ahead. Their path was blocked by two more of the bipeds. Others appeared behind them, two, three more, moving in on them cautiously.

'Coway,' Leia commented, bending to pick up a broken stalactite. She shifted it efficiently in her hand, holding it like a dagger as the humanoids stalked them.

Each was slim and covered with a fine grey down. Their eyes were shrunken, dark orbs. Yet they appeared to see Luke and the Princess clearly enough. Each wore a kind of abbreviated set of trousers from which dangled assorted primitive instruments and many charms. These were matched by others hanging from upper arms and neck.

All were armed with a long, thin stone spear made of flowstone. A couple also carried double-bladed axes. They displayed no fear of Luke's lightsabre, despite its recently demonstrated lethal qualities. This indicated either a fair knowledge of human technology from surface visits, or else a bravery born of ignorance.

Luckily their tactics were equally primitive. With a

rolling cry, the three behind all charged together while the two ahead rushed in several moments later. The slight difference in time was critical.

A single swipe of the sabre sliced two of the thrusting spears in half. The third jabbed at the Princess. She blocked the thrust with her stone, got her legs around the onrushing native's and sent it crashing to the ground. Rolling over on top of him, she brought the stalactite section down hard on its skull. There was a plastic breaking sound and blood gushed freely.

Luke ducked a wild axe swing and cut both legs out from under the wielder. By now the two latecomers had entered the fray. Luke dispatched one with a thrust that cut off the hand holding the spear above the wrist. Its owner collapsed on the ground, moaning and holding the cauterised stump.

More cautious than his companion, the second pulled up hastily. He started jabbing at Luke with his spear. Luke promptly cut off the spear point, whereupon its owner threw the shaft at Luke, spun and ran back the way it had come.

Luke turned to the Princess. She was adroitly dodging the alternating cuts and jabs of the remaining native, hunting for an opening. But when the creature saw Luke approaching, it turned to retreat.

Hefting the sabre carefully, Luke let the weapon fly. It passed completely through the Coway at the small of its back, until the solid pommel contacted flesh. It fell to the ground, instantly dead.

'Hurry!' the Princess urged, salvaging an axe from one of the fallen creatures. 'It mustn't get away to warn others.' Luke retrieved his sabre and hurried after her.

Together they ran in pursuit of the single remaining Coway.

In their rush, neither noticed immediately that they were travelling very slightly but unmistakably uphill for the first time since they'd abandoned the Thrella well.

A huge pile of rubble fallen from the ceiling lay ahead. The fleeing Coway reached it, started scrambling for the top. While still on the run, the Princess took aim and heaved the axe she carried with more force and accuracy than Luke (or anyone else) would have given her credit for. It struck the native on the right shoulder and sent it tumbling down the other side of the rock pile.

'You got him,' Luke exclaimed, 'you got him.'

Gasping for breath they started up the hill of broken stone. It seemed brighter on the far side. Probably, Luke mused absently, from denser growth of the light generating plants.

Mimbanian botany was otherwise far from his thoughts now. They had to catch and dispatch the wounded Coway before it brought an army of its fellows down on them. They topped the rise.

And paused there at the sight of what lay just beyond ...

□ X

THE cave opened out into an enormous circular amphitheatre, as large as the black lake only empty of water. High up on the far side of the cavern wall sat several small, single-storey structures. They were of the same construction as the city just behind them, perhaps some kind of gateway buildings. Only these were not nearly as run-down as the structures in the main part of the city. Someone had kept them reasonably intact. The ground around them had been cleared of debris, and walls and roofs were neatly, if crudely, patched. They gave every sign of being occupied.

Below, they saw the native the Princess had nicked with the axe holding his shoulder as he ran towards a great crowd of furred beings clustered in the cavern's centre. They stood around a modest pond, a depression kept full by seepage from the ceiling. A real bonfire blazed to the pond's left, fed by assorted yellow-brown substances which were not honest wood but which burned very efficiently.

Framed by pond and fire were three large stalagmites, to which were tied two growling Yuzzem and an old woman. Halla stood bound by several vine-like cords, while Hin and Kee were mummified by many more. Threepio and Artoo Detoo stood enveloped in vine-cords nearby.

At least two hundred Coway, including armed females and children, clustered around pond, fire and prisoners. The wounded relative running towards them was now yelling at the top of his lungs.

Luke started to turn. The Princess grabbed his arm,

staring hard at him. 'Where would we run to, Luke? They'll be after us in seconds, and they know these passages. If we have to fight and die I'd rather do it out in the open . . . and not on the lake.' She hefted the fallen axe.

'Leia, we—' But she was already scrambling down the rubble towards the cavern.

By this time the injured Coway had reached the crowd and was jabbering excitedly to several large males who wore unmistakable headdresses of stone, and other materials. Several cries came from backward-looking members of the assembly. All eyes shifted to the two beings walking towards them.

Luke held his lightsabre before him. The native Leia had wounded now pointed to the glowing weapon and muttered nervously.

As they neared the mob of assembled troglodytes Luke made what he hoped was a positive, confident gesture with the sabre. The crowd, muttering uncertainly, parted. Twitching internally, Luke and the Princess marched between the ranks of intent natives towards the three captives. While they respected the power of the lightsabre, Luke had the distinct impression they were anything but panicked by it.

'They're not sure what to do,' the Princess murmured, confirming his own thoughts. 'They seem to admire your sabre, but they're not going to grant you godhood.'

'They'll admire it more if they try and stop us,' Luke said grimly, with increasing confidence. He gestured sharply at one knot of Coways which were pressing a little close.

'Luke!' Halla yelped as the two drew near the captives. Both Yuzzem were chattering gleefully at Luke and to one another.

'Well, you met us,' he observed sardonically as he studied their bonds. 'You were right about that too, Halla.'

'Not quite the way I intended, boy.' She shouted something to the three splendidly attired natives the wounded one had approached, then resumed whispering to Luke. 'You realise we haven't much chance of getting out of here?'

'She's right, sir,' said Threepio. 'Try to save yourselves.'

'I didn't walk and row this far to end up sacrificed to some subterranean deity,' he shot back. Abruptly, he realized what had just happened. 'You can talk to them,' he stated in surprise.

'A little. Their language is a variant of the one the greenies use. It's not easy . . . sort of like talking under water. But I can make the chiefs understand me.'

'Chiefs?'

'It seems Coway tribes are ruled by a triumvirate,' she explained. 'Those three laughing boys in the bonnets over there. I just made them a proposal. If they're as noble, or sporting, as I think they are, we might have one chance.'

'Proposal? What proposal?' the Princess inquired suspiciously.

'I'll get to that shortly,' Halla told her evasively. 'We'd located the way down and were on our way to meet you when we were ambushed. It was in a narrow passageway, and in close quarters there were just too many of them. They used nets on your Yuzzem and 'droid friends, boy. We didn't have a chance.'

'We might if I set you free now,' Luke theorised. 'Where are your weapons?'

'Take it easy, Luke,' she admonished him. She jerked her head in the direction of a cluster of low-lying buildings, far off on the right side of the cavern. 'You'd never make it over there. Besides, I didn't see which house they put them in.

'Even if I knew exactly, you'd never be able to cut us free, get to them, and get back in time. You're pretty good with that lightsabre, I expect, but you can't fight a hundred spears all flying at you from different directions at once. Unless,' she brightened hopefully, 'that toy of yours generates a screen as well as a blade.'

'No,' Luke confessed, 'just the blade. How long have you been tied here?'

'About half a day, and my bladder's killing me,' she informed him. 'They've spent the time arguing about which way to go about killing us. They don't have any personal grudge against us ... they just don't like humans generally. Not surprising, if they've been able to observe how the miners treat the greenies. I don't think our Coway friends would be too upset if every human on Mimban suddenly picked up and left.'

'Tell them we're not like the local humans,' Luke insisted, eyeing the circle of hostile faces. 'Tell them that we don't want anything to do with the local people either.'

'This isn't a tribe of philosophers, Luke boy,' Halla explained patiently. 'Their concept of government is damned simple. You can't explain something like the Rebellion to the Coway. But I think,' she added, peering past Luke at the three chiefs who were still engaged in heated discussion among themselves, 'they'll give us one chance.'

'I don't believe it,' the Princess countered, glowering at the old woman. 'Would we give an enemy who'd already killed four of our own a second chance?'

'According to the fella with the gash in his shoulder who preceded you here,' Halla went on, 'you only killed two. The others are just wounded. Apparently the Coway treat death as an inevitable, everyday occurrence. Primitive society, remember? To their way of thinking the two you killed simply died a little earlier than they should have. One chief even berated the dead men just now for making a poor decision. Says they ought to have waited for reinforcements. He's arguing that the blame isn't yours, it's the dead ones', for acting stupid when they should have known better.'

'That's barbaric,' the Princess muttered.

Halla looked smug. 'What've I been telling you all along? Anyway, the one with the shoulder you sliced, Luke, is telling—'

'Not him,' objected the Princess, 'me.'

'Oh?' Halla's estimate of the Princess rose a notch. 'Well, he's been ranting on about what a great fighter Luke is.'

Luke looked distressed at this admiration of an action he'd despised. 'A lightsabre against spears and axes isn't a very fair fight.'

Halla nodded agreeably. 'That's what they're arguing about now.'

'I'm not sure I follow you, Halla.'

'I tried to tell them everything, Luke boy,' she explained, 'when you and the girl were climbing down this side of the rockfall. I tried to convince them that not only were we from off-planet and of a different variety of humanity from the miners, but that you were both fighting the humans on the surface and that if we won, you'd kick them off Mimban. Then the Coway could go back to roaming the surface whenever they pleased.

'One chief is all for it, the second thinks I'm the biggest liar in the history of their race, and the third is undecided. That's what all the noise is about: the first two are each trying to persuade the third to take his side.'

'What about this proposal?' the Princess wanted to know.

'Oh, that.' Halla managed to look embarrassed. 'I suggested that if they couldn't make up their minds as to what the truth was, they could let Canu decide. As near as I can figure, Canu's their local god in charge of adjudicating. All our greatest warrior has to do to convince Canu that we're telling the truth is to defeat one of their tribal champions.'

Luke blinked. 'Give me that again, Halla?'

'Don't worry,' Halla assured him, 'you have the Force on your side, remember?'

'Force? I'd rather have my sabre.'

She shook her head apologetically. 'Sorry, Luke boy. You said it yourself. Axes and spears against a sabre's not fair.'

Luke turned away, looked discouraged. 'I'm no fighter, Halla, and you overestimate the Force's usefulness.'

'Luke, these people are no giants.'

'They're not midgets, either. What happens if we agree to this contest and I happen to lose?'

Halla's answer was delivered with her usual aplomb. 'Then we'll likely have our throats cut in some uniquely primitive manner.' He kicked angrily at the ground. 'Please, Luke. I tried my best. It's our only possibility. They wouldn't agree to fight one of the Yuzzem. They don't think of them as intelligent.'

'Either that, or they're not as primitive as you think,' declared the Princess.

'It's not that so much, child, as the fact that it's we humans who are exploiting the surface. So we're the ones who have to prove ourselves before Canu.'

Further discussion was forestalled when the three chiefs abruptly broke off their conversation. One of them – Luke couldn't tell them apart – turned and called something out to Halla. She listened intently, then grinned.

'It's on. They're willing to abide by Canu's judgment.' She turned a concerned gaze to Luke. 'I'm an old woman, boy, but like I've told you, I still have a lot of living planned. Don't let me down.'

'You must win, Luke,' the Princess said. 'If I don't attend that meeting of the underground on Circarpous eventually our absence is likely to keep them from ever considering joining the Alliance.'

Luke's eyes moved from Halla to Leia. 'The Alliance? What about me? Don't let *you* down. Both of you listen.' He tapped his chest and regarded Leia. 'It's more important in the end that I go on living than it is for me to make some vague patriotic sacrifice. Or,' he continued, facing Halla, 'that I get you out of a jam that you should have been able to avoid. You're the one with all the Mimbanian experience.'

'Luke boy—' she started to argue.

He shut her up with a wave. 'Not now. It doesn't matter anymore.' He handed the lightsabre to the Princess. 'All right . . . what are the rules? And who do I fight? Let's finish this . . . one way or the other.'

'You fight,' Halla translated laboriously, listening to the chief's words, 'until one of you quits, or dies. The word for quit is *saen*. That doesn't matter, since you've nothing to gain by saying it.'

Luke merely grunted, walked towards the chiefs. The entire crowd was babbling now, apparently in anticipation of the imminent battle. Luke found that despite the coolness he was beginning to sweat.

The crowd parted and Luke had his first glimpse of the Coway he apparently was going to fight. Some of the tenseness left him. Though broader than he was the creature was the same height. He didn't appear especially ferocious, either. There were larger Coways in the crowd and more fearsome-looking ones. Yet this modest-appearing specimen was the chosen champion. There had to be a reason, which he was sure to discover sooner than he wished. He examined his opponent guardedly. For its part, the Coway stared back, gave him a profound bow and made an intricate movement with both arms.

Unable to duplicate the complex ritual, Luke gave the Alliance salute. What sounded like a murmur of approval issued from the crowd. It might also have been their way of saying that he was going to be torn to small furless bits, but he preferred to believe the other.

The Coway walked past him and stopped on the far

side of the pond. 'What do I do now?' Luke wondered, calling back to Halla.

'Walk to this side of the pond and face him,' he was told. 'When the second chief, that one in the middle with the blue spines sticking out of his collar, drops his right arm, the two of you go after each other.' Her voice held no humour now.

'Do we have to fight in the water?' he inquired worriedly.

'No one's said so.'

'That's good enough for me.'

A singularly chilling howl came from the crowd. It was followed by dead silence. The middle chief raised its arm, dropped it with a swipe. Immediately, the Coway started across the pond towards Luke.

Luke prowled his side of the water, trying to decide what to try. Should he strike at the head or body? It was impossible to detect any obvious vulnerable spot under that grey carpet of fur. Shouts from the onlookers thundered around the cavern walls.

'Why did you bother to tell Luke the word for quitting,' the Princess whispered to Halla, 'if he can't gain anything by using it?'

'I'm hoping he'll get in a tight spot and use it as a last resort,' Halla whispered back.

'But why?'

'Because it's not the Coway term for quitting. It's a local swear word. Has something to do with parentage, I think.'

Whirling, the Princess gave her a shocked look. 'In Alliance's cause, why'd you do that, old woman?'

'I thought it might do us some good if Luke yells something defiant while that brute is choking life out of him. We've nothing to lose by it. Luke doesn't either. The Coway admire spirit.'

The Princess was too shocked and disgusted to reply. Her obvious feelings had no effect on Halla. She was staring past her, towards the pond.

'If we're lucky he'll never have to say it,' she said blithely. 'In any case, there's nothing we can do about it now.'

Luke jumped around the edge of the water, trying to get some estimate of his rival's mobility. Either his opponent was too clever to respond, or more likely he just didn't care. The Coway headed relentlessly straight for Luke, splashing and kicking up water in a fine display of indifference to anything Luke chose to do.

As far as Luke was concerned, the Coway was far too enthusiastic about this contest. Its actions bespoke an assurance Luke couldn't begin to share.

If he remained where he was, Luke reflected frantically, the Coway would have to come upslope out of the water after him. It would give the worried youth a slight technical advantage. So he stopped moving around, checked his footing, and waited.

Arms outstretched for an unaffectionate embrace, the Coway charged.

Luke met directness with directness. As soon as the creature was close, he threw his best punch straight at the onrushing jaw. Maybe Coway had glass chins. As it turned out the metaphor was inappropriate. The Coway's lower jaw was made of solid granite, not glass. Even so, the force of Luke's blow stopped it. For a second.

When it came on at him again, Luke jabbed with his other fist at where the solar plexus would have been in a human. It didn't even slow the Coway. Luke tried to duck and roll under an outstretched arm, but the aborigine was startlingly quick. It grabbed Luke's shoulder and spun him around.

Luke desperately tried to backpedal but found himself in water. The pond bottom was slippery and he fell backward, landing with a splash. As the Coway threw himself at him he twisted in fear and found himself on *top* of his opponent.

With both hands he tried to force the furry head beneath the water. It wouldn't budge.

It was rapidly growing clear to Luke why the Coway had selected this slightly smaller version of themselves as their representative to Canu's court. He was lithe and agile and one big piece of muscle under all the deceptively soft-looking fuzz.

No other rules, he reminded himself. With one hand he hunted hopefully along the slick pond bottom for a rock, for anything solid and smaller than his fist. He encountered only sand, and all the probing unbalanced him. The Coway threw him off and fell on his chest. Unlike the native, Luke found his head easily forced under the surface.

A few centimetres of water served to turn the roars of the crowd to a muffled echo. He stared upward. Distorted by the water, the batrachian face of the Coway glared down at him. Inexorable pressure held him under as the native pressed him down with one hand and balanced itself with the other.

Desperately, Luke turned to the right. His mouth bumped against something warm and he bit down hard. With a jerk the Coway pulled its injured limb away. Luke's head broke water and he swallowed air gratefully. Like another opponent, the noise assailed him again. Through it he could hear Halla and Leia and Threepio screaming frantic encouragement. Both Yuzzem were hooting deafeningly, while Artoo beeped and whistled loud enough to drown out half the Coways.

If only Hin were in his place! The Coway above him wouldn't be grinning so easily. As the hand he'd bitten returned and tried to get a fresh grip on his skull, Luke twisted violently and probed with both hands. Fingers searched the creature's flanks, hunting for anything sensitive. Most of the regions Luke wanted to try were out of reach, however.

Impatient, the Coway brought its other hand over to

steady Luke's head so that the right hand could get a firm grip on it. Thus balanced, Luke discovered the water working to his advantage. He heaved and spun. The teetering native went over sideways into the pond.

Thoroughly soaked and half-drowned, Luke staggered to his feet. He eyed the Coway as it rose again, trying to think of something to attack next. Meanwhile the native lowered its shoulders and charged.

This time Luke used his right leg. As the youth put every ounce of his remaining strength into the kick, his foot fairly exploded out of the water. It caught the Coway in the mid-section, roughly where a human stomach would be located. Whether from the tremendous force of the kick or the fact that he'd struck a more vulnerable area, the Coway let out a startled *whoof*! and sat down hard in the water.

Stumbling towards it, Luke lifted his leg and kicked again. The Coway wasn't so stunned that it failed to raise an arm to block the kick. Simultaneously it grabbed the swinging leg and fell across it. Luke tried to turn over as the still sitting Coway pulled him towards itself by the one thrashing leg. If the creature could get its hands on him this time, Luke knew the matter would be ended. He was face down on the sand. There would be nothing he could do.

His dragging hands encountered something oblong and unyielding. A rock, but too large for him to get a hand around. He'd need both hands to raise anything so massive, and much better leverage than he possessed at the moment to make use of it.

The hand he feared came down on the back of his neck. It shoved downward, brutally hard; so hard that Luke's face plunged into the sandy bottom of the pond. He felt the clean grains pressing into his nostrils. Raised on a desert world, he was about to meet a sandy death damper than any he'd ever conceived of.

His thoughts became hazy as his blood scoured the last dregs of oxygen from his lungs. A voice sang fancifully in the back of his mind. It was exhorting him to relax. Well, that was simple enough to do, he reflected pleasantly. Relax he would. He was tired, so tired now.

The Coway took it for a ploy and didn't ease the pressure on Luke. If anything, it shoved harder, sensing victory. Then, miraculously, the pressure vanished from Luke's neck. Unable to think of turning to defend himself, of striking back, Luke shot to the surface.

Air! Most delicious of gases, it filled his starved lungs, those weakened bellows pumping harder with every fresh breath. Coughing up water, he stayed on his knees, delirious with the pleasure of being able to breathe again. Only when his system's panicky requests for oxygen faded did he think to turn and look for his opponent.

Blood trickled from the side of the Coway's head into the clear pond water. It was lying on its back, manifestly unconscious, maybe dead.

On hands and knees a thoroughly dazed and somewhat puzzled Luke crawled to the Coway's motionless side. With one hand he touched the other's face, raised a fist over it. But there was no movement. The Coway's distress was genuine and not some cat-and-mouse alien ploy. It did not rise to attack.

Another body was suddenly in the water beside him. 'You won, Luke, you beat him!' the Princess was shouting into his ear. She had both arms wrapped tightly around him and the pressure almost sent them both tumbling together into the water.

'Don't you understand?' she asked brightly. 'You won. We can all go free now. That is,' she continued in a more subdued voice, staring around at the silent crowd and trying not to show any fear, 'we can if these creatures have any sense of honour.'

'I wouldn't worry too much about that, Leia,' he advised her, wiping water from his face. 'Canu has judged, remember? Besides, it takes many thousands of years of advanced technological development for a society to reduce honour to an abstract moral truism devoid of real meaning.

'If this were an Imperial arena, then I'd be concerned.' He regarded the watching natives. 'I think the Coway keep their word.'

'We'll find out,' she assured him, wishing she could share his certainty. Putting his left arm around her shoulders, she helped him to his feet. As they started out of the pond Luke heard something burbling and snorting like a hog in heat. A glance to his left showed the twitching form of his opponent. He was gratified. The Coway wasn't dead.

As soon as this became apparent, several Coway broke from the assembled ranks and approached their injured relative. For a moment Luke felt concern. He'd heard of primitive societies where the vanquished or dishonoured representative of a tribe was put to death for his or her failure.

It looked as if the Coway were more mature than that. They lifted their defeated champion to a sitting position and held some kind of burning plant under his face. Luke caught a whiff of it and it helped him regain his strength. He tried to hurry past. Even if the Coway was dead, he decided only half-jokingly one breath of the incredible pungent burning substance would have aroused him.

Then something caught his eye and he paused, staring blankly at it. What had riveted his attention was not the Coway's continuing methods of medication, nor the vanquished warrior's convulsive reactions to them, but a large rock. As big as a man's head, it lay in the water close by the Coway's head.

His fingertips retained the memory of that stone. It was the one he'd encountered prior to passing out. Or had he passed out? It seemed as if something deep inside him, some resource of which he was unaware, had reacted on the brink of asphyxiation to help him raise the rock, turn and fling it at his tormentor.

Yet he couldn't recall even placing both hands around it, let alone lifting it clear of the water and throwing.

'How did I do it?' he asked the Princess.

She eyed him uncertainly. 'Do? Do what?'

'Beat . . . him,' he added exhaustedly, gesturing loosely towards the Coway fighter.

Her gaze travelling from the native back to Luke, the Princess permitted herself a frown. 'You mean you don't remember?' He shook his head. 'I thought everything was finished when you were pushed under the second time, Luke. I suppose I was worrying needlessly, but by staying under so long you had us all fooled.'

I wasn't fooling, Luke said to himself.

The Princess was smiling now. 'Then you threw that big rock. Caught him right in the temple. The creature wasn't expecting it. He didn't even try to duck. I didn't think you were that supple an in-fighter, Luke.'

Luke could have objected, could have mentioned that he wasn't expecting it either. Only the obvious admiration shining from the Princess's eyes kept him silent. They could discuss all that later, he argued with himself.

But one thing seemed unarguable – somehow, he *had* thrown the rock. By one method or another, he'd thrown it. That was the important thing. Now to find out if his evaluation of the Coway would make his mysterious effort worthwhile.

They reached Halla and the others. All were trying to congratulate him at once. Luke didn't reply. Retrieving his sabre from the Princess, he utilized it on low power to cut away the vines tying old Halla to the stalactites. The old woman nearly fell, momentarily incapacitated by lack of circulation to her bound legs. The Princess was there to steady her.

'Thank you, young lady.' Halla bent over and rubbed her thighs.

Luke moved to release the Yuzzem and the 'droids. As he did so one of the three chiefs, the one whose signal had initiated the fight, interposed itself between Luke and Kee. For an awful moment Luke felt he'd completely misjudged the Coway, that he'd taken a romantic instead of a realistic view of them. Was he going to have to fight again? Or possibly the Yuzzem, not being human, would have to perform some difficult feat of their own to gain their freedom? What unimaginable facet of subterranean law did they face now?

He needn't have troubled himself. The chief merely wished to illustrate Canu's judgment in a fashion clear to all. Luke watched tensely as the native slipped a sharp-bladed knife of volcanic glass from his garments, then relaxed when the blade was used to slice away first the Yuzzem's restraints and then the 'droids.

His relief faded when he heard a muttering sound and turned to see several Coway leading towards him the one he had fought. One supported the bandaged native at each arm. The champion shook off the pair of helpers as he neared Luke.

Muscles tight, Luke gripped the lightsabre firmly and waited. Kee chittered ominously but Luke put up a hand to quiet the Yuzzem.

Reaching with both arms, the Coway warrior clasped Luke around the shoulders and pulled. Luke thought he'd have to use the sabre after all, when the native pushed him away gently. Then it slapped him on one cheek.

Luke blinked. The blow had been nearly powerful enough to knock him out. The Coway murmured something, but somehow it didn't sound like a challenge.

'Don't just stand there,' an amused Halla instructed him, 'hit him back.'

'What?' Luke was confused and not ashamed to show it. 'I thought the fight was over.'

'It is,' she explained. 'It's his way of acknowledging that you're the stronger. Go on, hit him back.'

'Well . . .' Using his right hand, he belted the quiescent Coway hard enough to rattle the native's teeth. Despite Halla's assurances, he braced himself for some sort of violent response. Instead, the native displayed a satisfied expression and dropped to his knees before Luke as the crowd howled its approval.

After the warrior had moved to one side, a second chief drew close. It spoke solemnly, directing its words towards Luke.

'As near as I can figure him,' Halla translated softly, 'we're invited to stay for a feast tonight.'

'How can they tell tonight from today?' the Princess wanted to know.

'Probably they post watchers at their exits on the surface,' the old woman surmised. 'If they haven't always been underground dwellers, it's likely they'd retain surface methods of telling time.'

'Can't you refuse for us?' Luke asked hopefully. 'Tell them how badly we have to return to the world above.'

Halla muttered something at the chief, who replied readily. 'This isn't exactly a request, Luke. If we were to turn down the invitation, we'd apparently insult not only their hospitality but Canu's as well. We have our choice, of course. If we insist on refusing, all we have to do is pick a champion to fight one of theirs and then—'

Luke interrupted with, 'It's just occurred to me how hungry I am. . . .'

□ XI

THEY had no sense of night. When the time for the celebration finally arrived it was as bright in the huge cavern as ever. The phosphorescent plant life of internal Mimban functioned according to schedules that ignored the unseen motions of astronomical bodies.

Having dried his clothes by the permanent bonfire and then dressed again, Luke felt almost himself. Only his neck still bothered him. It ached at the back, where the Coway's unyielding fingers had pressed.

Large platters of exotic-looking foods were passed around a series of concentric circles around the pond. The visitors were entertained by endless dancing, made tolerable in spite of the wailing rhythmic music by the truly astonishing leaps and jumps of the spring-muscled Coway performers.

Halla pronounced judgment on each platter, indicating which foods were tolerable to the human organism and which were not. What went for man apparently served Yuzzem-kind as well, though they did encounter a couple of stomach-twisting exceptions, none fatal.

Luke ate with good grace. He considered Halla's evaluations severly deficient in a few instances, but he consumed enough food to please their anxious hosts and kept it all down.

While much of it tasted like reprocessed X-wing fuselage insulation, a couple of the subterranean gourmet delights were downright flavourful. He tried to concentrate on these. In actuality he ate a great deal more than he intended to. However alien their origin, the dishes set before him were fresh. They were a welcome change from the steady diet of concentrates he and Leia had been subsisting on.

For her part the Princess, seated on his immediate left, appeared to be enjoying the entertainment considerably. Apparently her feelings towards Mimban's surface didn't extend to criticism of its arts.

An inquiry produced a surprising response. 'That's one of the things that's so wrong with the Empire, Luke,' she commented enthusiastically. 'Its art has grown as decadent as the government. Both suffer from a lack of creative vitality. That's what originally drew me to the Alliance, not politics. Politically, I was probably almost as naive as you.'

'I don't quite see,' he said drily.

'When I was living in my father's palace, I was utterly bored, Luke. Examination of why I found nothing entertaining led me to discover how the Empire had stifled any original thought. Long-established totalitarian governments fear any kind of free expression. A sculpture can be a manifesto, a manuscripted adventure can double as a cry for rebellion. From corrupt aesthetics to corrupt politics was a smaller step than most people around me realized.'

Luke nodded, hoping he really understood. He wanted to, since what the Princess had just said was obviously very important to her.

From the platter nearest him he chose a small fruit resembling a miniature pink gourd. He bit into it experimentally. Blue juice gushed all over his front, eliciting immediate laughter from Halla and the Princess.

No, he reflected, he probably never would completely understand the Princess. What do you expect,' he mumbled, laughing at himself, 'from an untutored country boy?'

'I think,' the Princess responded softly, not looking

at him, 'that for an untutored country boy, you're one of the most sophisticated men I know.'

Primitive music and chanting faded into the background as he turned to her in surprise. Like a missile launcher sighting on its prey, his eyes contacted hers. There was a brief, silent explosion before she looked hurriedly away.

Thinking very hard about something he'd hardly dared think about for several years, he bit into the fruit again, more carefully this time.

Suddenly his hand opened as if he'd been shot. The pink bulb fell to the ground as Luke stood bolt upright, eyes open and staring. The Princess rose, trying to make something of the gaping expression on his face.

'Luke ... what's wrong?' He took a couple of unsteady steps.

'Was it the fruit, boy?' Halla looked equally concerned. 'Boy?'

Luke blinked, then turned slowly to face them all. 'What?'

'We were worried, Master Luke. You . . .' But Threepio broke off as Luke turned away to stare eastward.

'He's coming,' he murmured, every letter resounding. 'He's near, very near.'

'Luke boy, you'd better start making some sense or I'll have Hin hold you down and feed you dipills,' Halla said, 'Who's coming?'

'There was a stirring,' Luke whispered by way of reply. 'A profound disturbance in the Force. I've felt it before, weakly. I felt it most strongly when Ben Kenobi was killed.'

Leia inhaled in terror, her eyes widening. 'No, not him again, not here.'

'Something blacker than night stirs the Force, Leia,' Luke told her. 'This Governor Essada must have contacted him, sent him here. He'd be especially interested in locating you and me.'

'*Who* would?' Halla half-shouted in frustration.

'Lord Darth Vader,' Leia mumbled, barely audible. 'A dark lord of the Sith. We've ... met before.' Her hands were trembling. She fought to still them.

A shouting native voice broke the brief moment of desolate contemplation. The music ceased. The dancers halted their gravity-defying leaps and pirouettes. All three chiefs rose and stared at the native running towards the assembly. The runner collapsed in the arms of one chief. A short, mostly one-sided conversation followed. Then the chief left the courier gasping on hands and knees, turned and gesticulated wildly as he relayed the courier's information to his people.

Consternation replaced joy among the gathered Coway. Soon the orderly assembly had become a riot, natives rushing in every direction, hairy arms flying, eyes bulging in panic. Food, utensils, instruments were forgotten, were trampled or overturned.

Then the chief approached the non-Coway celebrants and chattered at Halla.

'What did he say?'

She turned to Luke and the others. 'Humans are coming. Hard-shell humans. Down the main passage from the surface. The way we came in.' She looked disgusted, angry. 'Many humans, carrying rods of death. They've already killed two Coway who were gathering food near the exit and tried to run from them.'

'Imperial troops, in armour,' Luke murmured with satisfaction. 'It has to be, given the other presence I sensed.'

'But how could Vader have found us down here?' the Princess demanded to know. 'How?' Luke was listening to something none of the others could hear, so she turned to Halla. 'Could our trail in the swamp crawler have been followed?'

Halla considered the impossible situation reluctantly. 'Possible, but I doubt it. There were a lot of places where we just about floated across the bog, and couldn't have left a trail. But it's conceivable a top-tracker could have plotted a rough course through the surface, making use of the traces we did leave. It seems incredible, though. I know all the Imperial terrain tracers and none of them are that good.'

'Even if one of them were,' the Princess rushed on, 'how could they go from the ruined crawler to the exit for the Coway cavern? How could they know we're down here?'

'Maybe they thought that after our crawler was destroyed we'd seek shelter underground,' Halla hypothesized. 'But I still don't understand how they knew we'd be in this particular cave.'

'I guess I'm probably the cause of that.' They all turned to face Luke. 'Just as I sensed Vader, he no doubt can sense me. He's had a lot more experience with the Force than I have, so his senses are probably stronger. Don't forget, he was a pupil of Obi-wan Kenobi.' He glanced back towards the shaft-tunnel leading to the surface of Mimban.

'He's coming for us.'

It was not possible for a 'droid to faint, but See Threepio managed a convincing imitation. Artoo chided his companion.

'Artoo's right, Threepio,' said Luke. 'Turning yourself off won't help anyone.'

'I . . . know that, sir,' the tall 'droid responded, 'but a dark lord, coming here. The very thought is enough to make my sensors go to overload.'

Luke smiled grimly. 'Mine too, Threepio.'

The two other chiefs joined the third member of the Coway triumvirate, started babbling at it. Their chatter was punctuated by innumerable gestures and much waving of hands. Luke had the impression many of the gestures and a good deal of the talk concerned the three humans standing nearby.

Finally the chiefs turned and stared expectantly at

Luke. Baffled, he looked at Halla for an explanation. He didn't much like the one she gave him.

'They say that since you defeated their champion, you are the greatest warrior present.'

'I was lucky,' Luke told her honestly.

'They don't understand luck,' Halla replied. 'Only results.' Luke shifted from one position to another. The unswerving stares of the three chiefs were making him acutely uncomfortable.

'Well, what do they expect me to do? They're not thinking of fighting, are they? Axes and spears against power rifles?'

'The differences may be great technologically,' the Princess countered, eyeing him hard, 'but I wouldn't sell these people short anywhere else. They caught two full-grown-Yuzzem without any sophisticated devices. I doubt a group of humans could have done better.

'And they know these passageways and tunnels, Luke! They know where the sinkholes are as opposed to solid ground. The Force isn't a geological phenomenon. . . . Maybe we have a chance.'

'The Coway'd be better off negotiating,' Luke mumbled, unconvinced.

'Sorry, Luke boy,' Halla apologized, after a brief exchange with one of the chiefs. 'An invasion in force is different from a couple of wanderers showing up. They want to fight. Canu,' she smiled, 'will judge.'

'I wish I had your confidence in aboriginal jurisprudence, Halla.'

'Don't fight it, boy. Old Canu did okay by you, didn't he?'

'Luke,' the Princess pleaded, 'we have no place to run to. You just said so yourself. If Vader knows you're here, then he probably knows I'm with you. He won't stop until he . . .' She hesitated, cleared her throat and went on. 'He won't stop, Luke. Even if he has to follow us to the centre of Mimban. You know that.

'We've no choice. We *have* to fight.'

'Maybe we do,' he admitted, 'but the Coway don't.'

'They will whether you do or not, Luke,' Halla assured him. 'We've already claimed we're against what the mining consortium here stands for. The chiefs want us to show them we mean it.'

Luke's thoughts raced crazily through his brain. Occasionally two or three would run into each other, creating further head havoc and making him wish only for a nice, quiet place to hide.

But . . .

He was tired of running.

Now that he reflected on it, they'd been running, Leia and he, ever since they'd touched the soil of this planet. He grew aware that Halla, Leia and the three Coway leaders were all anxiously awaiting some response from him. The Princess's expression was unreadable.

Naturally, he made the only decision he could. . . .

In the frenzy of preparation that ensued, Luke discovered that the Coway were not as helpless as he'd feared. So it was not too surprising to learn that the natives had experienced previous attacks from above before now, both from predatory carnivores and from other primitive tribes.

Most of the time Luke found himself looking on in admiration as the Coway readied themselves to counter the human invasion, rather than proposing suggestions of his own. They went about their preparations with enthusiasm and a grim delight.

Luke was thankful for both their competence and attitude. It alleviated a little of his principal concern: the fear that hundreds of Coway might die in defence of the Princess and himself. It was a good feeling to learn that they shared his anger at the shiny-suited figures descending from above.

Thanks to the tactics being employed by the Imperials, Luke discovered that the Princess was too furious to be really frightened. He tried to encourage her anger.

Anything that kept her from thinking of Vader was worthwhile.

'Using energy weapons on primitive sentients,' she muttered in outrage. 'Another gross violation of the original Imperial charter. Another reason for the Alliance to fight on.'

'The Coway wouldn't think much of your emoting, young lady,' Halla called out from nearby, 'since they consider us the primitives. And judging by the way Grammel and his toadies have behaved towards the local races, sociologically I'd have to side with our subsurface friends. . . .'

As the defenders polished their strategy for the coming assault, Luke and the Princess found themselves reduced to explaining the capabilities and limitations of the weapons all were likely to face.

At least, he mused, it wasn't to be all axes and spears. He hefted his pistol and luxuriated in its lethal weight. It had been one of the weapons taken from Halla and the Yuzzem on their capture, now returned to them.

Hin had promptly turned and handed his energy rifle to the Princess. He explained to Luke that he felt more comfortable with the enormous axe the Coway had provided for him. Kee's attitude was more civilised, and he elected to hang on to his rifle. Or perhaps 'civilised' wasn't the right word.

He was helping with the emplacement of the net when a reverberating crackle echoed like a thunder bolt down the winding approach tunnel. According to Halla, the invaders were at present about halfway between the cavern city and the surface exit.

'E-eleven trooper rifle,' the Princess commented expertly, as the last echoes of the shot died away, 'quarter-centimetre aperture, continuous fire on low power only.' She fought to shift the heavy weapon Hin had given her to a more comfortable ready position.

While their identification of the source of that roar was somewhat less precise than the Princess's, the

Coway recognised its ominousness. They embarked on a final frenzy of preparation.

A call came from a series of spread-out forward scouts. Coway started to vanish before Luke's eyes, moving, jumping, secreting themselves where no hiding place seemed possible. They disappeared into crevices and cracks, into the ground, slipped into holes in the cave ceiling, froze behind false flowstone curtains.

Luke and the Princess hurried to join up with Halla. Both Yuzzem were moving to their predetermined positions, mingling with the less concealed Coway. The two 'droids concealed themselves out of firing range.

Halla concluded her conversation with one of the three chiefs and turned to greet them.

'How many?' was Luke's first question.

'The scouts aren't sure,' she told them. 'For one thing, the Imperials have advance hunters out, too. That was the source of the shot we all heard. Also, they're backed up through the cave. But if I have Coway numerology figured right, they think seventy at least.'

'All on foot?' the Princess inquired.

'Yes. They've no choice, which is good for us. The tunnel is too choked with rubble and too narrow in many places for even a small personnel carrier to slip through.'

'That's something,' Luke observed, trying to bolster his own spirits as much as anyone else's. 'We won't have to cope with mobile armour or heavy weapons.'

Halla chuckled. 'Why would Grammel think they'd be needed? Not against our poor primitive Coway, certainly. Sixty, seventy Imperial troops equipped with energy weapons and personal armour ought to be suficient to capture a few poorly armed fugitives.'

'Sarcasm aside,' Luke pointed out unarguably, 'it's going to take more than bravery and courage to keep this from turning into a massacre of our friends.'

'I'd argue with you, Luke boy,' the old woman murmured pleasantly. 'Give me bravery and courage anytime.'

'Just give me one clear shot at Vader,' the Princess snarled, her hands tightening on the rifle stock. The hatred that flamed in those eyes belonged on a much less fragile face. 'Save that one chance, I ask nothing of life.'

Luke looked down at her and murmured with feeling, 'I hope you get it, Leia.'

'That brings up a distressing possibility,' she said later, as they climbed to take up places behind a bulwark of striped travertine. 'What if Vader doesn't come with the attacking force?'

'He's coming,' Luke assured her.

'The Force?'

He nodded slowly. 'Besides, as you pointed out before, he knows you and I are here. He'll come along to supervise the capture,' he said, then added after a knotted swallow, 'to make sure we're taken alive.'

Sighting the heavy rifle over the edge of the wall, Leia muttered forcefully, 'That's one thing he'll never do.' Then she relaxed slightly, her earnest gaze focusing unshakably on her companion. 'If it *should* come to that, Luke . . .'

'Come to what?'

'Being taken alive.' He indicated understanding and she went on. 'Promise me that out of any feeling you have for the Rebellion, out of any feeling you might have for me, that you'll put that sabre at your hip to my throat.'

Luke stared at her uncomfortably. 'Leia, I . . .'

'Swear it!' she demanded, her voice that of a steel kitten.

Luke mumbled something that satisfied her. They became aware a Coway was calling to them softly from above. Halla looked down from her position high on the cave wall to their left.

'Don't you two ever shut up? Hush now, children . . . company's coming.'

Silence reigned supreme in the tunnel. Luke strained until the muscles at the back of his eyes hurt, but the Coway concealment was perfect. Dozens were hidden within metres of him, but he could detect signs of only a few. Close by and evident were only Leia, Halla and Kee, the muzzle of his rifle protruding like a broken stone from between a pair of huge stalagmites. Of Hin there was no sign.

So clear and still was the dead air of the tunnel that Luke heard the metallic *pad-pad* of the first Imperial troops before he could see them. Shortly thereafter, the familiar robot-like forms came into view. Flesh and blood beneath the armour, the distant figures carried their own rifles casually, at waist level. Obviously, they were expecting little if any resistance.

As he studied them Luke realised that the Coway were right: in such close confinement the energy armour would work against the wearer. Such armour rendered the person inside it invulnerable to most energy weapons, save at vital points like the joints and the eyes where protection was necessarily weaker. More important, the armour also restricted its wearer's vision. Not so critical in a battle on a ship, say, with its wide, unobstructed corridors. But in the jumbled tunnel, vision was more vital than an extra shot.

As if on signal, four Coway, two on either side of the narrow pathway, materialized silently from invisible hiding places. The two advance scouts were dragged from view with astonishing speed. Not so astonishing to Luke, though. He'd experienced the power of Coway muscles. In the resulting silence he thought he could hear the cracking made by limbs and bone breaking inside restrictive armour.

Nervously, he waited for something to happen. Everyone knew that if the four Coway selected for the task of eliminating the scouts bungled their assignment, if they wasted even a few seconds, one of the scouts might have time to call to the troops behind him via his helmet communicator. Surprise, the defenders' most potent weapon, would be lost.

He was still waiting when the single Coway slipped up behind him, so quietly that Luke almost exclaimed aloud. The native made a quieting sound, performed a gesture with its facial muscles which might have been a smile, and vanished as silently as it'd come. It left behind two rifles and two pistols – the arms carried by the ambushed Imperial scouts.

Luke regarded the little arsenal joyfully. Slipping completely out of sight behind the travertine wall, he disengaged the power pack from one of the rifles and used it to bring his lightsabre up to maximum charge. Then he traded his pistol for a fresh one and resumed his place next to the vigilant Princess.

'We ought to get the other rifle to Hin,' he whispered to her, watching the tunnel.

'No time,' she disagreed reasonably. 'No telling where he is now. Can't risk it.'

'I suppose you're right.' He glanced down at the still half-charged rifle and its fully charged duplicate, plus the pair of pistols. 'At least we'll be well armed for a while longer than I thought.'

The rhythmic tread of metal-clad feet pounding rock finally reached them. All thoughts of conversation vanished as the main body of troops hove into view. They were marching cautiously, three and four abreast, as they rounded the same narrow place the two ill-fated scouts had entered moments before. The phosphorescent blue-yellow light of the growths in the tunnel gleamed off slick armour and immaculate weaponry.

Closer, closer they came, until Luke was afraid they would march right up to his wall before Halla and the chiefs agreed on the time to attack.

A strident, powerful voice boomed out in Coway.

The cavern dissolved into chaos. A waterfall of sound deluged the air where seconds before there had been only silence. Luke felt the noise itself, concentrated and magnified by the cave walls, would be sufficient to paralyse most men.

The soldiers caught in the maelstrom were Imperial troops. But they were not the Emperor's palace guard. They were men and women stationed too long on a backward, desolate world where discipline and training relaxed concurrently with morale. The screams of human and Coway howled through the cave.

Bursts of intense light from energy weapons created a berserk cat's cradle of destruction in the bottled-down tunnel. Luke found himself firing the pistol over and over. Next to him came steady, confident thrums as Leia pinched off bursts from the heavy rifle.

Higher up, Halla and Kee began pouring a murderous fire down on the mass of confused, densely packed troops. Soon they had to slacken their fire and pick targets with more care, as the Coway began erupting from beneath cloth covers camouflaged with sand to pull startled troopers into hidden pits, or coming out from behind half-stalagmites, or dropping from crevices in the ceiling.

Seeing friend and foe inextricably intermingled, Luke charged down the slight slope brandishing sabre in one hand and pistol in the other. Despite his admonitions, Leia had discarded her rifle. Pistol in hand, she was rushing after him to join in the hand-to-hand combat.

She passed him feet first, her kick all but decapitating a dazed soldier who didn't turn quite fast enough.

It was hellishly dangerous in the tunnel, what with energy bolts crackling wildly in all directions. Luke cut through the armoured legs of one soldier before the latter could bring his pistol to bear. Without realising it, he then swung blindly backward. The blue of his sabre intersected a beam fired point blank at him by an Imperial rifle.

Turning, he barely had time to utter a silent thanks to Ben Kenobi. The trooper was so shocked at the apparent coincidence of having his shot blocked that he didn't react in time. Thinking something had to be wrong with his weapon, he readjusted it to compensate for the imaginary fault. As he swung it upward again Luke jabbed him through the sternum.

Turning, he plunged back into the thickest fighting. He was hunting for one figure. It finally showed itself, standing aloof near the rear of the fighting crowd.

'Vader! Darth Vader!'

A wounded trooper charged him and he had to pause to deal with the more immediate threat.

But the Dark Lord had heard him. Surprised, the giant black shape activated his own sabre and strode into the mob, trying to cut his way clear to Luke.

The Princess was also trying to fight her way through the crowd. But she was not heading for Vader. Instead she was moving towards a stalagmite shattered at the top, a she-falcon flying for her prey-perch.

Under the direction of Captain-Supervisor Grammel, about ten of the troopers climbed for high ground intending to set up a covering fire the entire length of the tunnel. They achieved the summit of the small ridge and were lining up their weapons on the crowd below. Like hairy projectiles, Hin and several Coways dropped from hiding places above.

Roaring with delight, the huge Yuzzem grabbed two of the armoured troops at once and banged them together until their armour started to crack at the joints. Meanwhile, the muscular Coway wreaked havoc among the other soldiers.

Vader paused in the midst of his fighting, angrily evaluating the way the battle was going. He shook a threatening fist in Luke's general direction, then turned to the shaken officer nearby.

'Grammel! Re-form all survivors at the surface.'

'Yes, my Lord,' the distraught Captain-Supervisor acknowledged. Using his multiple-channel helmet unit, he signalled the retreat to his remaining troops.

Small clumps of soldiers began to break contact with the Coways and started rushing for the surface. Luke was startled to see how few remained.

The soldiers were pulling back in good order. At that point one of the Coway chiefs hiding high above rose and signalled. His order was relayed up the tunnel from one concealed native to the next. Several Coway pulled on a vine cable. Their action sent a pinned stalactite weighing several tons plunging from its eons-old growing place. It landed with a titanic crash. Half a dozen soldiers were mashed beneath it.

Further reduced in number, the troopers started to panic, to throw down their weapons and sprint up the passageway as fast as their armour would permit them. Most of them ran under the nets which waiting Coway dropped on them from above. Those same nets had held against Yuzzem. The troopers who lay flailing at the confining strands had no chance at all.

Leia Organa reached the top of the pinnacle, lay down across it and positioned the heavy rifle she'd retrieved. She fought to focus on a single, black-clad figure striding relentlessly and without panic up the tunnel. Vader was surrounded by Grammel and a few remaining soldiers. She couldn't wait. Soon the Dark Lord would pass from sight.

As she activated the trigger, Vader turned and gestured to the several troops lagging behind. A powerful beam of energy struck him in the side and sent him spinning to the ground. Leia smiled. Her joy turned to disappointment when she looked back through the blunt telescopic sight.

Vader had rolled over and was beating at the smoke issuing from his left side. There was a gaping hole in his protective cloak and the black armour beneath had been partly melted away. But the full force of the energy bolt had missed him.

The Dark Lord got to his feet and seemed for a second to be staring straight at her. Then he was moving again, still not in panic but with considerably more energy, up towards the way out.

Frantically the Princess re-aimed, fired ... just as Vader passed from view. The bolt exploded against the lowest part of the ceiling, annihilating rock and mineral but doing no damage to the evil figure beyond.

'Well, darn,' she said softly, irritated at herself. Picking up her pistol and leaving the rifle atop the stalagmite, she started to pick her way downward to rejoin the fight.

There wasn't much fighting left to rejoin. Caught completely by surprise, the soldiers had been decimated. Now the remnants, helpless and dispirited, were being cut down methodically by the victorious Coway. Those who tried to break from the fighting were picked off by well-aimed bolts from Kee and Halla.

She found Luke stalking wild-eyed among the carnage, trying to dissuade the hooting, yelping Coway from reducing the wounded to small pieces. Breathing out the nausea of battle, he jerked around and glared at her when she grabbed his arm.

'Forget it, Luke,' she advised him softly. 'Leave them alone.'

'They're killing the wounded,' he cried in anguish. 'Look at them ... look what they're doing!'

'Yes, it's almost human,' she commented, 'although the Imperials would have been a little neater.'

'You approve?' he said accusingly. She didn't reply, merely stared back at him until he sagged, utterly worn out and saddened.

'I'm sorry, Luke,' she told him gently, 'but there's very little in this universe that rises above the mean and petty. Maybe the stars themselves. Come,' she urged him with a cheering smile, 'let's find Hin and Kee and Halla and the 'droids and celebrate.'

'You go,' he told her, pulling his arm free authoritatively but without rancour. 'There's nothing here I want to celebrate.'

She looked after him as he went striding off through the residue of battle, ignoring the Coway intent on their massacre, drowning in his own unknowable thoughts. . . .

☐ XII

WHEN the last drop of blood had dried to a black crust on the cave floor, the refugees gathered together to decide what to do next.

Halla was talking to the Coway chiefs. 'They say that those who escaped have left one of their vehicles above, to watch the exit. Probably hoping we'll jump out into their sights.'

'Is there another way out?' Luke asked tiredly.

'Yes, close by.' One of the chiefs, ignoring its badly burnt arm, mumbled urgently at Halla: 'He wants to know if there's anything they can do to help us?'

'They can show us that other way out,' Luke informed her. 'They've done enough. We have to hurry. We have delayed too long already.'

'Too long for what?' the Princess inquired curiously. 'We'll be well away from here by the time Vader can return with reinforcements.' She looked thoughtful. 'I don't think he'll trouble the Coway. It's us and the crystal he wants.'

'That's what I'm talking about, Leia,' he replied worriedly. 'I don't think Vader's gone back to the town.' He pointed. 'When he passed from my mind, or rather, when the disturbance he generates in the Force passed from my mind, he was travelling *that* way. Not back towards the town, but towards the temple.'

'That's ridiculous,' Halla objected strenuously. 'He has no idea where the temple of Pomojema is.'

'Vader is much more attuned to the Force, albeit its dark side, than I am, Halla. It's likely that he can sense the crystal's natural disturbance. It would be faint, but someone as powerful as Vader *could* barely detect it. And he has more than that to go on. We were travelling in as straight a line as possible. He needs merely to plot along it and hunt for the crystal's effect when he angles off his course.

'He mustn't reach the temple before us.' He started off up the tunnel. Leia was quickly alongside matching him stride for anxious stride.

She beat at the dry cave air with a clenched fist. 'I had him, Luke! He was standing there in my scope and I missed him.' She hiked on, brooding on the nearness of the thing. 'I was too excited, too nervous. I didn't take enough time and I made a bad shot.'

'Your shooting, what I could see of it,' he countered, a mite jealously, 'was excellent. Better than I could have done.'

Leia said nothing for a moment, then added deferentially, 'I couldn't have survived that kind of intense infighting. Who taught you to use a lightsabre like that? Kenobi?'

Luke nodded. 'I owe everything to that old man, and wherever he's gone to, he knows it.' He patted the shaft of his father's weapon reassuringly.

'If we do catch up with Vader,' she went on, 'and we must, you're going to need both your skill with the sabre and the Force. If only I'd taken more time!'

Luke shushed her and the others. They were nearing the exit to the surface.

Dim, misty air filtered down to them. Even that dank light was intoxicating after so many days underground, travelling by the glow of unnatural vegetation. Several bodies lay scattered about, Imperial troopers too badly wounded to regain the surface.

The two Coway who'd come along directed them into a nearby crevice in the wall. Both Yuzzem grunted and had to inhale for all they were worth in order to fit through. They emerged behind a clump of thick brush at least twenty metres from the main entrance. One of the Coway pointed, indicating the location of the armoured vehicle on guard. Luke saw the squat shape, its muzzle angled directly down the mouth of the tunnel they'd been standing in only moments before. He shuddered.

With soft mumbles and alien gestures, the Coway took their leave, vanishing back down the hole. Luke crawled on his belly, freeing the exit for those behind him.

When all five were once again on the surface of Mimban, Luke turned to crawl clear.

'Just a darn minute, Luke boy!' Halla whispered. 'Do you think you can catch up with this Vader on foot?'

Luke paused, then returned to stare at the silent crawler poised over the Coway exit. 'All right, so what do we do, Halla? I agree . . . we have to have transportation. But that armed crawler happens to be full of Imperial troops.'

Halla studied the vehicle. 'Its upper port is wide open . . . big enough for two men. I can see two . . . no, one trooper with his head exposed. Probably giving information to those below.' The head disappeared. 'He's gone now. We should get in the branches hanging over it.'

'Then what?' the Princess asked. 'We jump inside?'

'Listen,' the old woman protested, 'I can't think of everything, can I? I don't know . . . drop an anti-personnel charge down them, or something!'

'Wonderful,' the Princess quipped. She looked from Halla to Luke. 'Now if one of you two magicians will use the Force to conjure up a convenient canister of explosive, I'll volunteer to do the dropping.' She folded her arms and gazed questioningly at them. 'Personally, I think I'm pretty safe in volunteering. Luke?'

He wasn't looking at her. 'We don't have any explosives, true, but we have something close.' She turned, saw what he was staring at, and found she had to agree. . . .

The Imperial sergeant had been fortunate to escape the underground ambush with his life, and he knew it. If he'd had any voice in the matter he never would have led his men beneath the surface. On Mimban, he was acutely uncomfortable whenever he had to leave the relative familiarity of the towns and venture out into the bog-ridden countryside.

It had been a terrible battle, terrible. They'd been overwhelmed and nearly wiped out to the last trooper. So many things had gone wrong.

The outcome of the engagement was decided in the first few minutes, when total surprise had belonged to the enemy. Even when it had dawned on the detachment that they were under attack, they still hadn't responded in the fashion Imperial troops were famous for.

There was no blaming the men, really. They were so accustomed to dealing with the subservient, pacific greenies that the concept of a fighting Mimbanite was unbelievable to most of them. They'd proven unprepared to cope with the reality.

Now, as he stared out the foreport at the ominous mouth of the cavern he'd retreated from with the rest of the survivors, he feasted on a single thought. If he knew the Captain-Supervisor at all, then as soon as he and the Dark Lord Vader returned from their journey, a retaliatory force would be organised. They would return here with heavy weapons, he mused grimly, and roast that cavern until every native male, woman and infant had been reduced to ashes.

Idly, he wondered where Grammel and the Dark Lord had taken themselves so hastily, and shuddered. He had no desire to accompany that tall, black-armoured spectral shape anywhere whatsoever. He preferred to speculate on the forthcoming massacre that would take place in the native warrens below. That favourable mental image mitigated his usually brusque call to the man posted in the open turret above.

The trooper heard the sergeant's order and turned to call downward that he saw nothing. It was an honest answer, the last one the trooper ever made. In glancing down into the armoured crawler he failed to see the bomb that fell from the large tree branch overhead.

A little over a metre and a half tall, the bomb was covered with short, bristly fur. It exploded on top of the trooper and yanked him clear of the turret. That left the opening clear for a second bipedal projectile to drop from the mist-enshrouded tree into the vehicle. It too erupted inside the personnel area.

Luke, the 'droids, Halla and the Princess watched from nearby, concealed by thick growth. There was a dull rumble as the crawler started moving. A great deal of shouting and screaming, muffled by metal and distance, came from within.

Halla sounded worried. 'They're taking longer than I thought, Luke boy. Are you sure of this?'

Luke threw her a confident glance before turning his attention back to the crawler, which was now travelling in erratic curves and circles. 'It was all I could think of,' he declared. 'In several ways this, if it works, is better than using an explosive. For one thing, we won't damage any of the crawler's instruments. No human can stand up to a Yuzzem in close quarters. Two Yuzzem in a confined space like that,' and he indicated the fitfully twisting vehicle, 'ought to be irresistible.'

Several seconds later, the crawler turned sharply to it right. Still travelling slowly, it slammed into a huge pseudo-cypress. A thick limb fell from the shaken tree. It struck the crawler with a metallic bong and tumbled to the earth.

Silence then. The crawler's engine whined, faded, finally stopped. After a few anxious moments Hin emerged from the turret opening, straining at the tight fit, and waved to them.

'They did it,' Luke observed with quiet excitement. The three observers left their place of concealment in the underbrush and hurried across the ground-bog. Broad, hairy hands extended to help them up the metal sides.

Hin grunted something to Luke, who nodded solemnly and turned away.

'What is it?' the Princess inquired impatiently. 'Why can't we go inside?' She glanced nervously at the silent, surrounding vegetation. 'There might be a few stragglers hiding out there.'

'I don't think so,' Luke disagreed. 'Hin suggests we look some other way while he and Kee clean out the crawler.'

'What for?' she demanded to know. 'I've seen all kinds of death and plenty recently.'

As she spoke, Hin reached down and took the first bit of what remained of the crawler's crew, rose and chucked the double handful over the side. It lay moist and glistening on the damp ground.

The Princess's face became slightly pale and she turned away to join Luke in contemplating the nearby trees. Several minutes later the ghastly cleanup was finished. They all dropped down to the crawler.

Even with two Yuzzem, they weren't crowded. The crawler was designed to carry ten full armoured troops. Less comforting was Luke's first inspection of the control panel. It was more complex than that of an X-wing fighter.

'Can you drive this?' Luke asked Halla, bewildered.

She grinned as she slid into the driver's seat, ignoring the stains on the padding. 'Why, Luke boy, I can operate any hunk of machine on this world.' She bent forward, studied the instrumentation and touched something on the rim of the driver's wheel.

The engine roared, lights flickered, and the crawler

promptly shot full-speed backwards to crash into a pair of entwined trees. There was a violent crackling noise and then two thunderous, reverberating booms as both boles fell on top of the idling vehicle.

When Luke's ears stopped ringing he shot Halla an accusing stare. She smiled wanly back at him. 'Of course,' she explained a mite lamely, 'that's not to say a little practice wouldn't smooth our ride.'

Once more she examined the controls, pursed her lips studiously. 'Let's see now . . . there, that's what I missed!' Again she activated switches and buttons before touching the control on the wheel's rim.

Moving in spasmodic jerks and stops, jumps and lunges, the crawler slid off into the mists. Save the pilot, all other occupants of the vehicle clung to something inflexible. Luke wondered if the trees ahead were as nervous as he was. . . .

'I'm sorry, my Lord, most sorry I am.' Captain-Supervisor Grammel looked up at Darth Vader from where he sat on one of the open benches of the big troop carrier. 'Who was to guess they were so well armed, or that the underground abos would put up such a battle?'

'The weapons were of small consequence,' Vader growled profoundly. 'A few guns, all in the hands of wanted criminals.' Grammel cringed as the grotesque breath mask dipped close. 'Admit it, Captain-Supervisor. Your troops were inadequately prepared, poorly trained. Discipline and morale were both absent and you were routed by a mob of ignorant savages!'

'They took us completely by surprise, my Lord,' Grammel argued strenuously. 'No native group has ever resisted the Imperial presence on Mimban before.'

'No native group previously had the benefit of human advice and aid,' Vader snapped back. 'They did not employ wholly aboriginal tactics. You should have recognised the differences early and taken appropriate countermeasures.' He looked away from Grammel to gaze significantly across the bogland. 'I know which parties were responsible for that. When I hold in my hand the balance of the crystal, I will mete out justice accordingly.'

'I'd hoped for that privilege myself,' a disgruntled Grammel muttered.

Vader turned a cool, metallic stare downwards and announced dangerously, 'You have no privileges, Captain-Supervisor Grammel. You have blundered badly. Not critically, I hope, but badly. I curse myself for being fool enough to assume that you knew what you were doing.'

'I told you, my Lord,' Grammel objected, at once angry and frightened, 'their surprise was complete.'

'I'm not interested in excuses for debacles, only successful results,' declared Vader. 'Grammel, your existence befouls me.'

'My Lord,' Grammel babbled desperately, rising from the bench, 'if I—'

Faster than a human eye could follow, Vader's lightsabre was up, activated and moving. Grammel's slashed form pitched wildly, stumbled backward and tumbled over the side of the crawler. There was a lull as the stunned driver looked on in terror.

Vader whirled, glowered down at him. 'We will travel faster without such dead weight to slow us, trooper. Return to your controls – now!'

'Y-yes, my Lord,' the man gulped, unable to keep from stuttering fearfully. Somehow he forced himself to turn back to the control board of the vehicle.

As they moved forward, Vader turned to glance back idly at the receding corpse of Captain-Supervisor Grammel. Already jungle scavengers were beginning to emerge from concealment to sniff hopefully at the body.

'Whoever is your lord now,' Vader murmured, 'it is not I.' Removing the shard of Kaiburr crystal from a sealed pocket, he held the glowing crimson splinter before his eyes, swaying slightly.

It was there ahead, somewhere ahead. He could sense it.

He would find it....

'Are we still travelling on the right track?' a weary Leia asked old Halla several days later. All of the crawler's occupants were dirty, discouraged and exhausted from racing nonstop through the misty landscape.

'Certain of it,' Halla replied with disgusting cheerfulness.

'We're getting close to something,' Luke ventured. 'It's ... peculiar. I've never felt anything like it before, not remotely.'

'*I* don't feel anything, except filthy,' countered the Princess.

'Leia,' Luke began, 'all I can say is—'

'I know, I know,' she interrupted him tiredly, ' "if I were a Force sensitive ..." '

Artoo beeped from the open turret. Luke rushed to the fore viewport, announced in hushed tones, 'There it is.'

Rising from the jungle growth ahead of them was a black apparition. A monstrous pyramidal ziggurat, it looked as if it were formed of cast iron. But metal it was not. Instead, the massive edifice had been built of great blocks of some volcanic stone.

For all its breadth, it was not very tall. Vines and creepers clung jealously to it in many places. As they ground nearer Luke saw that much of the stone was crumbling to fine powder. Fortunately the entrance was still visible, although the ten-metre-high curved archway was half collapsed and had filled the passageway with rubble to a height taller than two men.

'It doesn't look as if anything here's been disturbed for a million years,' the Princess murmured in awe. All her worries and uncertainties had been dissolved by the actual sight of the legendary temple.

Luke was moving rapidly from port to port. Now he turned to look back at her and when he did so, his eyes were shining. 'You realise, Leia, that Vader isn't here? He isn't here! We've beaten him!'

'Take it easy, Luke boy,' Halla advised him cautioningly. 'We can't be certain of that.'

'I can. I'm certain.' He urged Hin out of the way, mounted the turret ladder and exited from the crawler. It slowed to a stop. When Leia emerged from the turret top he was already walking confidently towards the temple entrance.

'He's not here!' he shouted back to her. 'There's no sign of a crawler or anything else.'

'We still have to find the crystal,' Halla called out to him as she followed Leia to the ground. But Luke's enthusiasm was contagious. She found herself forgetting the Dark Lord, forgetting her own fears and last-minute trepidations.

Here was the temple of Pomojema, the temple she'd been trying to reach for years. Hin and Kee flanked her as they moved towards the entranceway. Threepio and Artoo remained behind to guard the crawler.

Despite Luke's assurance that they were alone here, everyone kept a worried eye on the drifting fog. Anything imaginable and many things unimaginable could spring out of that cloaked haze at any minute.

Luke was waiting impatiently, standing on the topmost block of the rubble in the entrance. 'It's light inside,' he told them, after peering inside. His gaze went higher and he squinted. 'Part of the roof's caved in, too, but it looks solid enough.'

'Go ahead, boy,' Halla urged him, 'but quietly, quietly.'

'That's all right,' he said. Now that they had actually gained the temple, he wasn't about to steal the old woman's dream. This was her right as much as his. So he waited until the others had joined him. In a few moments all were standing silently inside the ancient structure.

There were two places above where the soaring, domed roof had fallen in. They admitted sufficient light to illuminate the temple's interior. Piles of broken stone lay splattered beneath each ragged hole.

Jungle growth had penetrated inside. Lianas and other parasitic plants lay everywhere, extending their tenacious embrace into all corners of the building. They spiralled skyward on the cylindrical bodies of towering obsidian pillars. These unyielding supports boasted intricate carved patterns and designs, whose meaning none now alive could properly appreciate.

Each swimming in his or her own thoughts, the five walked across the spacious floor towards the far side of the temple. A colossal statue was seated there against the dark wall. It represented a vaguely humanoid being seated on a carved throne. Leathery wings which might have been vestigial swept out in two awesome arcs to either side of the figure. Enormous claws thrust from feet and arms, the latter clinging to the ends of armrests on the throne. It had no face below slanted, accusing eyes – only a mass of Medusan, carved tentacles.

'Pomojema, god of the Kaiburr,' Halla whispered, without knowing why she was bothering to whisper. 'It almost seems familiar, somehow.' She chuckled nervously. 'That's crazy, of course.'

Then she was pointing excitedly, voice and hand trembling alike with the wonder of it. 'It's there ... I knew it, I knew it!'

In the centre of the grey stone chest of the statue lay a dimly pulsing light the hue of vanadinite.

'The crystal,' breathed the Princess softly.

Halla did not hear her. Mind and gaze remained focussed on an obsession become attainable.

Luke stopped, his eyes on the movement to the left of the leering stone figure. It was dark back there, and there was no telling how far the darkness stretched.

Then they all began backing away slowly. Halla's pistol was first to be aimed.

The creature moving out from behind the statue had a wide, wide mouth fringed with short sharp teeth now open in a batrachian grin. Small yellow eyes blinked dumbly at them. It moved on ponderous, warty legs like thick tree stumps.

Halla fired. The beam of energy had no visible effect on the creature, which continued lumbering towards them. Luke had his own pistol out, as did Leia. All three of them fired. If the joint barrage had any effect it was to irritate the sluggish beast. It blinked blood, then continued its bowlegged walk towards them at a faster pace.

They continued retreating towards the entrance. 'Hin, Kee,' Luke called to the Yuzzem. 'Go back to the crawler . . . get the rifles!'

Hin chittered a reply, then both Yuzzem were racing for the exit. Luke considered the crystal, receding behind the protective bulk of the monster. Taking his lightsabre from his belt, he activated the powerful blue beam and started cautiously forward.

'Luke, have you lost your mind?' the Princess shouted.

He reflected briefly that it wasn't impossible, and then dismissed the thought. If he paused to do much thinking, the steadily advancing carnivore would have him for a snack.

It hesitated within snapping distance, slightly hypnotised by the weaving beam of the sabre. Luke lunged forward. The sabre contacted the creature's chin. Intense energy punctuated a small hole in the wide lower jaw.

That produced a dimly outraged moan from the thing. Jaws parted to reveal a gullet high and wide enough to dance in. Luke saw something moving *inside*. Whether prodded by instinct or a good guess he threw himself sharply to his left and rolled rapidly.

The long pink tongue exploded outward, to pulverise a black boulder which had been just behind him. As he rolled to his feet and continued backing away, the creature spat out chunks of rock.

Before Luke could move out of range the thick tongue shot out again. Unable to dodge, he held his sabre tightly in front of him. It seemed pitifully inadequate against that pink pseudopod. But the sizzling sound was loud. Apparently he'd contacted sensitive tissue, because the creature let out a throaty yelp. With single-minded determination, it resumed stalking Luke. Death glinted in narrow yellow eyes.

Leia and Halla kept up a steady fire on the massive body, to no effect. 'Useless,' the Princess said tightly. She looked towards the entrance. There was no sign of movement there. 'Hin!' she shouted. 'Kee!' No response.

'They'll get here,' Halla advised her. 'They'd better.'

Unexpectedly, the monster hopped forward. Horizontal door-jaws snapped shut with a ringing thud as Luke ducked beneath the bite. His sabre cut a black line across the underside of the jaw as he stumbled clear, to bang into one of the thick pillars supporting the roof. One of the gaps in the soaring ceiling shone directly above.

He shot an anxious glance towards the entrance. Where were the Yuzzem? He couldn't worry about anything other than himself now. It was crawling for him once more. A quick glance at the ceiling, a quicker decision, and then he was swinging the lightsabre at the pillar's base.

Like an X-wing punching through atmosphere, the incredible energy beam sliced through the black stone. A rumbling noise followed, punctuated by explosive crackings.

'Halla, Leia . . . run!' he yelled. Then he was sprinting to join them.

Lumbering towards them, the lizard-creature never noticed the cracks in the ceiling overhead. They spread, multiplied, joined, and then the pillar disintegrated, bringing a section of roof as wide as the existing gap down on top of the monster. Gigantic blocks of curved stone crushed its front end to pulp, stilling the toothy grin forever.

As the rumbling echoes of the collapse subsided and the black dust began to settle, Luke, panting, paused to look behind him. There was no sign of the front end of the beast. It was buried completely beneath tons of volcanic rock. Twitching hind legs clawed futilely at the air for awhile. The massive scimitar tail smashed at the ground. Before very long, all movement ceased.

'What happened to Hin and Kee?' he finally asked. 'The thing had me cornered. I could've been a short meal.'

'They're probably arguing,' the Princess essayed in disgust. She eyed the entrance. 'Pretty soon they'll remember what they were sent for. Then they'll come rushing back in, begging your forgiveness.'

'I'll bawl them out then,' Luke sighed. 'Right now I'm—' He glanced around for Halla and saw her moving at a trot towards the distant idol. 'Halla!'

'Let her go,' the Princess advised him, with an indifferent wave of one hand. 'She's not running anywhere with it.' She started walking towards the far side of the temple. 'She'll need our help to get it down anyway.' When Luke didn't follow, she wondered aloud, 'Aren't you coming, too?'

'In a minute,' he assured her, his attention behind instead of in front of him. 'I want to make certain this thing is *dead*.'

As the Princess strolled without hurrying towards the statue, he moved to stand next to the visible portion of the hulk-corpse. He prodded it with his sabre, sinking the shaft of azure destruction into dark flesh up to the hilt. It didn't stir.

Satisfied, he turned to rejoin his companions. There was a faint, warning rumble and his gaze jerked skyward.

So did those of the Princess and Halla. 'Luke!' they shouted simultaneously.

He didn't need urging. What he did need was a second or two. The edges of the new hole in the ceiling were widening slightly.

Fate gave him the first second but begrudged him the second.

'Luke!' The Princess was running towards him now as the rumbling stopped and the last small stone fell heavily. Halla stood frozen, torn between the pile of rubble beneath which Luke was buried and the tantalizing proximity of the crystal. Drunk with its nearness she continued on towards the statue.

Leia reached the small hillock of fresh broken rock and looked around frantically.

'Over . . . here,' a voice murmured, slow and full of pain.

He lay nearby, pinned on his back. She shifted debris from him, ignoring the cloying dust and the scratches the sharp fragments made on her hands and arms. But she couldn't budge the massive block which had struck the temple floor and then tumbled to rest on his right thigh and calf.

'Try again,' he instructed her. They strained together. Leia put her back beneath one edge of the stone, thrust upwards with what little weight she had. The block did not move.

They rested, breathing hard. Luke's face was a mixture of fading pain and hope. 'It's not pressing on me with its full weight,' he told her. 'If it was I wouldn't have a leg to pull free now.' His gaze turned towards the silent entrance. 'Dammit, where are those two? They could move this thing easily.'

'I am afraid your slow-witted companions will no longer be able to help you or anyone else, Skywalker.'

Luke went cold all over. A tall, blood-chilling shape stood on top of the rubble in the entranceway. Clad completely in black armour, it stared down at them expectantly.

'They're both dead,' it informed them pleasantly, in a voice devoid of any spark of humanity. 'I killed them. As for your 'droids, they are conditioned to obey orders. I had them turn themselves off.'

Slowly Leia's mouth moved, forming a name. But no sound issued from between those perfect lips.

Moving leisurely down the pile of rubble, Darth Vader addressed them in a coldly conversational tone.

'You know, Skywalker, I had a difficult time finding out that it was you who shot up my tie fighter above the Death Star station. Rebellion spies are hard and expensive to come by. I also found out it was you who released the torpedo that destroyed the station. You have a great deal to atone for to me. I've waited a long time.'

Casually he drew his own lightsabre and began swinging the activated energy blade loosely back and forth, chopping playfully with bits of stone and carving.

'You were lucky that time in the snubship,' he went on, as Luke fought to pull his pinioned leg free. He dug at the stone until blood ran from beneath his nails. 'I probably won't have the patience to let you last as long as you deserve. You may consider yourself lucky.' His voice dropped to a toxic whisper. 'I expect no such difficulty in restraining myself where you are concerned, Leia Organa. In several ways, you are responsible for my setbacks much more than this simple boy.'

'*Monster,*' was all she could spit out, furious and afraid.

'Do you remember that day back on the station,' Vader mused, with deliberate patience, 'when the late

Governor Tarkin and I interviewed you?' He placed a peculiar stress on the word 'interviewed'.

Leia had both hands on opposite shoulders and was shivering as if from intense cold.

'Yes,' Vader observed, perverse amusement in his voice, 'I can see that you do. I am truly sorry I have nothing as elaborate to treat you to at this time. However,' he added, swinging his weapon lightly, 'one can do some interesting things with a sabre, you know. I'll do my best to show you all of them if you'll co-operate by not passing out.'

Leia's hands dropped to her sides. The fear did not leave her, but she forced it into the back alleys of her mind by sheer will. Running the few steps to Luke's side, she knelt and groped at his wrist. When she rose, she was holding the lightsabre carefully in one hand.

Vader looked on approvingly. 'You're going to fight. Good. That will make it interesting.'

She spat at the advancing giant, a pitifully feeble gesture as she brandished the lightsabre. 'The Force give me leave to kill you before I die,' she snarled.

An awful coughing laugh issued from behind the gargoylish breath mask. 'Foolish infant. The Force is with me, not you. But,' he shrugged amiably, 'we will see.' He assumed a position of readiness. 'Come, girl-woman . . . amuse me.'

Grimly determined, mouth clenched, she moved towards him. As she did so Vader abruptly let his arm fall, let the lambent beam of his sabre hang limply at his side.

'Leia, don't!' Luke yelled to her. 'It's a feint . . . he's daring you. Kill me, then yourself . . . it's hopeless now.'

Vader looked over at Luke contemptuously, then back at the Princess. 'Go on,' he told her, 'let him fight for you if you want. But I won't let you kill him. I've been robbed too often.'

Leia appeared to hesitate, then lunged straight at

Vader with the tip of the sabre. Simultaneously the Dark Lord brought his own beam up in lightning gesture to parry hers.

But Leia performed a spinning, twisting arc in the air and brought her sabre down in a slashing flare of blue light. Energy flashed as it contacted the Dark Lord's armoured breath mask. Only superhuman reflexes enabled him to avoid the full effect of the blow.

If there was anyone in the vast chamber more surprised than Vader, it was Luke. He fought to free his trapped leg with a slight twinge of hope.

'Almost, little Princess, almost,' Vader murmured without anger. 'I have been guilty of overconfidence before.' He adjusted his stance. 'I will not be guilty again.'

His sabre curled in, around, down. She barely managed to deflect the blow as she backpedalled. Again he advanced, swung; again she deflected the cut.

They duelled on, with Vader steadily pressing his attack. It required every bit of skill and strength the Princess possessed for her simply to defend herself. There was no thought of mounting an assault of her own.

One occupant of the temple chamber was not watching the fight. High above and far away from the duellists, Halla stood at face level with a pulsing, multifaceted crimson crystal as big as her head. With trembling hands she reached out, caressed it. A twist and pull brought it out of its socket in the statue with unexpected ease.

For a long moment she held the jewel in both hands, gazing deeply into a luminescence that was almost alive. Then she was picking her way back down the juts and thrusts of the idol, clutching the crystal light to her bosom with her right hand.

Vader cut down, the Princess brought her sabre up yet once more to parry, and Vader at the last instant changed his swing. The tip of the energy beam slashed across her midsection, slicing through her miner's suit to leave a black burn across her middle. She winced in pain, grabbed at the wound with her free hand. Vader allowed her no respite but continued to press forward.

Luke's efforts to pull himself free had left him as firmly pinned as ever, and utterly exhausted. He lay on the ground, fighting to get his breath and energy back, forced to watch helplessly as Vader continued his game of cat-and mouse with the Princess.

Another intricate swing-and-thrust. This time his sabre cut across her cheek, leaving another ugly scorch mark. Tears came as her free hand went to her burned cheek. She was moving more and more slowly now, the hand holding Luke's lightsabre shaking uncertainly.

'Come, Princess-Senator Organa, where is your noble fortitude, your traitor's determination?' Vader taunted her. 'Surely a few little burns cannot hurt so much?'

Enraged, she swung the sabre at him with fresh strength. Without straining, he blocked it completely and continued to move on to cut at her again. Though she blocked it, the force of the blow sent her tumbling, rolling to the ground. Vader followed relentlessly as she tried to crawl away and regain her feet. His sabre draw a long black gash down the back of her left leg.

Screaming, she rolled over somehow and ended up standing. Then she moved away from him with a limp, favouring the damaged leg.

Unable to watch any longer, Luke had his head buried in his hands. *Clink* – a sound of rock on rock. Raising his head and turning, he looked behind him. The sound was repeated. He tried to see around the stone trapping him.

A hand, seemingly independent of arm or body, worked its way with infinite slowness and determination over the side of the big block of volcanic stone. It was followed by a head. A terrible wound showed halfway through the upper portion of the skull.

'Hin!' Luke called softly, hardly daring to breathe. A quick glance showed Vader still fully intent on the Princess. The fatally injured Yuzzem put a hand to its snout ordering Luke to silence.

Crawling on hands and knees, Hin came around the stone until he was beneath an overhanging edge. Backing up against the supporting rocks, he started to rise. Massive bristled shoulders pressed upwards against the long rock, arms strained. The boulder did not move, and Hin fell to the floor. His breathing was laboured, his eyes half closed.

'Come on, Hin, come on!' Luke urged frantically, his gaze travelling from the fight on the floor back to the prone Yuzzem. 'You can move it . . . just a little is all. Try again, please!'

Hin blinked, seeming to stare at Luke without seeing him. Moving mechanically, it positioned heavy-muscled arms and shoulders underneath the edge once more.

'Come, little Princess. Now is the time for spirit,' he admonished her. 'You still have a chance.' He stalked her as she backed from him, threatening her with false cuts and thrusts that she tried to block feebly while limping on her damaged leg.

'Stand and fight,' he urged her. Another downward swing of the lethal sabre, this one cutting across her chest and through the suit. The Princess sucked in her breath with an agonised gasp, bent over and almost fell. Vader moved towards her.

There came a grinding sound loud enough to cause both of them to look up.

With a final effort Hin had shoved the huge stone block aside. He fell in a heap, the life already draining from him, as Luke desperately scrambled clear. The pressure on his leg had been just enough to restrain him, not enough to damage it. He was running towards the two combatants, favouring his right leg but feeling it grow stronger with every step.

'Leia!' She still retained enough presence of mind to switch off the sabre before throwing it to him even as Vader grabbed to intercept the weapon. The Dark Lord missed it by a finger-length but caught the Princess instead.

But the throw was weak. Luke tried to run faster and found his still-sore leg hobbled him slightly. Vader growled something unintelligible, shoved the Princess away from him with his free hand. She fell to the hard floor and lay there panting, exhausted.

Luke saw Vader closing the distance between them. The Dark Lord would reach the lightsabre first. He sprinted somehow, threw himself at the ground. He felt reborn as his fist closed around the sabre haft, then he rolled with renewed vigour to his right. Vader's blow was an instant late, cutting a deep furrow in the stone floor where Luke had fallen.

Then Luke was on his feet, the sabre now shining bright blue in his hand. His roll had taken him behind Vader. He stood between the Dark Lord and the Princess. Vader regarded him silently.

'Leia?' No answer. He glanced backwards. 'Princess?'

A thin, sorrowful voice. 'Don't worry about me, Luke.'

Vader appeared to inhale deeply. 'No, Skywalker,' he rumbled, 'don't worry about her. Worry about yourself.'

Luke felt a wild sense of elation as he brandished his father's weapon. 'I'm not worried about anything, Vader. Not now. I have no more worries and only one concern.' His voice held an unaccustomed hint of conviction. 'I'm going to kill you, Darth Vader.'

That humourless laugh again. 'What a high opinion you hold of yourself, Skywalker.'

'I'm . . . I'm Ben Kenobi,' Luke whispered in an odd way.

For just a moment Vader seemed shaken. 'Ben

Kenobi's dead. I killed him myself. You are simple Luke Skywalker, an ex-farm boy from Tatooine. You are no master of the Force and the equal of Ben Kenobi you will never be.'

'Ben Kenobi is with me, Vader,' Luke snarled, gaining confidence every second, 'and the Force is with me, too.'

'You do have something of the Force about you, boy,' Vader admitted. 'A master of it you are not, however. That dooms you. Only a master could do ... this.'

The Dark Lord lunged and Luke spun well clear. At the same time, Vader was staring not at Luke, but at the ground. A small fragment of the fallen ceiling rose, shot straight for Luke's head. Seeing it coming he reacted as Kenobi had taught him ... without thinking.

A much smaller stone lifted and intersected the path of the charging rock. The two met. Though Vader's missile was by far the larger, it was deflected just enough by Luke's rock to send it shooting past his shoulder harmlessly.

Panting, he stared challengingly back at Vader. 'Good, boy,' the Dark Lord confessed, 'very good. But my stone was the heavier. My powers are the stronger.'

'Not strong enough, Vader,' Luke insisted as he lunged forward. His thoughts were of Kenobi, of the techniques of sabre and Force the old Jedi knight had laboriously taught him. He tried to let the Force guide his arm.

Vader parried, blocked, parried again, and found himself being forced backwards by the aggressiveness and skill of Luke's demonic attack. The breath mask tilted back for a second. A section of heavy bas-relief on one of the supporting pillars was loosened, fell away.

At the last instant Luke sensed it, jumped backwards. The huge carved panel shattered between them. Both men rested uneasily as the dust settled. Luke gulped for air, while Vader showed less aplomb and increasing tension.

'You are good, Skywalker,' he declared. 'Very good indeed, for a child. But the end will be the same.' He raised his sabre and came charging over the broken panel.

Now it was the Dark Lord who initiated the assault. Luke found himself forced steadily backwards as Vader threw an unceasing blizzard of stone shards and sabre cuts at him. It was impossible to counter them all.

Somehow Luke did so.

They were circling in the centre of the temple floor now. Lying on her side, the Princess tried to turn and watch. The pain of her wounds rose about her like a steel wall. Around her thoughts the wall closed, and in response her eyes closed and she slumped back to the cold, cold stone.

Again the two enemies paused, only now it was Vader who was panting heavily. 'Kenobi . . . trained you . . . well,' the Dark Lord admitted admiringly. Some of his usual insouciance had been drained by the steady fighting. 'And you have some . . . natural ability of your own. You have proven a challenge. I enjoy . . . a challenge.'

Still unhurt, Luke whispered defiantly, 'Too much of . . . a challenge for . . . you!'

'No,' Vader assured him, 'no. You overestimate yourself, child.' The Dark Lord drew himself up to his full, awesome height. 'I have finished playing with you.'

Swinging his sabre until it was no more than a blue blur in the dank air of the temple, he leaped straight up into the air. It was more than a jump, less than levitation. Out of the blue circle of energy he flung the sabre.

Instinctively – he had no time to think – Luke parried. The Force inherent in the thrown sabre knocked

Luke's out of his hand. Both weapons flew off to the right and lay, still gleaming, still activated, on the ground, near a dark circular opening that gaped black in the floor.

As Vader drifted slowly back to the floor he grabbed his right wrist with his left hand, made a fist, and seemed to convulse like a man retching. A ball of pure white energy the size of his fist materialised in front of Vader's hands and moved down towards the wide-eyed Luke.

Something made Luke realise he could never reach his sabre before the white glove touched him. He threw up both hands and looked away. So he didn't see what happened.

His hands seemed to blur. The white glove struck, then bounced back, and contacted Vader gently as the latter touched the ground. There was a soft crack as of an explosion far in the distance. Vader was knocked head over heels and the glove vanished.

But when the white energy ball had touched Luke's hands, the power inherent in the kinetite, or restrained energy globe, had thrown him to the ground. Had he resisted it unsuccessfully it would have thrown him across the chamber and through the temple wall.

Now he lay on his belly while Vader rolled slowly on to his side, shaking his head in disbelief. His eyes focussed, to see a shaken but otherwise unharmed Luke crawling slowly towards his lightsabre.

'Not . . . possible!' Vader muttered, starting to crawl towards his own weapon. The left side of his body armour was dented inward as if by a giant's fist, where the kinetite had struck. 'Such power . . . in a child. Not possible!'

Luke had neither the strength nor the desire to argue. He saw only the sabre, felt only its smooth handle fitting compactly into his palm.

But by then Vader had reached his own weapon. With a supreme effort he tottered to his feet and turned to face Luke. Holding his father's sabre over his head, Luke rose, rushed at the Dark Lord and threw himself on the towering black figure.

There was a blinding flash of light as he made contact with Vader's sabre beam and slid on through with the blow. His sabre continued downward, pierced the stone floor. Luke's hand struck a rock and jarred his sabre loose.

He hit the ground hard, then rolled on to his back to see what had happened. What he saw was Vader staring at the floor. His right arm lay there, still gripping the glowing sabre. There was less blood than Luke would have expected. He tried to rise, failed. He no longer retained the strength to climb to his knees, let alone to regain his feet.

So he lay there completely exhausted. Slowly, in uneven, unsteady steps, the Dark Lord tottered to his severed arm. Amazingly, he bent down, lifted the amputated limb and detached the sabre from it. Holding it in his left hand he turned to face Luke. It was useless, he thought, as Vader raised the sabre over his head with his one remaining hand. The Dark Lord, Lord of the Sith, Master of the Dark Side of the Force, was invincible.

It was over.

'I'm sorry,' he murmured, turning his head to where the Princess lay crumpled on the temple floor. 'I'm sorry, Leia. I loved you.' He looked back up and found he hadn't the strength for a last curse.

The sabre soared above and behind Vader's head. The Dark Lord staggered drunkenly forward. He stumbled a couple of steps to the left.

And disappeared.

A dissonant, inhuman howling marked the descent of the Dark Lord down the black circle to Luke's right. Frowning painfully, hardly daring to believe, Luke crawled slowly over to the rim of the black circle, peered in and down.

He could not see the bottom of the pit, nor any sign of Darth Vader.

'He's gone,' he mumbled, dazed, hardly daring to believe it. 'Gone down to where he belongs, I hope.' He looked across the floor as he struggled to sit up, balancing himself on one arm. 'Leia, I did it! He's gone, Leia.' And yet ... there remained a stirring, a faint tremor in the Force, so light he could barely sense it, like a bad aftertaste in the mouth. But it was there ... *Vader was alive!*

Yet Vader was no threat to them. That was enough for him now. He was sobbing as he dragged his exhausted body across the floor. 'Leia, Leia!' Reaching her, he extended a questing palm, touched her forehead. She oppened her eyes and looked back at him. His tears fell uncontrollably as he probed gingerly at the terrible scars Vader's sabre had left on her body, her face.

'Luke?' she breathed, barely audible. She smiled at him, painfully. Taking her hand in his own, he slumped to the ground at her side.

At the top of the rubble blocking the temple entrance, Halla stopped to peer behind her. She saw the two figures lying hand in hand in the middle of the temple floor. Of the Dark Lord of the Sith there was no sign. She'd seen him fall down the sacrificial well of Pomojema's worshippers. She was free to go.

Her gaze turned downward, to stare into the glowing abyssal crimson of the Kaiburr crystal, then moved out to peer into the fog and mist of Mimban.

The personnel carrier they'd arrived in waited thereout. Hidden in it lay Kee, felled forever by a blow from Darth Vader. Luke's two 'droids sat motionless and deactivated nearby.

'Damn,' she murmured to herself. 'Aw, damn!'

Then she was scrambling down the pile of broken stone ... back into the temple.

'Luke!' She propped the limp form up, stared into

the somnolent face. 'Luke, boy? Come on, you're frightening old Halla.'

Eyes opened, turning to squint at her. 'Halla?'

She licked her lips, looked skyward, then placed the crystal in his lap, shoving it at him as if it were burning her. 'Here. I can't do much with it. I'm a faker, a charlatan of the Force, not a master. So I could do bigger and better parlour tricks . . . I'd waste it, and the Empire would find me soon anyway.'

Luke moved his gaze from her down to the pulsing silicate in his lap. 'The crystal magnifies the Force.' He chuckled, choked. 'What good is that now?'

'I don't know!' she shouted angrily. 'You wanted it, well there it is, dammit. What more do you want of me? What more can I do?' She shook both hands at him, furious at her own helplessness.

'Nothing, Halla.' He smiled gently at her. 'There's nothing more to be done, I guess.' He reached down, fondled the crystal. 'It feels warm . . . good.'

'You're crazy,' she snorted. 'It's a cold hunk of rock.'

'No . . . it's warm,' he insisted. 'Funny kind of warmth.'

Unconscious, he fell back, both hands still clamped tightly around the crystal.

Halla stood, turned away. 'Stupid old woman,' she cursed herself. 'Stupid, selfish old woman. I should have helped them when it might have done some good. I should have—' She hesitated, frowned uneasily. Was it growing lighter in the shadowed temple? She turned, and her eyes bulged.

Luke's motionless form was enveloped in a rich, red bath of light. In his hands the crystal shone with a brilliance unnatural. Nor was the light still. It shifted, fluttered, ran over him like a live thing. It sought out every extremity, each finger and follicle, like the St Elmo's fire of old on the rigging of a sailing ship.

After several long, rapturous moments the radiant

envelope shrank, sucked up by the crystal which resumed its normal colouring.

Luke sat up so abruptly that Halla was unable to repress a short screech. He blinked once, looked at her. Hesitantly, as though she were about to greet a ghost, she edged towards him.

'Luke boy?' she husked querulously.

'Halla. What happened? I ...' his head turned, his eyes coming to rest on the silent pit which had swallowed Darth Vader. 'I remember that. I also remember ... Halla, I died.'

'You must have found it boring,' she replied without smiling. 'It was the crystal ... something in the crystal. The Force ...'

'Don't remember,' he insisted, shaking his head dully. Then he reached down and touched the Princess's shoulder. 'Leia?'

'You were holding the crystal,' Halla explained slowly. 'In both hands. Remember the old legends ... how the temple priests could heal?'

'I don't understand,' Luke murmured. But he hefted the crystal again in both hands, closed his eyes and tried to concentrate and relax at the same time. The glow from the crystal intensified.

'I understand,' came a voice out of Luke's body, a voice that might or might not have been Luke's.

The crimson glow emerged from the crystal again. It started up Luke's arms, only to halt at the elbows. Holding the crystal with one hand, he opened his eyes. Like a man sleepwalking he reached down. One fingertip touched the Princess's face, tracing the scar left by Vader's sabre. As he traced it with the red glow, the scar vanished. Halla could see the skin moving, folding, healing behind it.

Slowly, wordlessly, as a rapt Halla watched, Luke proceeded to trace each of the wounds Vader had inflicted on the Princess. When he finished the final one, he placed his open palm first for a lingering moment over her heart, then her forehead. Then he sat back. The glow from the crystal subsided to normal.

Several more minutes passed. Uninjured, her beauty restored, Leia Organa slowly sat up. Both hands went to her head.

'Are you all right, Leia?' he asked solicitously.

She winced, stared at him. 'Luke, I have the most awful headache.'

'Headache,' he echoed. He turned, smiled at Halla. 'She has a headache.'

Halla grinned back at him, chuckled, then was roaring with relieved laughter. Luke joined in, his embarrassed, happy laughing interrupted only by an occasional cough. The crystal had repaired his injured insides, but he was still oxygen-weak.

The Princess looked suddenly uncertain. She glanced down at herself. Events returned with a rush as she felt her leg, her face.

'They're gone,' she murmured in disbelief. 'Healed. How?'

Luke turned serious. 'It was the crystal, Leia. It healed me, healed you, and I wasn't even aware it was doing so. Everything that Halla surmised about it is true. It *does* use the Force. The crystal healed you, Leia . . . not me.'

'Now, Luke boy,' Halla admonished him, 'you were the agent the crystal worked through. Without you, wouldn't be nothin' but rock.'

'Luke, we . . .' Leia stopped, stared around nervously. 'What about . . .?'

Luke reassured her. 'Down there.' He indicated the pit. 'I never heard him hit bottom. Vader's finished, Leia.' Yet . . . even as he said it there was the peculiar tingling in the Force again like a smell of sulphur.

She shattered that unwholesome train of thought. 'What about Threepio, and Artoo?'

'They're all right,' Halla responded. 'Leastwise, they looked fine to me when I was just now, uh, checking out the crawler to make sure it hadn't been booby-trapped by your Dark Lord. They're turned off, but no damage that I can see.'

Luke sighed with relief, put an arm around Leia. She didn't move to shrug it off.

'Here,' he said, handing the crystal to Halla. She eyed him uncertainly, then took it, held it with reverence. 'You might as well keep it for a while, since you're coming with us.'

'With you?' Halla looked wary. 'What do you want with a tired, old, woman? What good would I do you?'

'A world of good,' Luke assured her. 'A universe of good. We'll get you safely off Mimban with us. Then, if you still don't feel like joining the cause of a bunch of "outlaws", you don't have to.' He thought wistfully. 'I know another man, a smuggler and a pirate, who once thought the same way as you.'

'Don't compare me with any smugglers, and don't rush me,' she instructed him crossly. 'I might be persuaded . . . the Force knows what you want with me, though. But where am I going with you?'

Luke looked down at Leia, smiled. She leaned into his side and smiled in return. 'We're going to Circarpous IV,' he informed her. 'We're late for a very important date.' He turned to look at her. 'With an underground movement. We'll make an idealistic revolutionary out of you yet, Halla.'

'Not likely!' she snorted. But she didn't object further as she followed them outside the temple of Pomojema.

Back on the crawler, Luke adjusted the necessary switches. Artoo came back on first, followed by a startled Threepio.

'Oh, sir! Where is he? We couldn't escape him. He knew all the proper code words and commands. I tried to warn you, sir, but we couldn't—' He stopped and stared at them. 'Why are you all smiling?' Artoo beeped in exasperation. For a 'droid whose speciality was communicating, See Threepio could be mighty slow on the uptake.

'I beg your pardon, sir,' the tall, slim 'droid continued politely, 'but have I missed something important?'

'Artoo, start us up. We're getting out of here.'

The little Detoo unit plugged into the crawler's ignition. Immediately, the engine responded. Halla swung the massive machine around and it plunged into the surrounding jungle mists and cries of Mimban.

'Why,' the faint, receding voice of a certain 'droid could be heard to say, 'do I have the impression that everyone is laughing at me . . .?'

WHAT TURNS MEN INTO MEAT-HUNGRY SAVAGES . . .?

FAMINE

by GRAHAM MASTERTON

When the grain crop failed in Kansas it seemed like an isolated incident and no one took too much notice. Except Ed Hardesty. Then the blight spread to California's fruit harvest – and from there, like wildfire, throughout the nation . . .

'The Greek-looking man said: 'This food in here – you think that you're going to keep it all to yourself? All of it? Just because you're a store-keeper you think you've got some God-given right to survive while everybody else starves?'

Nicolas didn't even want to think about it. He said: 'I'm giving you three. You understand me? Three, and then I shoot.'

The first shot missed. The revolver bucked in his hands, and he heard the bang of broken glass at the back of the store, followed by a sudden rush of green olives from three broken jars. He fired again before he could allow himself to think, and the Greek's shoulder burst apart in a spray of gory catsup. And then there was a deep, deafening *bavvooom*! and Nicolas realized with strange slow horror that the Greek had fired back at him with his shotgun, and that he'd been hit, badly hit, in the belly and the thighs . . .

GENERAL FICTION 0 7221 6003 8 £1.75